PAYBACK

PAYBACK

ANIMUS™ BOOK ELEVEN

JOSHUA ANDERLE
MICHAEL ANDERLE

This book is a work of fiction.

All of the characters, organizations, and events portrayed in this novel are either products of the author's imagination or are used fictitiously. Sometimes both.

Cover Art by Jake @ J Caleb Design
http://jcalebdesign.com / jcalebdesign@gmail.com

A Michael Anderle Production

LMBPN Publishing
PMB 196, 2540 South Maryland Pkwy
Las Vegas, NV 89109

First US edition, February 2020
eBook ISBN: 978-1-64202-746-4
Print ISBN: 978-1-64202-747-1

THE PAYBACK TEAM

Thanks to the JIT Readers

Nicole Emens
John Ashmore
Kelly O'Donnell
Jeff Goode
Diane L. Smith
Dave Hicks
Jeff Eaton

If I've missed anyone, please let me know!

Editor
The Skyhunter Editing Team

DEDICATION

To Family, Friends and
Those Who Love
to Read.
May We All Enjoy Grace
to Live the Life We Are
Called.

CHAPTER ONE

A bleeding soldier with cracked armor and a half-destroyed helmet hobbled awkwardly to take refuge behind a piece of a wrecked ship. He sat, vented his rifle, tried to give himself a moment to recover.

The marksman's bullet sank into his head through the gap in his helmet and he fell before he vanished in a flash of white.

Flynn lowered his rifle as two other soldiers—a vanguard and a titan—swept the area. Two ships flew overhead and more engineers and soldiers dropped in. The marksman placed his rifle on his back, slid down the ridge he was perched on, and made his way carefully to his team.

He heard a yell and turned as two hostiles ran from a pursuing demolitionist. The heavy flipped a switch on his cannon, planted himself firmly, and pressed the trigger. A beam streaked from the barrel and both enemy soldiers cried out again when their chests were consumed by it. Their legs and heads fell while the rest of their frame melted away.

With a nod to the demolitionist, the sniper hefted his rifle. He felt like he knew the man, although he couldn't recall from where. A few random images flashed into his mind of a tall, broad-shouldered man with messy brown hair and a goofy grin. No name came with the snatched memories, though, so he put it out of his mind. There was no reason to know much about each other. They had a mission to complete and now wasn't the time for camaraderie.

An explosion in the distance made the man turn and he aimed his rifle in that direction to look through his scope. A small group of soldiers raced through the forest and trees toppled following another detonation. Enemy ships swooped over the mountains and one of them held a rod with a holographic emblem above it that displayed the Ultra Ark Academy logo.

It identified them immediately as the enemy.

Flynn located his team who waited for some direction from him. He raised a hand and pointed to the battle to indicate for them to join their comrades. They nodded and ran off, quick to enter the fray as their own fighters engaged the enemy dropships.

After a hasty scan of the area, he found a small space well-positioned for cover behind a small group of rocks and took aim. Before he could fire, however, he noticed an odd shimmer that seemed to move toward the demolitionist. He flipped a dial on the end of the scope to switch to thermal and confirmed the outline of an assassin who ran up behind the heavy.

He fired, clipped the shrouded figure in the shoulder,

and knocked her off her feet. If he'd shot through her, he would have struck her intended target as well. Still, it was enough to mark her and alert the demolitionist. The man spun as the assassin appeared when the cloak briefly gave way from the impact. She didn't have a chance to stand as he held his cannon above his head and raised a giant armored boot to drive it into her skull.

The marksman felt a small amount of satisfaction in that kill. For most people, identifying a cloaked soldier was almost impossible but for him, seeing the tell-tale shimmer had become almost mundane. The other way to know that an assassin was creeping up on you was to listen for unnatural sounds close to you—like the sudden snap of something trodden underfoot behind him.

He shortened the barrel as he lowered his head and rolled away. A plasma blade sliced over him and cut deeply into the stone he was hiding behind. Flynn fired at his attacker, but firing at close range—even with the shortened barrel—diminished the impact of his kinetic rounds. It was still enough to shatter the opponent's shields and knock them back, however. His attacker used the momentum to flip back and gain some distance between them. He tried to line up another shot, but the assassin threw a grenade.

As soon as he noticed it was a flash, he instinctively darkened his visor but was a second too late. Even with his eyes closed, the brightness of the flash disorientated and blinded him. He could hear the assassin approach but he felt no fear and instead, focused on the noise, dropped his rifle, and drew his blade and pistol.

While he waited for his adversary to creep closer, he

placed a finger against the lining of his belt and calmly tapped the switch positioned there for a moment. When he pressed it, his shields erupted and a crackling sound to his left confirmed that the barrier had thumped into his attacker.

Flynn deactivated his shield, swept a leg out, and tripped the assassin, who convulsed at his feet. He attacked immediately and thrust his blade down as his vision began to return to normal. It sank in but he ripped it free quickly before he stabbed again and repeated the process several times. Once his vision returned in full and he saw the chest of his victim no longer moving, he stood and activated the heat switch on his blade to burn the blood off. He flipped it to slide it back into its holster but suddenly, he couldn't move.

He hadn't been struck by a shock grenade, so perhaps it was a toxin? It was like his limbs no longer responded to his commands. He felt something strike the side of his head. With no shield to deflect the shot, his helmet proved useless. It was an energy shot, not kinetic, and simply burrowed through. In the next moment, the forest seemed to turn sideways before a flash of white faded and he found himself with only darkness all around.

Marlo received a message that the team leader was dead. The readout indicated a shot to the head, which probably meant a marksman had caught him in his sights. He felt a pang of pity but quickly let it go. His gaze scanned the field and drifted toward a ledge higher in the mountains, very obviously a sniper's nest.

The shots from his cannon would deteriorate over the distance, so he would need to call in some assistance. The demolitionist raised an arm and pointed to the location to mark it. After a few seconds, he received a confirmation message from fighter four. He picked his cannon up and continued up the path as the craft swooped past him and launched two missiles at the nest.

At least two marksmen tried to bail out but they were caught in the blast. It occurred to him that he should send a warning to the others to keep their surroundings clear. Who was the leader now? Was it him? Why was his memory fuzzy?

He shook his head in an effort to clear it. There was no time to worry about it and he'd have to make do and report the problem when they returned to base. For now, a mechanical whine echoed throughout the ridge and reminded him he had a job to do. Fortunately, it looked like he wouldn't have to run far as his job came to him.

A mech broke through the tree line and fired a beam at his teammates, but the vanguard in the group made a shield hastily to protect himself and the other soldiers. It wouldn't hold for long, however. Marlo adjusted the firing mode to charged shots and pressed the trigger to make it power up as he began to run. He activated his bounce jet and vaulted up to fire at the head of the mech. The blast knocked it back and it stumbled haphazardly. Its massive arm swept along the ground and almost caught its own allies, who were forced to jump or roll out of the way.

The demolitionist landed while he charged another shot, but the upper half of the mech spun and fired at him. He braced for the laser to melt him, exactly as he had done to his enemies, but instead, the vanguard now stood in front of him and intercepted the blast with a personal shield he'd formed around his armor.

Marlo rushed out from behind him and fired his shot at the mech's cannon. The blast destroyed the weapon and the blowback all but annihilated the rest of the arm. The vanguard's shield drained into his hands and he created an orb of energy that he threw at the mech's chest. When it struck, it launched the target off its feet and it careened into the enemy troops that approached from the end of the path.

The vanguard nodded to him and took point as the soldiers in the back ran up to release a sustained volley at the retreating enemy soldiers. The demolitionist vented his cannon and glanced up when a fireball crossed the sky. A dropship plummeted in flames and crashed on the left side of the battlefield, He paid it no mind at first and simply accepted that all occupants were killed, but a warning was quickly issued to challenge his assumption.

Alert. Havoc Droids. Alert. Havoc Droids.

Several droids emerged from the wreckage and immediately, chain guns and cannons ripped into the other soldiers. They were heavily armored, black in color with the exception of a golden circle with lines along the edges meeting in the middle—the insignia of the world military. It appeared they had finally begun to support the resistance groups, at least with bots and weapons.

He broke off from his unit and pushed forward to confront the droids. Yelling and pounding drew his attention to two more mechs that had joined the fight on the enemy's side. He looked around to confirm that they were now being forced back. He checked the unit readout, which told him they were down to fifty-two units and eight fighters in the sky. Marlo focused on his cannon, lifted it, and shut the vents before he retrieved a charged spike. He knew what had to be done.

As he ran into the middle of the fray while his cannon powered up, he sent a one-word warning to his comrades —*Zeus*. Many of his teammates broke away and others held the droids and enemy soldiers at bay while he bulldozed into the battle. He lifted the spike, activated it, and shoved it into the cannon's barrel. His shields soon burst and lasers struck his armor to melt through it and burn his skin. Kinetic shots penetrated too and continued through him. He drove his cannon into the ground and energy pulsed off it as he slid off it and fell. Soldiers on both sides now fled as the havoc droids tried to destroy the cannon and Marlo's life slipped away.

The weapon erupted, covered the field with a bright light, and melted anything caught within.

"We lost another," an Arbiter technician muttered and tapped the glass of Marlo's tube. "What do the reports say?"

"He eliminated a fair number and even sacrificed himself to pull off a Zeus maneuver. The battle might still be won, although they have far more soldiers than anticipated," a crewman commented as he walked down the line to compare the readouts on his tablet with the monitors next to the pods.

"Are there any issues with motor function?" the technician asked and made sure to monitor the demolitionist's vitals and brainwaves. "De-sync successful."

"Not with him, no, but the sniper, tracker, and titan all had issues. I think the sniper was actually caught because he froze."

He gave a throaty, frustrated huff as he turned away from the pod. "Keep those three on ice for now. It looks like four to five might be the limit. Prepare the demolitionist for another battle. He should be ready to sync with another golem in a couple of days."

"Do you think we'll keep doing this?" the other man asked. "All the soldiers we got from Ultra, Sol, Alpha, and the other Arks are already on missions. The Nexus students are the only ones we have to use golems for. They aren't working at peak efficiency, they can't use EIs—"

"Yes, I know," the technician grumbled to cut him short. "This was Keller's best option. The early experiments to simply force the change without the codex and Master EI proved...fatal. We still need the troops and even if they work at only seventy percent of their normal efficiency, these are Ark soldiers—the best of the best!"

"True enough, but we're wasting resources simply trying to determine who is what," the crewman pointed out. "Of the two hundred and something we snatched, only a hundred and fifty-seven have turned out to be soldiers, engineers, or techies. The others are logistics or medical and we can't do much with them or the less hands-on techs."

"Again, I am aware..." He sighed and rubbed the bridge of his nose. "Not that I am ungrateful for the help, but can I ask why you are here? You seem like you should be on the bridge or in engineering."

His companion chuckled. "I used to work here, although in a different division. My job became unnecessary once that fancy EI took control of so many things."

The technician looked up at an image of a wire-frame female face in one of the monitors, a reminder of the EI's ceaseless vigil over the ship. "She has made the flagship very efficient."

"Yeah, and left a number of us sitting around too. I've helped doing odd jobs on the bridge and in the bay and decided to come here for a while because the general...uh, is having something of a rough day."

"What's the matter now?"

"I couldn't tell ya. He's been doing so good lately and I haven't seen him act so self-assured and cocky in a long time. I think the attack on the ship a couple of days ago rattled him."

"That was hardly an attack." The technician scoffed. "More like a brief tantrum by rogue military members. Do you believe the general's ego has become so inflated that a minor scuffle would cause him to—"

"Attention all personnel." Nolan's voice boomed through the ship. "I have decided that due to the increased fighting and the various resistances that have cropped up since the day the Arbiter Organization revealed themselves to the world, we should make an example of these traitors of the human race. If they want oblivion, they shall have it. Prepare the cannon!"

The crewman looked at his companion, who almost dropped his tablet in shock. "He can't be serious, can he?" the technician asked. "We need all that humanity can offer. I know some loss of life is expected, but to simply destroy a city for purposes of intimidation?"

"Does that answer your question as to whether his ego has gotten too big?" The other man shrugged.

"Merrick will not stand for it."

"He ain't here," the crewman stated bluntly. "He's still trying to get the embassy to agree to follow his plans—the ones still alive, at least. If the general becomes too much of a problem, you can expect a visit from that personal assassin of his."

Dario looked out one of the side windows on the third floor of the colossus with a small frown. Nolan intended to destroy something? Without Merrick's permission? What a cheeky little general he had become.

He probably should be more concerned or angry at this unexpected development, but he could understand the man's plight. He hadn't been able to secure the codex or Master EI at Nexus, which made most of the captured students useless. He still had to share military power with Damyen and now, the Omega Horde as well. To add insult to injury, he was once again sent to Nexus to discover a lost device Merrick wanted but wasn't sure was still there.

The order basically made him an errand boy, if that. They at least knew what they are being told to do.

As he watched the clouds draw closer, he began to walk away to gain a little distance. If one were too close to the mouth of the cannon, one's body felt uncomfortably shaky for a while. Of course, he should probably say hello to Nolan and let him know he was on the ship, but it had been fun to see how he normally ran things when he thought no one was looking. Besides, he didn't sneak aboard to backseat strategize.

When he couldn't find Kaiden amongst the students captured, he worried he might have lost a fun new friend he never really had a second time with. The Gemini EI was never recovered either, so there was a good chance he was still alive. No doubt the fiery-blooded soldier would want another opportunity to destroy this ship and rescue all his mates, right?

The assassin was sure he would, and he was also sure he would be there to meet him once that happened.

Kaiden saw only the bodies of his comrades and grimaced when he realized his armor was shattered and Chief was unresponsive. He looked into the grey skies above as a massive vessel approached. A bright flash seared from the main cannon and heat enveloped him and his armor began to melt. In despair, he took one final look at the decaying bodies of his friends.

"Kaiden!" Chiyo shouted and the ace woke with a start.

He was dazed for a moment and struggled to focus in the dim light of the Emerald Lounge.

He rubbed his eyes. "Chi?" he asked. "What are you doing here? I thought you were working with Cyra."

"Come with me," she said and offered him a hand. He could see both grim determination and a hint of panic in her eyes. "You need to see this."

CHAPTER TWO

A group of several civilians ran desperately through the alleys and streets of the west side of Tacoma. Behind them, above and to their left, were the robots that had forced through the city barrier only a couple of days before and breached the defensive line. Anyone who set out to try to find friends or loved ones, recover supplies, or hell, simply catch a glimpse of the city away from the safety of one of the bunkers could potentially be vaporized or taken by one of these Arbiter droids.

One of the men screamed in mid-stride when a spike pierced his upper thigh and he fell and rolled. Two of the others turned quickly to help but retreated when more projectiles narrowly missed them. The wounded man told them to keep running through his pained grunts. They did and his cries and curses were silenced barely a few seconds after they had rounded the corner.

Only several yards farther, they encountered another group of droids and frantically increased their pace down the street. The mechanicals landed on the rooftops and leapt down in pursuit. The distance between them closed and the enemy straightened to their full height and extended their weapons toward the group.

Some of the civilians clung to others and shut their eyes. One stood with determination etched on his face and his chest out in defiance. He refused to die a coward, even if it was only for himself.

Before any of the enemy could attack, laser fire from above distracted them. Several officers dressed in medium armor with jetpacks flew above and directed a volley at the droids while they wove easily around their return fire. One of them landed among the group and fired his heavy pistol at the original group of mechanicals that had now caught up behind them. He took a spike from his belt and drove it into the ground, and a shield began to form around the civilians.

"Stay here," he ordered as he drew a second heavy pistol. "A dropship is on the way to evacuate you and we'll keep them at bay." With that, he took to the sky seconds before the dome closed. He headed to the west, firing at other mechanicals that had settled on the rooftops as two other officers joined him. "Wolfson, are you close by?"

"Aye, I dropped the last group off at the carriers. Do you have another?" the head officer of Nexus security responded and increased the speed of his ship as he closed in on their position.

"Yeah, a smaller group this time. I guess they were looking for supplies like the others," Haldt explained, settled on top of a nearby building, and fired several shots into a droid below him. "The droid infestation is worse. Are the police any closer to fixing the ba—"

At an explosion on the main street, the officer immediately moved in that direction. "Dammit. Please hurry, sir." He launched again when his pack fired and circled as quickly as he could to the street where he was greeted by the shattered bodies of two officers and the group of civilians huddled behind the shield while his remaining men struggle to maintain defensive fire. There were only two of them against several bots that were now backed up by one of the so-called elites, the enhanced versions of their mass-produced counterparts.

He holstered his pistols and drew his launcher from the back of his waist. "Get back! Charge your shots," he ordered both remaining officers as well as two others who had heard the commotion and raced to reinforce their teammates. He aimed the weapon carefully and fired to launch three thermals. They exploded to create a tall plume of fire and smoke as parts and rubble scattered through the street. The elite was still standing with its lights aglow and electricity sparked through the smoke as it fired at him through the haze.

"Its shields should be down. Fire!" he ordered as he dodged the shots. His officers responded with their charged or rapid shots and the barrage finally forced it to the ground before it burst apart from the damage sustained. He landed, checked on the civilians, and gave them a thumbs-up as a sign of safety.

"Look out!" one of them yelled and pointed into the distance. Haldt's eyes widened at a plasma orb that hurtled toward him. Instinctively, he flung himself aside and the projectile missed him by inches. He deactivated his jetpack and scrambled to his feet as the orb struck an abandoned vehicle behind him and erupted in a dome of blue light.

One of his men cursed and he whirled and echoed the exclamation when two more elites marched relentlessly down the street. The officers called out to one another as they took turns to vent their weapons. Two of them with personal shields landed in front of Haldt to protect him as he tried hastily to reload his launcher.

"Do you need help there, Haldt?" Wolfson asked a split-second before cannon fire streaked from above and hammered into the enhanced droids. Their shields held only momentarily against the assault before they failed and both machines were quickly obliterated. The defenders cheered as the head officer's ship circled to land swiftly. Haldt deactivated the shield protecting the civilians and escorted them hurriedly to the vessel as the pilot lowered the rear ramp.

"Good timing, sir," the officer complimented over the comms as he helped a limping woman aboard. "Did you see anyone else on the way here?"

"Nothing on visual or radar." Wolfson sounded regretful. "I think we've saved all we can in this sector. Another sweep couldn't hurt, but I did see another group of bots breaking through one of the weakened sections at the edge of town."

"We'll make it quick, then head over to section four and evacuate all the bunkers we can," Haldt promised. "Have you any word on what progress the commander has made in getting us military support?"

A long pause was broken by the head officer's heavy sigh. "Let's go with less than we hoped for."

"So there have been no changes since our last meeting?" Sasha asked General Hartman's hologram inside the makeshift office he had been allocated by the city council of Seattle.

The general shook his head. "We can provide a destroyer at the end of the week, but it is to remain in the city for defensive purposes. You must understand, Commander, we are planning a counterattack but cannot condone private citizens such as yourself setting out to fight the enemy on your own."

"You forget that the enemy doesn't give citizens much choice on whether or not they wish to fight or not. They must either fight for their lives or they are kidnapped and forced to fight for the enemy."

"That's only a theory at this point," the man retorted, his tone brisk. "Despite Merrick's ravings. So far, we have no proof that the soldiers fighting for the Arbiter Organization do so against their will."

"That's the official stance—what you tell the media to calm the public and the soldiers so they don't hesitate in battle." He folded his arms and stared at the general. "Tell me, as neither one of those, what is the real truth? You didn't request Laurie's help for nothing."

"Why? What did he tell you?" Hartman asked and a trace of anger edged his voice.

"He didn't tell me anything other than that he was leaving, but it was in his demeanor and the tone of his voice." He thought back to the downcast expression Laurie had worn as he boarded the military vessel. Given the circumstances, it wasn't a surprise to see he wasn't in good spirits, but this was the face of a man who had only recently been shaken to his core. He recalled that the last time he saw it was when he felt responsible for Gin's sabotage of the Animus system. "So tell me, General, what and who are we facing?"

Hartman sighed and adjusted the cuffs of his jacket out of annoyance or nervous habit. "The soldiers out of the sixth Ark Academy—the first one that was to be officially under the jurisdiction of the WC and headed by the now traitor Damyen Orlov—all seem to be volunteers. They show loyalty that the other soldiers do not as well as a certain...intelligence."

"Intelligence?" Sasha questioned. "In what manner? Mods or drug-enhanced brain activity?"

"Not exactly," the man said evasively. "They obviously didn't have the student numbers schools like Ultra or Nexus have. They were only open on a trial basis to get everything into place—proof of concept and all of that,"

"It sounds like you are rambling," he pointed out brusquely. "What does this have to do with the differences between them and the others?"

The general grimaced and picked a tablet up off-screen. "They were all handpicked by Damyen. From what we've been able to discern from raids on the facility in the last few weeks was that they've been on an accelerated program working solely on combat, assassination, and weapons expertise, with the only deviation being courses on vehicle skills and knowledge for both large and small craft. Given that they stole our ships, it's easy to see what that was for."

"Even so, if it's only been a smaller group of students over a couple of years, they shouldn't be able to take on a military force with such ease. They're working on a version of Animus that's only several updates newer than those I used when I attended Nexus."

"That would be one of the complications. It appears they somehow got their hands on the current patch of the Animus software—or a cracked version of it, rather—designed to further increase the students' abilities and performance and trade out the talent system for a pure experience increase."

The commander was aghast, both at the fact that they had the Nexus' version of the Animus system—something only Laurie should have access to—and the information on how the students were so advanced so soon. "Doing something like that could yield good results but it is much too dangerous. You're basically forcing the mind to accept these rapid changes at gunpoint. The stress and potential for sync issues are immense."

"That would be one of the reasons we called the professor in. We need his help to determine how they found a way around it. As you can guess, reports say they should have had many casualties using this method but from what we can tell, they've only had a few." Hartman lowered the tablet. "Although it's the other thing that we are concerned about—the intelligence."

"And what would that be?" Sasha frowned and tried to grasp what was inferred.

Hartman looked to either side, his demeanor cautious. "You are alone, aren't you?"

He nodded and the other man returned the gesture. "This is not for you to talk about to anyone, understood? I'm telling you this in confidence."

The chancellor folded his arms. "Very well. Let me hear it, General."

The general drew a deep breath as he locked eyes with Sasha. "I'm sure you've seen the Ark soldiers without their helmets—the white eyes and faint glowing lines. We all thought it was some kind of augmentation. It is more akin to biological modification, the result of special chemicals that have been absorbed by these soldiers."

"What are the chemicals for?"

"To help with the integration of the chips." Hartman moved his hand beyond the frame again to retrieve a small box and opened it to reveal a coin-sized chip. "We've found them at the base of the skull of several soldiers, both Damyen's and others. It seems similar to the device the WC used in the golem program."

"Which was secretly the Arbiter's program," the commander—now chancellor of Nexus—said flatly.

The other man frowned but continued. "They do receive orders and messages, but they also intertwine the functions of an OS with the human mind."

"Do what? An OS? Like an operating system?" Sasha demanded, appalled. "That can't be—what good would it do? If anything, it sounds like it would cause massive mental—" The pieces clicked as he spoke his thoughts aloud and his eyes widened.

"Indeed. It's a grim picture isn't it?" The general closed

the box and put it aside. "Damyen's soldiers have used it to get around the complications of their misuse of the Animus. The OS in the chip is what would have been their EIs. They act as a filter, disperse the information absorbed in the Animus, and allocate it somewhat safely to the soldiers. That's why they don't have a high mortality rate."

"But what does this have to do with the other students?" he asked. "They bond with their EIs over the years, certainly. But this shouldn't be possible. Even Laurie couldn't make it work until he met someone with the Gemini syndrome."

"His purpose was to make a harmonious connection between a human and an EI," Harman stated bluntly. "The chip cares little for either. From what we can tell, when an Ark student from any other school is put through this procedure, their EI is broken down to its base systems. All are focused to not only enhance the human but mute their free thought. In other words, they keep the skills, training, and experience of the person and even improve them but leave their personality suppressed."

The commander grimaced at a sudden sense of weakness in his legs, no doubt the effect of shock at the revelations. "So they become golems, then?"

"Except golems are fragile. They have a shelf life and can only perform actions within reason. Essentially, they have no real skill of their own and it's all downloaded and not ingrained," Hartman corrected. "But these are Ark students who have trained for years—specialists, in many cases. This process makes them super-soldiers. They may feel pain and may tire, but their command pushes them on so they ignore those weaknesses or they compensate with mods and armor. They are super-soldiers."

"And that's what they are doing? They are taking the Ark students—my students—to simply turn them into grunts?" Sasha stared at the general in shock and disbelief.

Hartman nodded grimly. "They want your soldiers, Sasha. They have no interest in the people."

CHAPTER THREE

The enormous ship pierced the clouds, which warped and swirled around the massive hull as it broke into visibility. The townspeople below looked up in horror as a vessel almost half the size of their city hovered menacingly above them. Some began to run but others fell to their knees in shock. Police tried to hurry as many as they could to safety and what few fighters they had quickly tried to engage, no matter how fruitless that would have been, even if they had the time.

Energy coalesced in the main cannon of the colossus and created what appeared to be a miniature star at its peak. The light was absorbed into the lining of the weapon before it fired and found its target in the middle of the city center. A wave of energy surged in all directions like a ripple of death and anyone and anything caught in it was instantly turned to plasma. The land itself blackened and a thin sheet of glass formed as the energy wave subsided.

In a single stroke of unrestrained power, the city of Centennial was no more.

Kaiden slammed the tablet on the table and dragged a breath through clenched teeth. "They aren't even pretending this is about the greater good anymore, are they?"

"From what we can gather, this wasn't ordered by Merrick," Cyra explained and took the now damaged tablet away from him. "We believe it was in retaliation for an attack on the ship a couple of days ago. Centennial had a small military base stationed near the city."

"They destroyed the entire city!" he protested and pushed up from the edge of the table. "It seems a little drastic, don't you think?"

"I would argue that everything that has happened during the last couple of months can be classified as drastic, Kaiden," Chiyo pointed out.

He almost snapped at her, offended by what appeared to be an attempt at humor. When he looked up, the retort ready, he saw the helplessness in her eyes. She plainly struggled not to give in to despair or worse, apathy. This might have been the most devastating report recently but tragic reports had become commonplace. Even victories against the Arbiter Organization, big and small, elicited only momentary joy before they encountered two or three setbacks or losses in quick succession.

The ace sighed and ran a hand through his hair. "I can't let this get to me. After all that shit I talked after the invasion, I can't show that they have beaten me before I've even fought them properly."

"Exactly," Cyra agreed. "Remember to give it back to

them twice as hard for everything they've done when you get the chance."

"Right, but when will that be?" he asked and looked from one woman to the other. "This is the second time the colossus has returned since the invasion. Last time, it was only here for a few days. How long will it stay this time?"

Cyra looked at Chiyo, who approached Kaiden and opened a holoscreen. "From what we can tell, the flagship makes stops to reinforce certain cities and battle zones. At this rate, it probably won't return to the Academy for a few more days."

"Assuming they can resist the temptation to destroy another city along the way," he muttered.

The infiltrator frowned. "Speaking...purely scientifically, it would be in their best interest to do so. Not only for their personal mission statement to 'save' humanity"—he almost spat at the idea—"but also because this colossus was based off an old model, one that was decommissioned. While I can't tell what they've changed or improved, one of the biggest issues was the blowback on both the structure of the ship and the power core from using the cannon. From what the engineers have told me, using the weapon frequently—and by frequently, I mean even once every couple of weeks—could lead to massive damage to the vessel."

Kaiden thought about what he'd learned about the usage of the cannon and realized that even with that in mind, they still used it for such a petty reason. "It sounds like the guy in charge is losing it."

"It's a possibility," she agreed. "Which would be fortunate for us. At this point, we can use every possible little advantage."

He merely nodded in silence because he hated the feeling of agreeing with something that sounded so desperate. "If we have a chance now, I want to take it," he announced and folded his arms. "Is Genos around? I want to hear what the engineers have tinkered with to get back into the Academy."

"I can put you in touch with the professor. He's helped with the project today since Genos left," Cyra offered.

"Genos left? Where did he go?"

Chiyo changed the screen to display a map of a snowy locale. "He and Jaxon left on a mission. There was an opportunity to recover a device the Omega Horde stole from a military facility in the Arctic."

Jaxon and Genos leapt out of the dropship and observed their surroundings as soon as they landed. It was nighttime and they stood on a frozen tundra in a few feet of snow, surrounded by large frosted trees and low ridges.

"Remember to be cautious, kin. We may handle the cold better than humans, but should our armor be compromised or heaters destroyed, we will experience difficulty," Genos advised.

"I agree, although the mercenaries are probably the most pressing concern right now," the ace replied and closed the mission details screen. "We are to make our way to a stronghold approximately twenty-two miles from our current location. Once there, we are to retrieve the sat-marker and disable the base if we can. Destruction has been authorized."

"Understood," mechanist acknowledged as he took his machine gun off his back. "Where shall we start?"

Jaxon drew his blade and flipped it as he examined it. "You take point."

"Pardon?" Genos asked in obvious confusion.

"I wish to see how you handle command for now. We haven't had a chance to examine one another since the invasion. I was always curious."

"And you think now would be a good time for that? Although I am not saying I am not up to the challenge."

The Tsuna ace nodded and slid his blade into its sheath. "Let me know when we can begin."

Genos raised his head when both heard a low rumble in the distance. They ran up the closest hill and immediately saw lights approaching. "They have responded rather soon, it seems," he muttered and pointed to the vehicle. "I assume they must have seen the dropship on approach."

"It makes this much faster—if you work quickly," his companion said and they crouched to conceal themselves behind the ridge of snow. "Can you disable the vehicle without destruction?"

The mechanist drew his long-distance pistol. "Of course," he said. "You know I am always prepared, kin."

"We have company! Repeat, we have hos—" The Omega Horde merc's warning cut short when Jaxon's pistol thumped into the back of his head. He toppled and joined the other two unconscious figures in the snow.

"I'm finished." The ace turned to where Genos crouched over a fourth man a few yards away. "I see you managed yours with ease but I didn't hear you fire a shot."

"That would be because I didn't," the engineer admitted and held his pistol up. "I locked his armor and recorded his voice as he yelled obscenities."

"For amusement?" his teammate asked as he holstered his weapon.

"For emulation. It will make it easier to get inside the base as infiltrators rather than fighting our way through."

"Like our coop test."

Genos tilted his head as he thought back. "Similar, yes."

"An omen, perhaps." Jaxon pressed his boot on the merc's chest as he drew his blade. "Stand back, kin. I have my own ways to get what we need."

The other Tsuna regarded him in silence for a moment, then nodded and stood. "Very well. I think it would be most interesting to see whose methods are quicker. But try to make it clear and understandable. Viola can take care of the rest." He turned away and plugged a wire from his gauntlet into the helmet. "Oh, and please do try to not wear him down too much. We need it to sound convincing."

The ace flipped his blade and nodded as he leaned over to get to work. His teammate briefly turned on the sound dampeners in his helmet and sent a message to Chiyo that they had begun their mission and should hopefully have the sat-marker in their possession soon but would go dark for now.

He sent the message and turned his dampeners off. The

mercenary retched. "That should be enough for now, kin." He tapped the Tsuna ace on the shoulder.

"Are you sure, Genos?" Jaxon released the man's now three-fingered hand as he stood. "These Omega Horde members can be quite difficult to negotiate with."

"I think he understands the situation and we only need a few words." He held his gauntlet up and the claw grip activated. "And if he needs more convincing, I shall do it myself."

CHAPTER FOUR

The Omega Horde merc stationed at the gate looked up when an alert sounded. One of their Charger vehicles moved slowly toward the base through the snow. The problem was that they expected no arrivals, even if it appeared to be one of their own.

He watched the vehicle suspiciously but one of the windows lowered and an armed grunt presented his keycard. The guard nodded, leaned back, and opened the gate. The Charger drove in slowly and the man at the gate returned his attention to the game on his tablet.

The vehicle's heater must have stopped working because he thought some of the guys' flesh looked a little blue from the frost. No wonder they returned to base.

"This Omega Horde is not the smartest group," Genos commented as he straightened, removed the merc helmet, and looked out the window. "After all that work, he simply handed us a keycard. I feel somewhat annoyed that my efforts went to waste."

"You may have a chance to take that frustration out on the rest," Jaxon reassured him.

The engineer nodded. "This base isn't well defended but they have only occupied it for a few weeks." Another glance out the window revealed that the wind had picked up and the snow fell a little harder. "We may have some cover to assist our mission."

"A blizzard?" the ace asked and received a nod in response. "That is an omen indeed. From the looks of things, I should be able to get inside and deal with any forces within, assuming you can keep the ones outside distracted."

The Tsuna engineer looked at the vehicle's dashboard and pressed a few tabs on the monitor to get a readout. "This is equipped with cannons, boosters, and a few missiles as well. I believe I can make that work."

"Do you know how to handle this vehicle?" Jaxon asked.

"I have small-vehicle talents up to level five, although I haven't had much experience. Despite that, I believe I can drive it better than any of the mercenaries here."

"Understood." His teammate nodded, confident in the assurance.

The base was a lone grey-and-white rectangular building. Icicles had formed along the edges and snow and ice covered the few windows. A few droids paced the area and a couple of dozen mercs were in evidence around the site.

"Are you ready to begin, kin?" Jaxon asked. Perhaps Genos would have an easier time than he thought despite two more Chargers that appeared, obviously patrolling the area.

The engineer nodded, retrieved a couple of nano grenades, and handed them to the ace. "Take these, they may prove useful."

"I appreciate it," he acknowledged and stowed them for easy access. "Let us begin."

"Hey," an Omega merc began and thumped the back of his hand against the chest of another as he nodded to another merc in the distance. "Where the hell did he get armor like that?"

His comrade whistled. "I don't know. He must have spent a good chunk of his shares to get that getup. Look at that rifle. Shit, only a company man would invest that much into his gear."

"Or he likes strutting." The first man chuckled. "I need to find out who he is. He's possibly one of the outpost boys. Maybe I can borrow it if I ask him when we get some time to ourselves."

Another merc, the taskmaster of the group, joined and stared at the person of interest as he strode into the main building. "He ain't one of us," he said quickly. "I know everyone on this mission and no one is kitted out like that. Hit the alarms."

The other two jumped to their feet. "Right! I'll go and —" He was interrupted when a Charger slid in front of their station before the cannons emerged and lit up. "Shit,

hit the floor!" the merc shouted as it fired into their canopy.

The few mercs who whispered about Jaxon as he walked calmly into the building were startled out of their curiosity by a large explosion. They were immediately on alert and some reached for their weapons when the alarms sounded. Several rushed past him and he drew his heavy pistol and turned to fire. His precise shots felled five of the mercs as they ran to the exit.

"We've been tricked!" a man shouted as the Tsuna traded his pistol for his rifle. He fired two shots and caught a merc in the chest with both. Quickly, he fired a third to strike another in the side of the head. He made his way deeper into the base as the foundation shook. Genos had no doubt fired two missiles, probably at another Charger, so he had to work quickly.

He continued down the hall and behind him, snow drifted in from the storm through the now-broken windows. Some of the walls had cracks and holes from laser fire, although he assumed those were from the battle when the mercs took the base.

The sound of assault droids activating had become commonplace and he recognized it instantly and stopped. He retrieved the nano grenades Genos had given him and peered around the corner as the droids jumped from pods and turned toward him. Calmly, he pressed the switches on both grenades and lobbed them. They burst seconds later and only a few shots were fired by the droids before they fell silent. His HUD displayed several green dots, the sign that they were his to command.

A group of Omegas entered the hall but stopped when they saw the droids standing idle and yelled at them to move. The mechanicals turned and fired on their erstwhile allies and Jaxon nodded in approval as he continued to run through the building.

The ace opened the map of the building in his HUD. It had been provided by the military contacts who had given them the mission and it confirmed that he was close to the last area the object had been in. He hoped the mercs hadn't had a reason to use it or worse, break it down for parts or in a drunken stupor. A warning flash of a shot from his left stopped him in midstride and he ducked as two troop droids clunked toward him.

They bore the logo of the station but had obviously been stolen from somewhere and hacked. Their movements were slightly slow and there seemed to be a hesitation in their actions. He aimed and fired to eliminate one as the other returned fire. All he had to do was simply step to the side to avoid the blast before he felled the last mechanical with a shot to the head.

He moved past their remains and hurried up the hall. When he found the research area, he put his rifle away and identified two shadows through the door window before he drew his pistol and kicked the door in. Two guards spun with shotguns, but neither had a chance to fire before his shots struck home and ended their defensive efforts.

Jaxon stepped over them and scanned several boxes strewn around the room. Once he'd replaced the map with a picture of the sat-marker and its container, he examined the room until he located a silver box with the station's logo stamped on it. This one had a unique lock, which set it apart from the rest. He spun the dial on the box three times to the left and twice to the right, then pushed it in and the box opened to reveal their prize.

Another large explosion outside reminded him that he needed to get out. Even with the aid of the Charger, there were more dangers than either had anticipated. He prepared to head out of the room but stopped when he noticed a row of windows in the lab.

"Locked-on. Firing," Viola, Genos' EI, stated and two missiles left the launch tubes of the Tsuna's Charger. They rocketed into the side of the enemy vehicle and the fiery wreck rolled onto a group of attacking mercs and droids. *"We are now out of missiles, Genos."*

"Understood, Viola," he acknowledged. "We only need to hold out for a while longer. I'm sure kin Jaxon is almost —" Laser fire erupted from the building on his left, followed by a person who flung themselves out of the damaged windows, landed in the snow, and waved at him. It was Jaxon and he held the case they had come for.

"Oh, most fortuitous," Genos said approvingly, leaned over, and opened the passenger door. His teammate dove in as mercs fired a concerted barrage. The engineer shut the automated door and as the vehicle raced toward the gates, he fired at them with his cannons and pressed the boost to plow through the snowbanks. The blizzard finally struck in full and obscured their escape.

"Welcome back, kin Jaxon," he said and glanced quickly at the case. "The sat-marker, I take it?"

"It is. Pull over for a moment," the ace requested. His teammate nodded and halted the vehicle. Jaxon opened his door as he accessed the case and removed the device. It looked similar to a launcher but with a mirror-like end to the barrel and a large, complex scope. "We still need to destroy the base," he pointed out and dropped to one knee to rest the marker over his shoulder and look through the scope. "And they did say we could test it if need be."

Genos looked at the dim outline of the base through the drifting snow as his teammate held the trigger. A green light flared for a moment in the scope before Jaxon stood and put it away.

"Did it not work?" the engineer asked.

"It will work soon," the ace replied, clicked the case shut, and tossed it in the back of the vehicle before he slid into his seat and shut the door. "Onward to the extraction."

"At once." Genos turned away and drove off. Behind them, a large beam seared from the skies and pierced the Omega-occupied base to create a large explosion that neither Tsuna paid much mind to.

CHAPTER FIVE

When Sasha stepped out of his temporary office, Kaiden was there to greet him. The determined glare and fidgeting movement indicated that he wasn't there for idle chat or even an update. The chancellor knew what the young ace wanted, although he was still hesitant to okay it.

He didn't know how much longer he could continue to find relatively safe missions for the soldier, nor did he know how much longer he would accept them, albeit unwillingly. It seemed he'd have to do his best to delay that moment once again.

"Still nothing from the military?" the young man asked and joined him as he walked down the hall.

The commander kept most of the discoveries to himself and simply replied, "They will send us more reinforcements, a full destroyer deployment this time. But they will not join us on any raid or mission outside the city."

Kaiden shook his head. "That's no surprise." He looked

expectantly at the older man. "All right, enough small talk. I'm sure you know why I'm here."

"I really hoped it was for small talk," Sasha retorted as they made their way into the elevator. "So I'm not so fortunate that you wish to simply ask me about my week?"

"When is my next mission?" the ace asked, folded his arms, and leaned against the wall. "Julio is busy running supplies so I can't get into the merc net—if that is still even an option right now. The military guys around the city only have me doing grunt work, and the stuff I'm getting here isn't much better."

"Kaiden—"

"And yet it seems like every day, I hear my friends are sent off on actual missions that not only help but are really dangerous. They often go in without the proper numbers or gear. Did you know Genos and Jaxon left for Alaska last night? Only the two of them and a pilot."

"Are you saying they are not prepared for such tasks?" the commander asked.

"Hell no, of course they are," he countered and stared at the lowering numbers above the elevator doors. "But it makes me wonder if you don't think I am."

"We discussed this a week ago, Kaiden." He fixed the impatient man with a stern look. "You brought this group together and are more of a figurehead than I am—or Wolfson or any one of us. The others need that morale, that rock to keep this together. They stay with us instead of joining the military or setting off on their own because they have a stake in our mission to reclaim the Academy."

"Wouldn't I set a better example if I was actually out there fighting?" Kaiden challenged. "I don't mind the patrols and the occasional rescue mission. But like you said, our plan is to take the Academy. We know the ship is on its way and I don't hear a real plan from anyone."

"If you have an idea, I'll listen," Sasha responded as the elevator reached the ground floor and they walked out the doors and through the lobby. "Those missions your friends and fellow students have run are to retrieve devices, supplies, and data from the enemy that we can use. It does not seem like we will receive any assistance from the military at this point."

"You'd think they'd be more open considering they've finally beaten back most of the terrorist groups and we have a pact now."

"That's a formality," he countered. "They said they would work with resistance groups in this time of crisis. But how integrated we are or if they see us as equals depends on who we work with. I think we may actually be one of the lucky ones at the moment."

"I'd hate to see what a lousy coop looks like." The ace sighed. "I haven't had much luck reaching out to all the gangs. The Fire Riders, Skyway Kings, and even the Halos are all silent so far. Wolfson said he can't get in touch with Raza either. My guess is it's because the gates are closed."

"It sounds like we have the odds against us at the moment," the commander said and studied his companion. "But that's been the case often before."

Kaiden finally cracked a small grin. "I'm glad to see you haven't given into the doom and gloom thus far."

"I have too much work to do," he explained only half-jokingly. "I'm sure I can catch up with it with a bottle of liquor or three after this is all over. For now, we all have our jobs to do."

"And is mine to sit on my hands?" he asked. His expression manifested a kind of morose acceptance as if he'd resigned himself to disappointment yet again.

Sasha sighed. He had to admit, the ace was far more patient than he had expected. He didn't want to tell him but it wasn't only for morale that he didn't want him to face the enemy quite yet. Laurie had told him in private that without Aurora, Chief was the best EI they had, probably in the world. The Arbiter Organization had already shown that they wanted him and from what the general had told him, he was even more reluctant to send him out and have him possibly be captured.

But that wasn't only his decision, and if he didn't give him something to do, even if only vent his frustrations, the young man's patience might finally wear out and he could take matters into his own hands. There was a limit to how much someone as volatile as he was could bottle up. The commander retrieved a commlink and placed it in his ear. "Isaac, call Wolfson."

They both stopped in the middle of the plaza when the call finally went through and Wolfson answered. "Aye, Sasha. We're about to head back now. Do you have something for us?"

"Not for there but when you return, how long will you need for recovery?" he asked.

"I'm good to go. Haldt and his team did most of the fighting this time. I provided air support with these new cannons the military provided. I'm telling ya, I was purring." The Head Officer chuckled.

"Then when you return, Kaiden will join you on a recon mission to the Axiom lab in California. There have been sightings of the Omega Horde in the area and given that it has come to light that Axiom labs have links to the AO, we feel it's worth having a look to see what, if anything, is left in there."

"You're sending both of us over there for a quick look about?" The man sounded surprised. "Is that really the best allocation of resources, Chancellor?"

"I expect you will run into said Horde while you're there," he replied and glanced at Kaiden. "It would be beneficial if they no longer bothered anyone. I'm sure you can merely ask nicely."

The ace smirked when Wolfson uttered another throaty chuckle. "All right, we'll pop past and have a look, then find any of the Omegas and have that nice chat."

"Hey, are you sure you want to freeze that marksman?" the crewman asked the technician at the console.

"It's probably best we do it now. At most, we can have one or two more runs with him before there is permanent damage and we either have to freeze him for a much longer period or simply terminate him," he replied before he thought it over and turned to look at the other man. "Why?"

"We had a request from one of those Omega Horde guys. He says a team is heading over to Oakland but they're low on members. They have a couple of golems ready and wanted a sniper, at least, and he's the only one available right now."

"Can't they use any of the actual Arbiter soldiers?" The technician sighed. "I suppose they are mostly used to fight the military right now. Fine but keep an eye on him. If it gets too much, eject him manually."

"I'll see to it." The crewman nodded. "I'll send C12 into the other body. He's just finished a week of rest. It shouldn't be a big deal anyway. The area is deserted after the evacuations. Who are they gonna run into?"

CHAPTER SIX

Two guards stationed outside the hastily erected barricade tensed and drew their weapons when the sound of footsteps crunched on the gravel. Cautiously, one turned a light on the approaching soldier. The slender figure held her hands up and flashed the light on her shoulder pad three times, the signal of a runner.

"Oh, good, a friendly," he said wearily with no sarcasm in his tone as they holstered their pistols. He was tired and grew more so by the hour. "Did you have any luck out there?"

"I've found some supplies." Izzy nodded and removed her sack from over her shoulder. "Mostly food and other bits and pieces. I checked the residential areas and the only weapons I could find were a couple of pistols that were left behind. There are a few light kinetic rounds to go with them as well."

"Still, it's a good haul for one person. The others are still out there," the guard told her and handed the sack to the other guard, who took it into the camp grounds. "It's brave of your group to split up like this. You certainly find more items that way, but it's a hell of a lot riskier than staying together."

She shrugged and glanced at the darkness behind her. "It's calm for the most part. Besides, if we were caught, they could kill all five of us in one."

"Five Nexus trained scouts?" He chuckled. "I'd like to see them try."

He had merely tried to be supportive, she knew that, but as she walked past him, she couldn't help but lower her head and made no effort to respond. The guard realized what he had said and looked away a little guiltily. The enemy had already proven they could eliminate Nexus scouts—and many others too.

Izzy made her way across the wooded area to the bunker stairs. She descended to where several soldiers and officials paced the halls. They exchanged cursory greetings and she moved on to the makeshift medical center and opened the door. Amber looked up from where she worked on a patient.

"Is your arm better?" the battle medic asked and the soldier nodded as he ran a hand over the darkened area.

"I can move it now so that's a hell of an improvement," he confirmed and stood from the bed.

"It will still be tender for a couple of days. Take this." Amber handed him a vial of gel. "Apply it gently to the wound once a day and it will clear up soon." He thanked her as he put the vial away and shook her hand with his good arm before he left. "I wish I could simply use my stem-pack or emitter." She sighed and plopped onto the bed. "I think most of them understand that we're strapped and they should be saved for bigger battles, but we're all used to being able to fix laser wounds in seconds."

Izzy took a seat beside her. "So are we spoiled because we can heal serious wounds so quickly, or do we suffer because we're so used to it?"

Her friend chuckled at the dark joke. "I won't say they cancel each other out, but it is rather confounding, isn't it?"

"I merely try not to get wounded either way," she admitted, opened a small satchel on her belt, and removed a small package in a pink wrapper. "I found these while out on patrol and thought you would like them."

Amber took it and unwrapped it. Inside were several small macarons, each a different bright color. "It's been a while since I've seen something so joyful-looking." She smiled and hugged her friend. "Thanks, Izzy."

"Don't mention it. Thanks for coming back." They broke from the hug, both thankful for friendship in these dark times. The medic offered her a confection and she took a green one while her companion chose a red. Both bit into them at the same time with a small smile.

"I'm surprised at how many have stayed in Bellingham," Izzy stated once she'd swallowed. "With so much activity down here and in the campsite above, you wouldn't think we worked only with a skeleton crew."

"To be fair, that's only because our group came in last week," Amber reasoned. "Those other guys—the military officials—are only here to confirm when the colossus returns. I don't know if they will stay or not."

"They haven't exactly been chatty with anyone, have they?" The scout huffed and pushed a strand of hair out of her face. "It feels like we have the same enemy but different objectives."

"That is probably exactly the way it is." Amber sighed and focused her gaze on the box of pastries. "I'm worried that...they only want to destroy the colossus. I don't think they are thinking of any of the prisoners inside."

Izzy frowned and drew her legs up to her chest. "Are you sure they are still on board?"

The medic nodded and placed the box on the bed beside her. "Chiyo and Cyra told me that with the codex the comm—chancellor was able to sneak away with, they were able to locate the signals of every student and staff aboard. They were very faint but they were there. If it had changed, I think they would have told everyone."

"Then when the time comes, we'll have the be the first to make a move," she stated firmly. "Everyone is working on missions to prepare what we need to retake the Academy and rescue the others but we need to be patient for a little while longer. If Kaiden and Luke can hold their impatience in check for now, I think we can manage."

"But will the military stop us?" Amber asked, her voice much quieter as if to make sure it couldn't be heard by any outside listeners. "They want their revenge. I can understand that, given all the loss of life and the destruction of Terra, but if they try to pull rank when we try to mount an offensive..." She shook her head despondently.

"I don't think they'll try," Izzy replied to reassure her. "Sasha has been in talks with a General and several other high-ranking members of the military. With the embassy still in limbo right now, those have to be guys who are temporarily in charge, right? If they intended to stop us, they would have said something by now. I'm actually more worried that they plan to use us as a smokescreen so while the AO is dealing with us, they spring their own trap and we'll have no support."

"I'm not sure about the smokescreen idea, but I think we have already accepted the idea that the military won't help us, at least." With a heavy sigh, the medic stretched her arms back and let the top half of her body fall onto the cot. "If so, then fine. This is what we've trained for, and when we get the chance, we will get our friends back."

"Damn right." She nodded emphatically and lay beside her friend.

"Speaking of Kaiden and Luke, do you happen to know how they are doing?" Amber asked and glanced quickly at her. "I've been so busy that I haven't stayed in contact all that much. Have you?"

"I check in with Chiyo and Silas when I get bored out on patrol. It's probably not the safest time, admittedly, but whatever works, right?" The scout clasped her hands together and stretched them above her. "Kaiden is very restless, the last Chi told me, and he's probably badgering Sasha to send him on a mission. As for Luke...well, I can't talk about him specifically, but Silas told me that a few of them were headed to Oakland."

The titan roared as he brought his hammer down to demolish an elite droid with one blow. "Who's next?" he shouted and focused on the targets his EI marked to indicate several other droids close by.

"It looks like they are," Silas muttered as he and Cameron changed their kinetic ammo cartridges. "Mack, are your shields up?"

"Energy is building," he answered and thumped his fists together. "I have enough if they want another round."

"Feel free to—" Before he could finish, Luke activated his bounce jets and leapt at the advancing droids that were almost within range.

"Uh…feel free to go second," the bounty hunter muttered as he raised his rifle. The group now faced the third group of droids in a row and they knew there were many more ahead.

CHAPTER SEVEN

Luke drove his hammer into the doors of the ground level of the tower. "So have we simply thrown stealth out the window?" Cameron asked snidely.

"Do you honestly think it's still an option right now?" Mack asked as he walked past with his shield up and brightened its light as they walked into the lobby. Silas took point and scrutinized the various cracks, burns, and destroyed ornaments and walls in the area. If there was anyone hiding out in there, they hadn't been present when the Horde invaded.

"Cam, do you have any readings on the droids?" the enforcer asked from his point position. He glanced over his shoulder at the bounty hunter, who retrieved his tablet and studied his map.

"There are a few along the edge of the sector, about twelve miles out where we started. I don't think there are many left, though. The Omegas have been the ones making runs through here."

Silas looked around and listened intently. "Which

means we have different targets to worry about, ones that can't be tracked as easily."

"Hey, I'm working with what I have. Blame Raul for taking that gig with Julius and Otto. I think he wanted something cushy," Cameron muttered as he stowed the tablet.

"Let's make this quick—split up and search but stay in contact and let us know what you find," the enforcer ordered and held his shotgun in the port arms position as he made his way to the stairs on the right.

Luke and Mack nodded. The bounty hunter looked up to confirm that he had a clear shot to the floors above. He raised his arm, fired his grappling hook from his armor, and hauled himself quickly to the sixth floor.

Silas walked through what was his fourth hallway thus far. He had heard nothing since he entered, but cuts had been etched into doors and along a few of the walls, obviously from metal blades rather than plasma. They wouldn't be so clean, otherwise.

What concerned him was the dried blood and other fluids but no bodies thus far. He wasn't sure what had happened there and whether the Horde or the droids had arrived first. Not only that, there was no way to tell if their purpose had been to capture or simply terminate the occupants.

None of those options were easy to swallow, especially given the hope that this would be a rescue mission.

He stopped in front of the door at the end of the hall. A

window in the middle was partially broken but faded lettering on it indicated that this was the main work floor, clearly some kind of assembly plant. A few dim lights were on, the only signs he'd seen of activity or an indication that someone might be there. A couple of small belt lines were within, worn but still functional, and his keen gaze noticed something robotic hanging off one of them.

Cautiously, he pushed the door open and walked in and crossed to the conveyor belt. On the end was the partially disintegrated arm of a droid—not an Arbiter droid but a Guardian droid, so it must have been the company's. Something was odd, however, and he studied it intently. It hadn't been damaged by a blade or blast or even by something like a force hammer. Instead, it looked like the metal plating around the arm had been crushed and then pulled from the body. Was this done by another droid? If so, why were there splotches of blood along the frame?

A rattle from the other side of the room was followed by a growl.

It sounded like a sickly inhale and he looked up from the arm, instantly alert. A monster—there really was no other way to describe it—moved into the dim illumination of one of the lights hung overhead. It was gaunt with long spindly arms and a black-and-gray body, but wispy lines of purple energy wove through its entire being, similar to veins. The face, however, was what terrified him.

The skin resembled pale, ragged leather stretched over a sunken skull. On the top of its head, it wound together into a crescent-like shape that was mirrored beneath its chin to a long, sharp point. Jagged sockets with eyes of pure white reflected an artificial glow beneath and it approached with its mouth agape to reveal splintered, broken teeth.

Silas didn't back away and simply stood and observed as it inched closer. He glanced up when something tapped against metal and he identified another one that walked on the railings above and stared at him, either with curiosity or hunger.

The creature in front of him uttered a shriek and attacked. He raised his shotgun and used it to block the attempt to take hold of him. The ghoul pushed him back but he planted his feet quickly and they both came to a halt with his attacker pressed against the gun. The weapon thankfully didn't buckle beneath its abnormal strength. It stretched its head back to lash out and tear into his face. He responded by headbutting it first and thrust it back before he kicked it into the conveyor line. It impacted with a solid thump and fell.

The ghoul above took the opportunity to jump with a low growl but Silas raised his shotgun and fired. Several lines of light burrowed into the fiend in midair and he stepped back and stared as its eyes darkened and it sailed past him. The creature was dead when it landed, but its comrade had found its feet and turned to strike. His plasma blade emerged from his gauntlet and he swung to sever its raised arm, caught it in his other hand, and spun to whip it against his attacker's face before he hurled it aside.

With a malevolent hiss, the creature recoiled and clutched the massive wound. Silas ran up to it with his shotgun raised and pounded it into its chest. The monster wheezed and snarled, but the synthetic light in its eyes began to dim. He pulled the trigger and the force of the strike catapulted it into several machines behind them.

Above him, something clanged against the metal railing and he looked up. The figure of a thin man with cropped hair was visible in the shadows. He tapped the edge of what looked like a curved dagger against the railing.

"Silas, what the hell is going on?" Cameron asked over the comms.

His gaze remained focused on the walkway. "I found a little trouble and I'll take care of it, but stay alert. There might be more."

"More of what?"

He looked hastily from the man above to the two humanoid creatures nearby. "I'll have to get back to you on that. Give me a minute." The enforcer vented his weapon as he took a couple of steps forward and once again focused on the man on the walkway. "Is that your way to applaud me?" he asked and flipped his weapon so it rested on his shoulder.

"It was a good show—very brief, but you made it look good," the man replied in a gruff Australian accent.

"Are you an Omega?"

"I am. My name's Dred," he stated and crouched with one hand holding the railing above him. "Might I ask who you are and to what I owe the pleasure of your little visit here?"

Silas pressed the switch to close the vents with his thumb. "I'm Silas, a soldier trained at the Nexus. I'm here on a rescue mission."

"Is that right?" Dred chuckled. "I'm not sure if you noticed but you might be a little late."

The enforcer stopped and pointed to the corpses, which now seemed to smolder, for some reason. "What the hell are those things?"

"Heh, to be honest, I'm not so sure myself." The man's current position enabled Silas to see his features more clearly in the light—tanned skin, brown eyes, and a crooked smile above a dark brown goatee, with several small scars across his forehead and his mouth. "Me and my boys were sent to test them. They're some kind of golem, I think. I don't know what they did to them, but the fucking things act like zombies now. Well, they did before, but that was metaphorical. Now, it's almost quite literal in this case."

"You unleashed these monsters on innocent civilians?" Silas demanded, his voice almost a growl.

"Calm down there, mate. By the time we arrived, the only guys walking around here were military. I guess that's not much better, but not civvies, at least." He tapped the blade against his jaw as if in thought. "If it makes you feel better, we don't exactly have a great record controlling them and they killed a couple of my boys too. I was given the order to exterminate this batch. You might have finished the job for us, but we forgot how many came along. The guy keeping track of that was one of the first to go."

"So there are both other Omegas in here and these golems?" he asked.

"You walked into the lion's den, huh?" The man laughed mockingly.

"It looks like it." The enforcer flipped his shotgun into the ready position and aimed it at the man. "I guess it's a good thing I brought this." He pulled the trigger and the man leapt into the shadows. "Guys, we have both Omegas and feral golems on the premises. I'm calling a retreat," he ordered and held his shotgun in both hands as he ran deeper into the room. "I'll join you soon. This won't take long."

CHAPTER EIGHT

Although Cameron heard Silas' order, he didn't respond immediately. Instead, he raced down the hallway of the eighth floor toward the edge, vaulted over it, and fired his grappling hook to descend to the fourth level where loud blasts and the clash of metal indicated a battle in progress. It sounded like his teammates were already engaged with someone or something—whatever a feral golem was. He released the line and landed smoothly, then sprinted deep into the west wing and finally located his teammates in what looked like a large office.

Mack and Luke both fought heavies dressed in the Omega Hordes black and dark-red armor. Luke faced an enemy titan who wielded a spiked mace rather than a hammer, and as both men exchanged blows, the clash of their weapons rumbled through the room. His large teammate's opponent was a demolitionist who fired a huge cannon that put severe strain on the vanguard's shields until he condensed them and hurled the energy forward.

The force thrust the demolitionist away and gave him time to attack.

The bounty hunter looked around the room but saw nothing that might fit the feral golem mentioned. A hasty peek behind him still revealed nothing and he reminded himself that he should hurry to achieve his other objective. Otherwise, his paranoia over possible monsters would get the better of him.

The battle looked fun and all, but they needed to end it. He traded out his laser fire, pressed a switch on his rifle as he shoved an ammo cartridge into his gun, and aimed at the demolitionist.

"Mack, get down!" he shouted. The vanguard immediately stopped and ducked as Cameron fired. He caught the enemy heavy with four shots and at first, they seemed to have no effect. Seconds later, they erupted into a large foam-like bubble that essentially glued him in place.

"Luke, your turn!" The bounty hunter turned as the titan flipped the switch on his hammer to release a wave of energy. His large adversary attempted to attack, only to be knocked back when Cameron fired four more shots to trap him in the same way as his comrade. He struggled uselessly against the restraint and yelled curses.

"What the hell are those?" Mack asked and gaped at the two disabled heavies.

"It's something Raul suggested. I guess I'll have to give him my compliments when we get back," Cameron admitted and gestured for the others to follow. "Come on, let's save Silas."

Dred uttered a low, mocking chuckle as the enforcer pursued him across the factory. The merc flung several blades at him but he rolled beneath them and fired a shot. His adversary's coarse laugh echoed as he disappeared. He picked up and examined one of the blades and once he zoomed in, he identified smaller rotating blades along the edge. "Nano-blades."

"Fancy, huh?" Silas spun as Dred stepped out of the corner with a manic grin on his face as he twirled his main blade. He wore light armor colored in random patches of black and crimson. His weapon was indeed a curved dagger with a silver hilt, but the blade appeared to be made out of some kind of black metal. It was surprisingly long, around eleven inches, with several tally marks along the side.

There wouldn't be any prizes for guessing what those meant.

"I was already gonna snuff you for what you saw here. We still need the element of surprise for now while our current boss is doing the whole diplomatic thing—not that it's done much good as far as I can see," the man stated and continued to twirl his blade carelessly. "But now, I'm a little mad that you keep shooting at me and I'm starting to take it personal."

Silas readied his weapon and Dred studied it for a moment. "Nice gun you have there. I thought only the military had all the good stuff," he said with a whistle of approval. The shotgun pulsed with a red light as he pulled the trigger slowly. "Pity about the damage on the body. It would fetch a nice price otherwise."

"I can't tell if you're a serial killer or a pirate," he retorted.

"I have many interests and as many vices too." The merc flipped his dagger in the air, caught it by the blade, and presented the side to his opponent. "You probably saw the tally on the blade, right? That's a little low, huh?" He smiled, let the blade fall, and grasped it by the hilt. "This one is new. I have two others on the ship, both marked up to fifty."

"Why do you knife and sword guys always have to say dumb shit about your weapons?" His aim remained steady. "Use them, why don't you?" He fired and Dred's shields took the hit but he immediately disappeared once again.

Silas placed his right foot forward and drew his gun back, prepared for a strike.

Dred chuckled. "Do me a favor and last at least a few minutes, won't ya?" His voice seemed to emanate from the entire room

"If you keep talking, you won't last one," he warned, a little concerned as to why he couldn't pick up anything on thermal. He knew it must be some kind of mod, but he should also pick up an energy reading if it was a stealth generator, so what the hell was going on?

Something thrust into his back and his shields ruptured to knock the attacker off him. He spun as Dred grunted and leaned forward. The enforcer prepared to counter when he charged but instead, the man smiled, slipped into the shadows, and seemed to melt into the wall behind him.

Hastily, he checked his sides but the merc was nowhere to be seen. In the next moment, the hanging light above him plummeted. He flung himself aside and glanced up when something flashed above him to sever the cords to all the lights around him.

"Ya can't figure it out, can ya?" Dred yelled as the last of the fittings shattered on the floor. Silas held his shotgun in one hand and slid his blade out. "With all your fancy tech, you can't respect the classics."

Something sliced into his side and he clenched his teeth and spun as he slashed with his blade, but to no effect. He removed three small orbs from his pouch, activated them, and threw them out. They flared to life and illuminated his surroundings seconds before Dred faded into a pillar. No, not the pillar, his brain corrected. The man vanished into the shadows themselves but his previous scornful comment triggered something now that he had a moment to think. Respect for the classics... He could have sworn he remembered a piece of tech Flynn had told him about. Then, it clicked into focus.

"I see your gimmick," he muttered and held his blade ready.

"It won't help you," Dred countered. The merc's blade cut cleanly into Silas' shoulder and blood sprayed onto the wall behind him and onto his face.

He fell back, yanked several rods from his belt, and tightened his grasp to break their casing. When they lit up, he threw them around him in a circular perimeter and stretched a hand to his belt for a grenade. Shit, he only had one, he realized. Well, he had to make it count, then.

"Do you think a few lights will help you?" his adversary questioned mockingly. "I guess you're looking for anything to help, aren't ya? But you can't run, not in here and not from me."

"What kind of things have you done with that blade to make you talk about it so lovingly?" Silas chided.

"What I've done to you. I've done it for years now," the man replied and again, his voice seemed to echo all around him.

The lights on the rods were bright but they wouldn't last too long. While they were still working, the area they illuminated would soon shrink. His safe zone had already decreased. He stumbled when something thumped into his arm and he scowled at an old gear on the ground, thrown from the darkness.

"So you're down to throwing trash?" he said, his tone edged with a challenge. "You can't fight me unless you're cloaked in darkness."

"Look who's talking about their happy place," Dred mocked. "But all right, have it your way."

Silas looked up to the only place his enemy could safely attack from. His intuition was right as the killer plunged toward him. The enforcer dropped his shotgun and stabbed above him with his own blade. Dred met the strike with his dagger and parried it deftly. The man landed and rolled and he tried to stab into his shoulder while he was distracted, but his adversary recovered quickly enough to sidestep it. The merc tried to cut him and he blocked hastily and the blade slid along the edge of his knife.

Dred pushed him off before he kneed him in the stomach and drove the hilt of his dagger into his temple. The enforcer fell heavily and grasped the gear before his attacker could thrust forward to deliver the final blow. He threw it hard and caught the Omega in the chest. The man toppled onto his knees and coughed as he tried to vanish once again.

"I got you now, Omega scum!" He snatched the grenade from his belt and lobbed it high. It detonated into a bright light and the merc shouted in surprise as the entire room lit up. Silas scrambled to his feet, his visor shaded, and surged forward into the attack. Dred, blinded, spun and raised his blade for a strike.

An agonized yell issued from the merc when the light flared brightly for a moment before it began to dim rapidly. He curled on the floor and held what was now the stump of a leg.

"Damn," Silas muttered and gaped at the pool of blade surrounding his opponent.

"What the hell did you do?" the man cried in rage and pain.

"It's a spark grenade. Some call it an artificial sun," Silas said casually. "I can see why."

"You cut my bleedin' foot off, you bastard!" he retorted angrily.

"And you want me to feel bad about that?" The enforcer glanced around for the severed appendage. "Weren't you talking about snuffing me?"

Dred continued to moan and curse and spat on Silas' boot. He repaid the act by stabbing him in one of his arms, which triggered another wave of insults. "I can keep this going, or you can buy yourself more time by telling me what your plans are."

The Omega rolled over and extended his hand, which held another blade. "To hell with you! I won't tell you a damn thing even if it costs me my life."

"I never said that was the deal," he pointed out and drew his heavy pistol. "I'll make it quicker if you tell me where they are making those golems."

In response, the man clenched his teeth and rolled over to finally reveal the device on the back of his belt. The shadow reflector was an old model of stealth generator that used special lighting to warp darkness and shadows to make the user almost invisible. "Sod off! You won't get me to talk and you won't catch me."

"It won't matter. You won't escape." With that, Silas fired several shots into Dred's body that was now partially in and out of the shadows. It slumped, motionless, and the raider lowered his weapon.

Satisfied with the result, he turned to locate his shotgun but paused to answer a call on his comm.

"Hello? Silas?" Cameron asked. "Are you dead yet?"

"Not quite. The other guy is, however." He winced when he tried to roll his shoulder and glanced at Dred's corpse "I tried to talk it out but it didn't go so well."

"Ah, shit. I guess that means we have to keep at least one of our guys?" The bounty hunter sighed.

"One of your— Are you guys all right?" He walked quickly to retrieve his shotgun. "You didn't run into any of those golems, did you?"

"No, we didn't. Not yet, anyway, and I'm not sure I want to," his teammate admitted.

"You really don't," he replied and holstered his weapon on his back. "They aren't hard to kill but damn if they aren't unsettling."

"Make sure to get pictures if you can. Maybe we can bring one of the bodies."

"I should have video of them, but I'm actually almost at the place where I —" When he approached the far side where he'd left the corpses, a terrible stench permeated the air and almost choked him, even with his helmet on. "God, what the hell is that?" He gaped at where the bodies of the ghouls should be but instead, there was nothing but the suits and murky puddles of a white liquid tinged with streaks of red. "Dammit."

"What's wrong?"

"I wanted to take a flesh sample, at least, but it doesn't look like I'll get even that much." Silas took a vial from his belt and fought to suppress his gag reflex as he scooped some of the liquid and capped the vial hastily.

"When we get these Omegas to base, do you wanna take a ship and head over to that lab we saw?" Cameron asked. "I checked my messages and it looks like the commander sent someone to take a look. We could back them up."

"If they already have someone on it, we should focus on continuing rescue efforts," Silas replied, but as he exited the room, a thought occurred to him. "Wait, Chancellor Sasha sent a message directly to us?" He opened his own messages and saw the one Cameron had mentioned. "He would usually send a message to the outpost and they would tell us. It makes me wonder—"

"Who is going to the lab?" the bounty hunter interjected. "Do you wanna take a guess?"

Silas didn't have to guess as he read to the bottom of the message. "Okay, a change of plans. It's been a while since we've worked together with him."

CHAPTER NINE

"This ship is cramped," Kaiden muttered as he adjusted his seat. They currently crossed Californian skies but not in Wolfson's drop ship or any other for that matter. Instead, they used a two-seat fighter craft, a Corsair model on loan from one of Julio's acquaintances and one of a number of ships they borrowed from or through their friend and contact.

"This ship was built with two pilots wearing G-suits in mind," Wolfson said and thumped the chest of his armor a couple of times. "Not two soldiers in full gear."

"And the reason Haldt had to take your ship and we couldn't?" The ace shifted one leg against the side of the wall in an effort to adjust his position. "There were numerous Nexus shuttles available. I don't see why it had to be yours."

"None of the armed shuttles were available and I wouldn't send him and his team out with no guns," the head officer replied and checked one of the screens. "Not where they are going."

"They were headed to Chicago, right?" he asked Chief in a quieter tone.

"Yeah, and that was one of the places battered by Black Lake during the initial invasion," Chief stated. *"They had deaths in the five digits in only a week in the early stages of fighting. After evac and everything, the west side is mostly deserted except for the Omega Horde and other mercs out to make some quick cash courtesy of our new buddies."*

Kaiden clenched his teeth and restrained a growl when he thought of their enemy. "I think I liked the AO better when they were only a conspiracy." He sighed.

"Honestly, so did I," Wolfson agreed and pulled the ace out of his thoughts. "I'd much rather I was the crazy one, not the world."

The younger man looked out the window. The sun set on the horizon as they flew over a highway littered with abandoned vehicles. Wrecks of ships and buildings were visible too as if to reinforce the impression of utter devastation. "They don't have the whole planet, right? Some places have to have peace."

"I'm sure there are many. They've focused on the major cities but we're fighting to make sure they get no farther and to kick them back." Wolfson looked at him. "Right, boyo?"

He nodded grimly but before he could respond, he received a message. "Silas? He's the one who reported the lab in the first place, right?"

"Yeah," Chief said. *"I'll put him...huh, something is wrong. I have trouble holding a connection."*

"Kaid...we...can you..." Silas' voice came in clipped fragments and sounded quiet like he spoke at distance from his mic. The connection ended abruptly only seconds later.

"What's happening, Chief?" Kaiden asked as he straightened and retrieved his rifle. It was awkward in the cramped space but he'd rather have it in hand than be caught weaponless. He glanced at his companion, then looked around the cockpit. "There's a jammer or something nearby."

"I have a feeling similar to that distorter at the Academy," the EI explained.

"Ah, shit. Wolfson, how's the ship?" He squinted and tried to look at the console over the massive shoulder plate of the other soldier.

"Better than you would think it would be," the man muttered and tapped the various screens displayed. "There's definitely a dip in power and comms are out, but the disrupter was able to scuttle the entire island back then. We're not plummeting yet, though."

"It's certainly the same wave but it isn't as powerful... although I feel more of them the closer we get," Chief clarified. *"My guess would be they've made smaller versions, probably for portability and so they wouldn't be as easy to detect until you stumbled into their field."*

"Are you doing all right, Chief?" the ace asked, although he noticed his HUD had so far remained unaffected.

"Yeah, I'm good."

"Have you built a tolerance after having to deal with it a couple of times?"

"Nah...well, kinda. These are weaker, for one. But I learned how to counteract them by shifting my own channels. The waves work by essentially giving an electronic device what you could

describe as a nervous breakdown by— What's with that weird look?"

Kaiden shook his head. "Sorry, but you learned how to do this from where? Did Laurie have a chance to upgrade you before they jetted him out?"

"It's from Aurora's files," the EI answered. *"The ones he said he wanted us to look at since she was taken and I was now...well, the closest thing we had to a second option."*

"Ah, right." He sighed. "I guess the bright side is that you won't be all that easy to hack, huh?"

Chief's eye narrowed. *"It was believed she wouldn't be either."*

The ace slowly nodded and cradled his weapon closer to his chest. "True, but you can't be stolen so easily. You're a part of me, so unless they crack my skull open and dig out your chip—"

"Or they find a way to absorb me like they did her and you suddenly go brain-dead when the pathways I help to maintain suddenly give out."

An uncomfortable silence followed. This was an option he hadn't really given much thought to. "Stick around in here unless I say otherwise."

"That's the usual plan, partner."

"I'm losing more power," Wolfson stated. "We need to find a place to land as we're close now and will be in the Omega Horde's territory soon."

"We'll keep a lookout, then. Chief, is there any way you can help while our radar is on the fritz?"

"The most I can do right now is try to boost the radar's capabilities while we ride through the disruption waves. When I have

to switch my channels constantly, I can't access most of my fancier abilities."

Kaiden bit his lip in annoyance. "When we get on the ground, we need to try to destroy these things."

"I guess from all that mutterin', Chief can't help?" Wolfson asked.

The ace shifted to peer out the window. "He said he'll boost the radar which would hopefully broaden the range and keep it stable. But that's all he can do right now. Of course, that only matters as long as we have power."

"I think if we lose power, we'll have more to worry about than if the radar is working." The head officer chuckled. "Keep your eyes open, Kaiden. Make yourself useful and look for somewhere we might be able to land."

He leaned forward and peered below to see more destruction, this time of Oakland itself. Buildings lay shambles and a few fires trailed smoke. He noticed glints amongst the carnage and hoped it wasn't the lights of Arbiter droids.

"Before we get there, is there anything else you can tell me about this device we're supposed to retrieve?" Wolfson asked.

"Sasha sent you the briefing, didn't he?"

"I don't read and fly, boy," the man retorted. "Fill me in."

"You really are relying on my multitasking aren't you?" he said and moved his gaze from the landscape to the sky. "It's some kind of experimental energy drainer."

"A shield stripper?"

"From what I understand, it affects all kinds and completely nullifies power sources if you get it close enough.

But you're supposed to place it on barriers, and it will break through with ease. They were working on a function that would even allow it to control the flow of the energy, although I'm not quite sure what that is supposed to do. It's probably something Chiyo and Genos would have more use for."

"Still, even with the bare details, it sounds like something that would be better in our hands than theirs, yeah?"

Kaiden nodded as he focused on the skyscrapers in the distance. "I would say that every piece of tech is better in our— Wolfson, something is approaching."

"An Omega ship?" the man asked and glanced to the left of the cockpit. Both men located a small glowing light that moved rapidly toward their vessel.

"No— Shit, that's a missile!" the ace shouted and bracing himself as Wolfson immediately banked the craft in an evasive maneuver.

"There's no ship around so it must be from an anti-air launcher." The head officer moved to activate the boost but hesitated for a moment. "Dammit, do you think a boost would drain the energy we have?"

"Chief?"

"Probably. Let me in the system," the EI instructed.

"It's all yours. And Wolfson, serpentine!" The man responded immediately and jerked the vessel into a series of zig-zags. A loud pop behind them was followed by several hissing sounds. "What the hell is that?

"More projectiles—it's a cluster missile," Chief responded and appeared on the main monitor. *"Hit it, Wolfson. I can't promise to carry us far but it'll be far enough away from the missiles."*

"That's fine by me!" The pilot activated the boost and

Kaiden was thrust into the back of his seat when the Corsair cut through the sky. As it increased speed, however, it also began to descend slowly.

"Do we have a safe place to land?" the ace asked.

"We'll be lucky to find a place to land amongst all this rubble," Wolfson yelled.

"Would now be a bad time to mention the droids?"

"Droids?" both men exclaimed and twisted slightly to stare out the windows. A group of Arbiter droids was positioned in the distance and, it seemed, were already prepared to fire at the approaching ship.

"Dammit, Wolfson. Pull up or away or something."

The head officer didn't comply, however, and in fact, accelerated the craft even more. "You have all your gear on, right?" he asked and slid his hand to the ejection lever on the side of his chair as he pressed a button on the console. The roof detached and spun away.

Kaiden twisted hurriedly and snagged the case he had brought with them as Chief reappeared in his HUD. "I'm set."

"I'll give the call!" the head officer roared. Even with their helmets on and speaking through comms it was hard to be heard above the rushing wind. When they were only seconds from impact, the droids began to fire their cannons. "Now!" he bellowed

They both pulled their ejection levers and launched up and back as their ship spun out of control from the impacts of the plasma fire. It plowed into the enemy before they released a second volley and erupted in flames as the two men plummeted, neither having a parachute or jetpack.

CHAPTER TEN

Kaiden managed to flip to prepare to land as he continued to plunge closer to the earth.

"Shock mod activated," Chief informed him. *"Wolfson does have shocks in his armor too, right?"*

He thought about it and shook his head. "I don't know his specs but he damn well better. This was his idea."

"Then what is he doing over there?"

The ace managed to swivel a little to look at the security officer who appeared to have curled into himself. What looked like straps or locks connected at different points on his armor. "What the hell?"

Chief's eye widened in surprise. *"Oh, wow...that's...uh, a classic."*

"What's going on?" he asked as a light flashed in his HUD.

"Later. Focus on landing now," the EI advised.

The warning was well-timed and he sucked in a deep breath and relaxed his legs as he made impact. The ground beneath him shuddered, although he only felt a small jostle along his legs and back as the dampeners in the armor absorbed the tremendous impact. Wolfson, however, landed with a massive thump several yards away. Kaiden stood, adjusted his hold on the gear case, and pulled Sire off his back as he ran to the other man.

When he arrived at the crater, he gaped as the latches on Wolfson's armor uncoupled and the old soldier stretched with a flurry of quiet curses over the comms. "Wolfson, what the hell was that?"

"That was the old way of making emergency landings for heavies," the man muttered. "We called them comet drops back then."

"That's one way to look at it, I guess." He walked up and offered him a hand. "It looks like you're alive, though, and it only cost you your dignity."

"Shut the hell up, boy." The head officer grunted, took his hand, and allowed him to hoist him to his feet.

"I guess I should be quiet given that your landing probably alerted any hostile within ten miles." The ace chuckled, straightened, and looked around. They were in a residential area that seemed rather upmarket considering the area. The lab was visible in the distance and an oddly familiar logo as well. "Ramses? What the hell? I thought this was another company—Metta Labs or something."

Wolfson checked his shotgun before he turned his attention to the building. "It might have been bought out before the attack or maybe it's a different division. Who knows?"

"It's kind of odd to place it directly behind a residential neighborhood," he commented.

"Everyone around here probably works there—

company villas and all that. It was how this city became a powerhouse over the last century." The older man held his weapon ready and nodded toward the building. "Come on, lad. This area is probably about to crawl with droids or those Horde lackeys. Let's move while we still have breathing space."

"Hold up. I need to dump this before we head out." Kaiden dropped the case at his feet and opened it to reveal ammo, grenades, different gadgets, and tools. "Take what you can. We'll have to blow the rest."

"It seems a waste." The security officer grunted disapproval, although he did take a couple of containers of grenades along with a few gadgets and different ammo cartridges for his weapon. "Were we supposed to keep the rest in the ship?"

"Yeah. It's not an option anymore, is it now?" he quipped in response and glanced over his shoulder at the fire that still burned. He turned and began to remove different explosives and shield batteries for his armor. All in all, they were able to make use of most of the case, but there was still almost a third of the gear left. Wolfson selected a large explosive and placed it on top of the others that remained.

The sound of an approaching ship caught Kaiden's attention. "Wolfson, there is a patrol coming this way."

The man looked nonchalantly at the small shuttle that hovered slowly over the neighborhood and swept the area with searchlights. He held his shotgun out. "Hold this for a second." Kaiden did so and the security officer shut the container and took it in both hands before he walked up the street. As the ship drew closer, he began to spin with the case held out, then released it with perfect timing to hurl it directly into the ship. It didn't break through the shuttle's cockpit glass but did embed itself into it. He was swept by the beam of a spotlight almost immediately but simply held a trigger up and pressed the switch. The case erupted and the explosion swallowed the front half of the craft. The remaining section crashed into the street behind him as he walked to his teammate.

"You know, I planned to ask if we should focus on stealth this time around," Kaiden quipped as he held the shotgun out for Wolfson to take.

The officer shook his head. "I'm sure they know we're here anyway so there's no need to be too coy." He rested the shotgun over his shoulder and stared at the lab in the distance. "Besides, you wanted a mission so you could blow off steam, right?"

Kaiden smiled when he caught a glint in the shadows of the second story in a house behind Wolfson. He flipped a switch on Sire to narrow the barrel, aimed carefully, and fired a single laser bolt instead of a charged orb. A brief flare indicated that he'd found his target before the top half of a droid toppled out of the window with a hole in the left side of its head.

"More droids?" his companion muttered. "I'd hoped for something more substantial."

"You'll get quantity if not quality," Chief warned through their comms. *"I have several readings within fifty meters. I can't reach as far as usual right now but I'm sure there are more coming."*

The head officer nodded to Kaiden and both jogged down the street. "You'd best keep a tally, boyo!" he jeered.

"I'm already one up. Are you sure about that?" he retorted.

Wolfson swapped his shotgun for his launcher and loaded it with a thermal. A little farther ahead, a small group of droids either sprinted around the corner or leapt on top of the roof of the house at the end of the street. The large man took aim and fired at the edge of the structure. The resultant blast not only eliminated the droids on the roof but caused the side of the building to collapse on those below.

"I think that was about five," he estimated and loaded another thermal. "Not counting the shuttle, of course. You shouldn't get so cocky about a little lead that actually isn't one."

The ace frowned and was about to respond when Chief pointed out two droids in the distance that vaulted between rooftops. He took aim and fired two shots to catch them both in midair and followed the slow tumble of their bodies through his scope. "You should take your own advice, big guy."

The head officer chortled, held his launcher in one hand, and drew his shotgun to hold it in the other. "Don't dawdle and try to bolster your score. We have a mission to complete." A bolt seared from behind and pounded into him, but the soldier's shields and heavy armor were barely affected and he merely aimed his shotgun behind him and fired several shots. "You have ten minutes to reach the lab."

"And you want to talk speed while you're wearing all that?" Kaiden questioned.

Wolfson nodded. "I know I can make it despite my armor." He glanced back at two droids now full of holes and out of the equation. "So you have no excuse. That makes seven, by the way."

The ace flipped the switch on his rifle to revert it to charged mode. "I'll get there in five," he challenged and pushed forward, his speed augmented by his armor. His companion smiled. It was good to see a little spirit in the boy again. But when he glanced at the lab ahead, a small ship now hovered over the roof and several figures exited. Shit, his teammate probably won't notice them now that he was all twitchy and he cursed briefly when he realized he should have considered that.

Several shots thudded into the back of his armor and he turned swiftly. A number of Scarab droids crawled along the ground and the side of houses toward him. He sighed and aimed the launcher at them. While he wanted to enjoy this, he now had to make sure to catch up with Kaiden before he did something too stupid.

Ah well, he'll still enjoy this brief moment, at least. He pulled the trigger and the thermal struck the street and exploded to destroy most of the Scarabs and scatter the remainder before he turned away and pushed into a brisk jog toward the lab.

CHAPTER ELEVEN

"Where the hell is he?" Kaiden growled his irritation and drove his armored boot down on the destroyed droid's head for the third time. "He said he would have no problem getting here in ten minutes and it's been fifteen." He kicked the scraps of metal away and scowled at the building. "I wonder how long it'll take to find this—wait, do you think he died? Can you find him, Chief?"

"He's not dead, only slow," the EI answered. *"Pipe down for a moment, would ya? I'm trying to do something."*

The ace studied the building through his scope to see if he could see anyone through the windows. "What would this something be?"

"There's some kind of connection device nearby. I think it might be linked to the disruptors as it emits a frequency similar to the waves to counteract them. I've almost...got it... There!"

His HUD cleared a little and he noticed that he suddenly felt lighter as well. "Huh. Did you stop those disruptors?"

"Only the ones nearby, at least for now. Someone could probably flip a switch and change that."

"Why does that affect my armor? I thought you said you found a way around it?"

Chief rolled his eye. *"I had to make sure I didn't short out and I told you I wasn't operating at my peak. Now that I am, can calibrate your armor systems like normal."*

"Ah, thank Christ!" Wolfson exclaimed as he lumbered over to him. "I'm finally back to normal."

"Back to normal?" Kaiden asked. "Where have you been? Does this explain why you're late?"

"I've tried to make contact for the last several minutes. My weight distribution mod suddenly gave out," the officer explained, his voice somewhat weary, and drew deep breaths as he put his launcher away. "I had to…haul this armor along through sheer will."

"Isn't all that stuff like a few hundred pounds?" the ace asked. "All right, I can see why you might have lagged behind."

"Those disruption signals were picking up strength so might have actually become a real problem if I wasn't able to shut them down."

"It was certainly a neat trick," he admitted and scanned the grounds outside the lab. "I don't see this device you mentioned."

"It's inside the building, about seven floors up. My guess is it's in the lab where our device is."

"And you can access it from out here?" He was actually quite impressed. "Well, I'm glad you're putting those Aurora notes to use."

"One of us has to keep us alive, right?" Chief retorted.

Kaiden shook his head and grasped his rifle in both hands. "Smart-ass." He began to move forward and craned his neck to look at Wolfson. "Let's head inside."

The giant nodded and rolled his shoulders. "Yeah, right. I'm...uh, catching my breath." He caught up and placed a hand on the younger man's shoulder. "One thing, Kaiden—did you see the shuttle dropping soldiers?"

"What shuttle?" he asked. "I haven't seen any ships since you blew that one out of the sky earlier."

"I thought as much." The head officer held his weapon ready as he walked passed him. "Stay close. There's at least one enemy squad running through here."

The two approached a door at the back of the facility. Wolfson held an arm out and looked at Kaiden, who nodded. The large man shattered the barrier with a single blow and his teammate whipped forward to take point, entered quickly, and his gaze swept the interior. It was dark inside but appeared relatively undamaged thus far. "They must have cut the power or have control of the systems," Kaiden muttered as a thought occurred to him. "Hey, Chief, do you think you could—"

"I already thought of it," the EI answered. "I'm still working through it all, but they never relocked the system so I have easy access."

"Can we get some light?" he asked and a few small lights in the hallway turned on. "All right, how about internal defenses? Are there any bots or gates we can use?"

"It looks like there might be some—ah, hell, get down!" The lights above them grew brighter and hotter before they

erupted. More lights activated and did the same throughout the hall. Sizzles, crackles, and buzzes followed in rapid succession as numerous machines shorted out through the building around and above them.

"What's going on?" Wolfson shouted and scanned their surroundings with his shotgun at the ready. Sparks and glass cascaded off his armor.

"Someone overloaded the central power and blew almost everything connected to it, my guess is to expunge me from the systems" Chief explained. *"It's fairly rudimentary, but I sure as hell ain't in the system anymore."*

"It means they know we're here then," Kaiden reasoned and hefted his rifle. "Stay alert. Chief, lead us to the—"

A little farther ahead down the hall, the roof caved in and a heavily armored soldier fell through. The two teammates prepared to fire as the man stood, wearing bulky red-and-black armor with a domed helmet, and aimed a cannon at them.

"Bastard!" Wolfson shouted but the ace held him back as he retrieved a shield emitter, pressed the switch, and threw it. The barrier expanded to fit against the walls on either side. The enemy heavy fired and an orb of red light careened forward and broke the shield.

The head officer held his arm out and his plasma ax slid from the bottom of his gauntlet and into his hand. He swung quickly and threw the weapon at the merc. It sliced not only into his chest but also gouged the cannon on its way and a red gas-like emission flowed out of the gash. The heavy ripped the ax out of his armor but when he saw the damage to his cannon, he tried to drop his weapon and back away. An explosion of red plasma obliterated his section of the corridor and catapulted the man back and out of the building.

"Let's get moving before we're cornered by more—" Several shots, both kinetic and energy, streaked out of the dust and red clouds. Kaiden ducked and returned fire. "Do these assholes only show up when I mention them?"

"Up the stairs!" Chief ordered. The two men walked backward while they fired at the four enemy soldiers who stepped out of the smoke and dust. All wore the Omega Horde black and red colors.

The ace was the first to head up and he opened a pouch on his belt to remove four small disks. "Sync in, Chief."

"Already done," the EI acknowledged.

He tossed them along the walls and stairway. Wolfson followed hard on his heels and readied his launcher, although Kaiden stopped him from firing. "Lure them up," he shouted to the officer.

The man looked at the disks, nodded, and vented his shotgun once he'd put his launcher away again. "Come and get me, you kronidiots!" he bellowed and thumped his chest as he ran up the stairs.

They reached the next floor and the ace identified two silhouettes in his HUD beneath them. "Hit it, Chief!"

The two teammates were almost toppled by the blast but the mercs met their end when the stairs behind them shattered and gave way.

"That got 'em." Chief chuckled, although his eye shrank quickly in surprise. *"Or two of them at least. I still read at least four more, and worse news is that there's an enemy ship on the way."*

"Fucking fantastic," the ace bemoaned, although Wolfson clapped him on the shoulder.

"It is fantastic!" he bellowed. "We need a ship, after all."

He nodded as he thought it over. "Do you think you can take it while I get the device?"

The giant nodded, thumped his shoulder, and walked away. "You have ten minutes," he said cheerfully.

CHAPTER TWELVE

He inched his hands into the container and lifted the device slowly out of the box. His role had begun even before the others arrived and he'd already spent more than a week trying to bypass the vault. They now drove the enemy forces back while he focused on breaking through the final lock, but they had their objective.

When the device was secured in his case, he closed it and took it with him out of the vault. He sent a message to the pilot that they were ready to leave. His smile faded, however, when he heard two shots followed by the distinctive clank of metal as the two droids stationed outside collapsed. They were honestly useless, he thought for not the first time.

Without hesitation, he approached a group of machines, slipped the case between two of them, and looked around him for a perch. Normal protocol was to alert the pilot that there would be a delay, but he wouldn't be long.

Kaiden pushed the door open cautiously, checked the room, and immediately noticed that the lab was unlike the rest of the building, which had been largely undamaged. Whatever the reason for that, it did not extend to the main laboratory. Pieces of the wall were ripped out or cracked and many of the machines were also torn apart or battered.

"I guess it took them a while to find it," Chief commented as he studied the destruction.

"It looks more like they came here to loot than to retrieve a single device," the ace stated and grimaced when the floor beneath him groaned as he walked over the scattered debris, rubble, and parts. He reached a large door which he assumed was a vault. Several machines, laser drills, and claws lay abandoned beside it. They had obviously spent considerable time accessing the secure area. Ordinarily, he would have no objection to the fact that the enemy had done all the work while he retrieved what he came for. This time, however, there was a slight problem. One glance confirmed that the vault was almost empty. He noticed a cube-like container in the center and scowled. It was open and when he checked inside, it was empty.

"Ah, hell, did they take it already?" he asked and shoved the container onto its side in frustration.

"Hold on a moment, Kaiden. There's a signal coming off the box," Chief warned.

"Signal?"

"A silent alarm sending out a message. I can pick it up...it's an alert that it was opened without authorization. But it was only a couple of minutes ago. Right before we came in, actually."

"So unless the guy who took it can teleport—" Kaiden held his rifle ready as he exited the vault. "He should still be in he—"

Chief's eye enlarged rapidly in surprise. *"Kaiden, roll —now!"*

The ace immediately complied and rolled behind a console as two shots struck the floor behind him. "A sniper?" he asked and huddled against his temporary defense as he pressed the switch on his rifle and held the trigger to charge a shot.

"He has a damn good stealth generator too. That's why I didn't detect him. I only picked up the energy from his rifle when he was about to shoot," Chief explained. "Get moving. He's trying something. I'm picking up a spike."

He pushed himself away from the console and darted across the laboratory floor as the sniper fired at his previous position. A visible blue light streaked from the top of a large machine, which identified his attacker's position. When the man fired, however, the shot struck the floor and erupted. A wave of energy cascaded to hurl Kaiden off his feet and his shot rocked toward the foot of the machine. It blasted the edge, tipped it, and forced the sniper out of his perch. The man became more visible as he leapt from the machine to the floor.

"What the hell was that?" the ace asked as he pushed to his feet and pressed the trigger of his rifle. "A nova bullet?"

"These guys are outfitted well, at least," Chief muttered. *"I had a glimpse of our shooter and it looks like he's using a Dybbuk model generator. It works best when you're still but can't keep it up in motion. If nothing else, blow the place apart."*

"I can work with that plan." He dug out a few more

explosive disks. "Where did you last see him?" Chief displayed an arrow on the HUD that pointed to a corner. He raised Sire and fired and the sniper darted out of the way and attempted a shot while in mid-air. Kaiden whipped around, dodged the shot, and tossed the disks to scatter them in different directions. "Blow them, Chief!" he ordered.

The explosions were small but covered a wide area between the several he had thrown. When he saw a figure enveloped in the smoke of the blast, he fired Sire but instead of striking the target, the marksman threw a small orb to meet the blast. A cloud of orange gas erupted, blinding Kaiden. "Dammit!"

"Kaiden, fall back!" Chief shouted. *"This guy isn't simply some random merc."*

A loud bang was immediately followed by a solid thump of something into his helmet. He fell back, his visor cracked, and a partial warning popped up to warn him of impact to the skull. As he forced himself up, he dropped Sire and fumbled for one of the shield batteries on his belt.

"Keep your head down, Kaiden. You're exposed!"

He knew that, but more importantly, he would have to abandon his helmet as he could no longer see clearly through his visor. First, though he needed to get this gas away from him in case it was poisonous. He tossed the shield battery up, drew Debonair, and fired at it. The explosion wasn't lethal but the shield energy erupted in a sphere, scattered the gas, and hopefully, pushed the sniper back, even if only a little.

The ace unlatched his helmet and discarded it. A swirl of gas contorted around an object that wasn't visible to his left and he instinctively dropped to one knee and fired several shots. The sniper's cloak dropped as his light shield was destroyed and Debonair's shots burned into his armor.

Kaiden retrieved one of his last two disks and prepared to throw it. The marksman came out of his stupor and stared at him, and in a low, droning voice, he muttered. "Kaiden?"

This caused the ace a moment of hesitation. Even with that almost disembodied tone, it sounded like a call of familiarity, not like someone identifying a target or person of interest. But in the next moment, the man shook his head and raised his rifle with one arm. The ace reacted quickly and tossed the disc as he fired. The eruption engulfed them both.

CHAPTER THIRTEEN

Wolfson sprinted up the stairs, the four remaining enemy soldiers hot on his trail. He had almost reached the top and needed only a few more minutes, he told himself as he clutched the container of thermals on his belt. Only a few more would do it. His pace rhythmic and measured, he continued the ascent to the next floor as he closed the vent on his gun and held it aloft, then pushed on to the ninth and top floor.

He pressed the switch and hurled the container of thermals down the steps as he pushed toward the roof access. They detonated but he had no way to confirm any deaths right now. It would be better to get the ship and get out than stay and let them regroup or call reinforcements.

The door to the roof gave in to his single kick. He sprinted over to the landing pad but stopped in bewilderment when the expected craft was nowhere to be seen. Anger and confusion surged over him. He had seen them land there but the shuttle appeared to have vanished. Was it simply patrolling the skies and waiting for a call? Maybe the pilot saw the fighting and left? It wasn't exactly professional, but he wouldn't put it past these honorless bastards.

As he turned to retrace his path to the stairs, an odd whoosh behind him made him whirl in alarm. The shuttle banked sharply to face in his direction. For a moment, he wondered if the bastards had come for him simply because he thought about them. While he did feel a brief moment of satisfaction at the fact that he hadn't imagined the vessel, it quickly vanished when it aimed its guns at him.

The head officer flung himself off the landing pad as the craft opened fire. He landed heavily and a spray of large kinetic rounds punctured the roof and landing pad. With a string of colorful curses, he pushed to his feet and held his left gauntlet up to activate the personal shield emitter and generate a large rectangular shield in front of him to intercept the assault.

He was able to walk himself back and found shelter behind a cooling tower. The shuttle drifted to the side to gain time for its guns to cool. Wolfson planted his shield, detached the emitter from his gauntlet, and hunkered behind it as he ran a hasty weapons check. He had his shotgun, his launcher, one more ax, one shield spike, and a container of shock grenades. It felt like a damn waste now to have used his last container of thermals on the pursuing soldiers.

The ship fired at him again and he studied it quickly, knowing his shield was on its last legs. He recognized the model, which appeared to be a Mako although painted and modified somewhat. If he could get under it, his shotgun should have enough punching power to destroy the balance drive beneath. That would cause the pilot to lose control and crash, hopefully on the ground below instead of on top of him.

It would also mean they would have to find another mode of transport out of there, but that seemed moot. This shuttle wasn't much of an option now, anyway. He unlatched his shoulder pads from his armor along with his gauntlets, leg guards, and chest plate. For what he had planned, he would need speed and had to take the risk.

Wolfson loaded his launcher with three shock grenades. He holstered his shotgun and took his second ax out, then drew a deep breath as his shield broke and the firing stopped. His mind worked quickly to determine that he had to get the craft back to the landing pad as he would need the height.

He broke cover from behind the tower and raced along the roof as the ship pursued him. Without slowing, he fired one of the shock grenades behind him, more to confuse or anger the pilot than damage the ship. He reached the landing pad and confirmed that the shuttle continued its approach. Calmly, he retrieved the spike and drove it into the ground to cover himself in a domed shield. In perfect alignment with his plan, the shuttle passed overhead.

The vessel spun to fire on the stationary target, but Wolfson raced beyond his shield and fired both remaining shock grenades at it before he flung the launcher to the side. The shocks struck forcefully and stalled the craft temporarily while the guns seized. The pilot attempted to force it to move as the head officer pushed into a sprint. Once he reached the edge of the landing platform, he vaulted as high as he could and raised his ax over his head as he fell from his arc toward the front of the ship. The pilot regained control and pulled up, but the ax blade sank into the metal.

He held on as the pilot whipped the craft in an effort to dislodge him. Wolfson drew his shotgun with his free hand and located the rectangular compartment that housed the balance drive. He fired once and the plating was blown free. The ax slipped a little but retained its hold as he aimed again and fired and blasted the drive completely off.

The recoil from the shotgun's second shot was enough to thrust him free. He fell about fifteen feet and barely out of reach of the edge of the roof. Fortunately, he'd managed to retain the ax and he swung it again, embedded the blade in the rooftop, and hauled himself up. Behind him, the shuttle spiraled out of control. The pilot seemed to attempt an escape but the ship spun too quickly and instead of a clean jump, he was thrown out of the side door as soon as he opened it and had no opportunity to activate his bounce pack on the way down.

The head officer climbed stiffly to his feet, grunted, and rolled his shoulders. He had begun to feel his age over the last few weeks and while it wouldn't stop him, it certainly made the missions more of a pain.

Three soldiers drew his attention as they barreled out of the door leading to the roof. *Damn, they're persistent.* He scowled belligerently

Wolfson readied his ax and shotgun. If they didn't have the good manners to die in the explosion, he'd make them regret their rudeness. He surged forward, his weapons ready, and one of his adversaries responded quickly to swing his rifle toward him.

The enemy soldier yelled in surprise a split-second

before he was obliterated by a large blast. Equally startled, the head officer darted to the side and glanced over his shoulder at a shuttle that approached while it fired at his adversaries. As it drew closer, the Nexus logo confirmed that the new arrivals were reinforcements. The side door opened and two soldiers—one in medium armor the other in heavy—jumped out and onto the roof.

"Officer Wolfson?" Silas asked.

"Aye!" he shouted merrily and rested his ax over his shoulder. "Not to sound ungrateful, but what brings you here?"

"We tried messaging Kaiden earlier but couldn't get through," the younger man replied. "I assumed something must have happened and am glad it wasn't as bad as I expected. We only picked up your signal a few minutes ago."

"We had interference. You boys came at a good time, though."

"It seems to me we came at a bad time." Mack chuckled. "By the looks of it, there's no more fun to be had."

"I don't know about that," Wolfson confessed and lowered his ax to rest it on the ground. "Kaiden still hasn't made contact with me and it's well past ten minutes."

CHAPTER FOURTEEN

Kaiden coughed as he tried to expel the smoke in his lungs. He moved his hand instinctively to his face when a burning pain traced along the bottom of his neck to his left cheek. "What a bastard!" he muttered belligerently as he stood clumsily. "I have all my limbs, right?"

"Yep, all five," Chief announced.

He checked his arms and legs. "I thought it was only four?"

"I would also count your d—" A gurgled, wheezing noise interrupted him. He picked Debonair up and waved the smoke and dust out of his face. The sniper hobbled painfully a few yards away and looked far worse than he did. Most of his upper armor was shattered and the right half of his helmet was gone to reveal a pale, fleshy, and grotesque but familiar visage.

"A golem," he exclaimed in a low tone and aimed his weapon. "It kind of pisses me off that this one gave me so much trouble."

"Hold up a second, partner," Chief cautioned.

The ace eased the pressure on the trigger but didn't aim the gun away. "What? It's dazed or something. Let's finish it off."

"We still need the device, right?" the EI reminded him. *"And those golems are controlled remotely—they're basically fleshy robots. I'll see if I can get into it and locate the device, then sever his connection. Kill two birds and all that."*

Kaiden frowned but acquiesced and lowered his pistol. "Fine, that's a good point. We might as well give it a shot."

"Good man," Chief responded cheerfully. *"Give me a minute."*

Although he nodded, he retained Debonair's readiness, especially when the golem glanced occasionally at him and simply stared. The blank, white eyes unnerved him, but he was too cautious to look away.

"Chief, could you hurry and either find the device or let me shoot this thing? It's creepy." He walked to the side and the golem watched his every step.

"Kaiden, I know who is controlling this golem." Chief's voice had lost its brightness and was now replaced by a disturbing grimness.

"What do you mean, who is controlling this? I thought they were controlled by a program or something," he reminded him. "Unless it was like the golems Nexus tried to use, but that required the Animus or an EI connection didn't it?"

"Exactly. Kaiden, this is Flynn."

"What?" He immediately strode up to it but it didn't move to walk away or even try to attack. Instead, it simply continued to stare as he grasped its shoulders. "This thing is Flynn?"

"No. Flynn is controlling the golem, Kaiden. I'm in its chip and the code in here is an EI pattern—specifically, Jeeves' EI pattern."

"Flynn's EI," he whispered. "If this is Flynn, why did he attack us? Are they forcing him?"

"Obviously, there are directives and other programs in here. He doesn't have complete control. Memories and personal thoughts are being blocked. They are manipulating him to fight, probably along with every student they have."

The ace released the golem and walked away for a moment to collect his thoughts. "So when he said my name it was because he recognized me, right?"

"If only for a moment," he explained. *"Like when there is a hole in a firewall, it is found and patched. He may have recognized you, but as long as he's connected into—"*

"Then disconnect him!" he ordered. "He'll know it's me then, right?"

"Kaiden. I only have partial access. They could pull the plug at any second."

"We were gonna sever it anyway. If I can talk for a couple of minutes, it's worth it."

Chief's avatar appeared in his vision and he nodded before he drifted to Flynn. *"All right. I don't mean to twist the knife, partner, but remember to make it quick. I'm not sure what his mental state will be."*

The EI disappeared and the golem collapsed. Kaiden hurried toward it. "Chief, what happened?" he asked and knelt beside the slumped figure. "Did it work? Chief?" The golem's eyes closed, then opened. "Flynn?"

"Kai?" it responded and dragged in ragged, pained

gasps. Even with its bland, emotionless voice, he detected a hint of the Australian accent of his friend.

"Flynn! I'm here. Are you okay?" he asked and supported the almost dead weight against him.

The golem wheezed, placed an arm against the ace's chest, and pushed him back weakly. "You have to get out, Kaiden…a bomb."

"A bomb?"

It nodded slowly. "Meant to destroy the base when we left…they can still detonate it remotely. You have to go…" It pointed behind them to a group of machines. "The draining device is in a case over there…have to break the lock…take it and go."

He nodded. "They still have you on the ship, right? We'll come—"

"Kaiden, don't say anything," Chief warned. *"They can still comb through the memories. I severed control."*

Kaiden bit his lip but nodded. "We'll save you, all right?"

The golem nodded again and managed a small smile. "I look forward to it, mate." The body twitched and its arms spasmed for a moment. He released his hold as it shriveled in the armor and the skin turned ashen before it crumbled.

"All right, he's flushed," the technician said. "I wonder what disrupted the connection."

"I don't know, but the other golems are dead as well and I can't reach any of the Omega Horde squad members." The lead technician huffed his frustration. "It's best to play it safe, contact one of the outpost leaders in the area, and have them blow the building. The bomb should be set, at least."

"A bomb?" Wolfson asked over the comms and directed Silas and Mack up the stairs. "Did Chief pick it up?"

"No, it was— Look it's complicated right now. You have the ship, right?" Kaiden asked, snagged the case Flynn had told him about, and headed to the door. He retrieved Sire from the floor along the way.

"Actually, your pals handled that," the head officer said as they ascended to the roof. "They came looking for us after their call didn't connect. Nice of them, wasn't it?"

"I'll thank them in person when I get to ya," he promised. "Now, hurry. They can detonate the bomb remotely so I don't think we have much—" He was cut off as a large explosion rocked the building from below. "Shit!"

"Get to the shuttle!" Wolfson shouted. "Kaiden, get out of the building!"

"Yeah, Wolfson, that's the plan. I like living," he yelled and sprinted down the hall while the floor shuddered and walls crumbled. He drew Debonair and fired at the window at the end of the hall, shattered the glass, and shielded his face with the case as he launched himself out seconds before the building collapsed behind him.

"Your shocks aren't exactly in a great condition after being blown around in that fight," Chief warned. *"Try to make a good landing."*

"We're coming for you, Kaiden," Silas shouted and the ace twisted in mid-air to locate the ship that descended toward him. It would be close, he realized, retrieved another shield battery, and threw it far enough to blast it. The force hurled him a few dozen feet upward. He flipped so his feet were pointed at the ground and when the ship flew under him, he landed on the top and clutched the lever for the hatch as they accelerated away from the destruction.

"Are you all right, boyo?" Wolfson asked as the vessel slowed once they were at a safe distance. The ace pulled the lever and opened the hatch to drop into the shuttle where he was greeted by Mack, Cameron, and Luke.

"Nice of you to drop in, Kai!" Luke laughed and clapped him on the back. "A job well done?"

"That was a tough landing there, amigo." Cameron chuckled and glanced at the box Kaiden held. "All that for a little gadget? Was it worth it?"

He nodded, looked at the prize, and thought of Flynn and all the students still locked away in the AO's hands. "Yeah. If it will get us on that ship, it was definitely worth it."

CHAPTER FIFTEEN

"While I have to commend your tenacity, Ambassador," Merrick said, and the clear agitation in his voice let the Korean ambassador know what he would say next. "You're trying my patience."

"As I imagine most of my fellow ambassadors have done," she retorted. "I will not be the first to break."

"This isn't an interrogation," he snapped and pounded a fist on the table. He trembled slightly but composed himself quickly. "I am not trying to break you or anyone else here."

She pushed to her feet and glared daggers at the Arbiter Organization leader despite the fact that the Omega Horde guards reached their hands to their sidearms. "You have kept us trapped here for months. You attack any vessel that attempts to come close to the embassy and you shut the gates. The Tsuna, Mirus, and Sauren will declare war if they cannot contact their delegates."

"And how soon do you think they can get here without the gates operational?" he asked, although it seemed to be more of a rhetorical question he asked out loud as much to himself as her. "It matters not. They are of more use to us remaining on their planets. They will buy us time."

"To fight this threat you constantly prattle on about?" she demanded. "You have not given me a straight answer. From what I've heard, you haven't given anyone a straight answer on what this threat is. Is it so much worse than a madman leading a cabal to take control of our planet? To attempt to upend the government we have spent more than a century putting in place? For nothing more than a vision?"

"It wasn't a vision." Merrick slid slowly into his chair. His hand covered his face and one eye peered at her from between his pointer and middle finger. It narrowed in frustration, but for brief spurts, it would widen in truly terrified recollection. "It was a warning. Whether a beast we are unaware of or an invading force not even the other aliens know about, they will come." He lowered his hand slowly and he stared at the ambassador, his lips pursed. "You say you won't be the first to break? I'm not asking for simple submission. Be the first among you to show wisdom."

She closed her eyes and drew a deep breath before she sat once again. "Only if you first show sanity, Merrick. You obviously still have intelligence—you could not accomplish all this otherwise—but you are not well. You need help—"

"I am well aware of that. What do you think I have tried to convince you of all this time?" he retorted and his features settled into their usual calm. "I do need help—the help of this entire species. At one particular point in our history, I would not have run into such resistance as I have thus far."

The ambassador uttered a sound that was somewhere between a disgusted growl and a disbelieving laugh. "No matter how turbulent our history is as a species, I cannot think of any point in time where the leaders would roll over for a would-be megalomaniac dictator who uses anarchic prophecy to try to convince us that his cause is righteous. The people of Terra would certainly not."

Something changed in the Arbiter leader's demeanor after she mentioned that and it went from pensive, to calm, to an oddly thoughtful look. He nodded slowly, stood, and tapped a finger on the edge of the conference table. "I suggested that I would not have such a difficult time convincing others that aliens are a threat. In fact, the infrastructure that led to the Ark Academies was put in place because of that very concern."

"We will not make progress being xenophobic, Merrick," she snapped.

He held a hand up to stop her. "I do not fear or hate our alien allies but they are not my concern. You believe that I am simply here as an attempted usurper. I am trying to make sure there is something—a form of life—left in this universe once it comes."

The ambassador rubbed her temple. "You have no proof of this...thing, Merrick. I cannot be the only one who has reminded you of that. And if you truly believed it to be as terrifying as you say, we should be working together to take it on."

"We are the only thing that can stop it," he stated flatly as nothing more than fact.

Now, it was the ambassador who slammed her fists down. "And why is that? Because of another of your visions? I would have thought someone of your pedigree would understand how to debate. You do nothing but—"

"We still have the most room to adapt and evolve," Merrick continued and simply brushed her protest aside. "The Animus has proved that. The Mirus—I heard they were considered the most advanced of the races—die if they try to use it. The Sauren are incapable as well and can't even establish a link. Despite being a space-faring people, they are brutish at heart." He walked around the table and focused on the ceiling as he continued in a nonchalant tone. "The Tsuna have made strides but they do not gain synapse at the rate human students do, and all progress on better integration with the Animus has stalled, hasn't it?"

She followed his movement and turned her head slowly as he moved closer. "And what is your point? You send those students out right now as soldiers and not even under their own control. You have stripped them of their will and made them no better than husks. Is that how you see the army of the future? You obviously have an army of machines, so use them. Or can you not see value in your soldiers unless you see a battlefield mired in blood?"

The man rounded the corner of the table and clasped his hands together as he stopped only a few feet from her. "The army I see is undefeatable, a perfect militia of potentially millions who are all physically and mentally perfect. The ones we have now...well, they are a regrettable compromise. I want them to know what they are doing, what and who they fight for. I do not see them as simple tools. I see no one like that. If I did, why would I fight so hard to save humanity? That is why I reach out to you—to all the ambassadors. With the world council gone, you stand as the representatives of your people. We can begin to centralize our society even further and hold it together by our might, not through niceties and vague promises. In time, I can show you what we can truly achieve with everything in place."

Although she did not respond, Merrick could tell from her scowl that she still did not approve. He sighed and motioned to one of the guards. "Well, perhaps I have been too lenient. You were right about one of my actions, Ambassador. The people of Terra will not forgive me." The Omega merc stepped forward and brandished a pistol, and her eyes widened in shock. "But no dead person can forgive me or scorn me regardless."

The guard fired before she could even protest or voice one more insult. She toppled off the chair and he sighed. "The reality of the situation is that even with all my games and resources, I truly don't have the might needed to take this world by force. At least not right now, but I'm sure you were aware of that as many of your colleagues are too." The executioner signaled for others to remove the corpse. "It is easier to start a new regime with established and knowledgeable candidates. I had hoped that at least a few could see reason. But perhaps I have been too inviting, too kind, and some of you have seen that as weakness and exploited it. I did not give the council the same benefit because I knew of their games. They were beyond redemption. I had hoped for better here. At least in my former time as a member, there seemed to be more honor. It appears that may be lost."

He paused as the door to the room opened for two guards to exit with the body. "Make sure to keep a DNA sample in case we need access to any systems of hers. There's a chute down the hall that leads to the incinerator. Leave nothing behind."

They nodded. "Understood, sir," one acknowledged as the door closed to leave Merrick alone. He sat in the ambassador's former chair and glanced at her blood on the surface. He leaned his head back and wondered how long it would take the other ambassadors, delegates, and various embassy staff to realize she was gone and that his patience was now thin. His eyes closed. He had talked to these various ambassadors one on one for the last couple of weeks between delegating the issues that needed attention on Earth. Sleep was never in abundance for him but he'd had even less than normal ever since he'd stepped aboard the embassy. There was still so much more that needed to be done, but for a moment, he let himself drift off.

A black void was illuminated by countless stars, some in different colored hues like small jewels amongst pearls. They cleared and became more defined as planets that swirled around the stars. More appeared and stars faded and lit anew. A sapphire and emerald glint in the distance caught his eye. Although quite far away, it was unmistakable. It was his home, Earth, and around it, several rigs began to orbit—the first stations—like an artificial crown adorning the planet, a mixture of the natural beauty and advancement of the human race. All seemed to be in place.

But a darkness grew to overshadow it all and he looked at a bright, piercing light. At the center was a maw of darkness, impossibly darker than the abyss of space itself. A low, droning echo rattled his chest but in a moment, it ceased and seemingly absorbed all noise as it vanished. A pulsing crackle of energy erupted like something seemingly ripped at the very fabric of reality as it reached into the universe from the center of the darkness within the light. That brightness faded rapidly as the pitch-black heart streaked into the galaxy to absorb planets, asteroids, moons, and even stars.

Some were consumed by this darkness while others were passed over but left either barren or contaminated by this vile ebony power. He wanted to leave and felt too close to this horrifying apparition that would swallow him soon. The process seemed both inevitable and futile because there was no driving desire. It was simply instinct as if this was what it was meant to do.

He seemed to shift to watch from the other end of the galaxy now. Earth hung suspended in front of him and far in the distance were millions of stars. He felt safe, but only for a mere moment because those began to fade as they were consumed. The darkness surged in, faster and faster, and was now at the edge of their system. Neptune, Uranus, and Saturn all vanished in what seemed an instant. He looked at his home in horror. There was no reaction to the threat and nothing seemed to be done—were they oblivious? Did they not see the terror approaching? Was it too fast? Maybe they had but were resigned to their fate. He never received an answer.

His vision spiraled and when it cleared, he stood on Earth in a field of green as the sky darkened and he looked up as the darkness surrounded the sun. He closed his eyes as the strange, horrifying drone filled his ears, followed by the screams of billions before he felt a sudden chill and his body split apart.

"Sir, there is a call,"

Merrick awoke with a start and rubbed his sleeve along his forehead, where beads of sweat had gathered. "What... What did you say?" he asked and focused on his EI in his ocular lenses.

"A call. I am sorry to disturb your rest, sir, but it is Dario and it sounds urgent."

"Connect me, then," he ordered. His assistant appeared quickly onscreen and for once, he wasn't smiling, at least not outright. He seemed pensive, which was something of a concern. "What's wrong, Dario?"

"Well, I originally intended to call you and leave a message as it is time for my latest report," the assassin replied with a frown. "But there's been a rather interesting development in the last couple of minutes."

"And what is that?" he asked and recognized the edge of irritation that seeped through his drowsy tone. "Surely Nolan can handle any complications by now."

"Perhaps, but I think the sudden appearance of eight destroyers would be a tricky complication for anyone."

"What?" he shouted. "Eight destroyers?"

Dario looked down and shook his head. "I'm sorry, I was wrong there, *capo*. Two more jumped in," he clarified and folded his arms. "So its ten and a Dreadnaught is close behind."

CHAPTER SIXTEEN

"Two more destroyers have arrived, sir," the ensign shouted as the alarms blared through the command deck and the rest of the colossus. "The Dreadnaught is closing in."

"How were they able to jump into our space without a warning?" Nolan demanded and looked from Aurora's wireframe form on one of the monitors above his chair to the row of technicians several yards away. Finally, his gaze settled on Lana, who scanned her tablet hastily.

"I detected no warp pulses or channels opened," Aurora stated. *"My observation would be that they were lying in wait and used their jump ability from a nearby location for an ambush rather than pursue us."*

"Dammit. And they have a Dreadnaught." He growled annoyance. "I was assured there were none in this sector."

"Either hidden with an energy mask or maybe it got here through a gate?" Lana suggested.

"A gate? Merrick already made sure they were all either destroyed or shut down. It was Damyen's responsibility to raid military bases and outposts to be sure they had nothing to surprise us with." The general took a deep breath as the colossus sustained a powerful strike on their port side. "Bastards. Get all fighters in the air. I want the main cannon set to a scattershot."

"The cannon is still recharging, sir," one of the technicians called in response. "It won't be fully operational for at least an hour."

"We don't need it to be fully operational." He seethed with suppressed rage. "A close-range scattershot only requires a third of the energy output. Aurora, when can it be done?"

"With proper configuration, I will have it ready in fifteen minutes," she responded. *"However, I am also managing the shields and other ship weapons. If these tasks can be taken over temporarily, I can bring the main cannon online in less than ten."*

"Do it," he ordered. "All technicians and gunners to their stations. Get the droid transports in the air. Fighters, be sure to guide them to the enemy ships."

"The transports?" Lana asked. "Will you drop the droids on the destroyers?"

Nolan glared at her but nodded. "That is exactly right. Now, contact the containment unit, check the number of golems we have available, and put the pilots into those skin suits."

Arbiter fighters, both manned and automated, deployed from the hangars in droves and were met in the air by a smaller force of WCM fighters deployed from the destroyers. In pure numbers, the AO still held a slight advantage but the destroyers were damn close to the colossus, and their guns fired not only on their main target but backed their fighters up as well. Some of the Arbiter craft were eliminated only seconds after exiting the bay. While there were turrets along the side of the colossus, most of the guns were either along the top or bottom of the massive ship. The larger guns located on the front were busy firing at the destroyers in an effort to destroy their shields. The droid transports launched quickly into the fray, escorted by automated fighters.

Although some of the WCM pilots noticed them and warned the destroyers, the frenzy of battle proved to be an effective enough cloak for the transports. A few were shot down but several made it to two of the targeted vessels, both of which had their shields ruptured by the colossus' barrage. The transports dropped parties of droids onto the surface of the ships but also fired pods into the hull.

WCM soldiers raced frantically through their ships to intercept the mechanical intruders, but these weren't interested in military tactics or trying to take the ship. As soon as the top of the pods opened, they leapt out of the containers and attempted to crush, slash, or blast a path of destruction through the soldiers. Resistance was fierce and coordinated despite the unexpected infiltration, and the droids suffered severe losses once their initial advantage of surprise was lost.

Flying sentries were deployed from the colossus. These were much faster than any fighter, although their guns were hardly any better than a simple distraction. Their intention was not to engage the enemy. Instead, they would find a target and pursue until they could sink a grappling spear into a WCM fighter's plating and pull themselves in. Once attached, they exploded. Or, at least, that was the plan. Instead, whenever a sentry connected with a fighter, the WCM pilots purged their shields to knock them away as their self-destruct sequence activated, and they simply exploded in the sky. Occasionally, a pilot would be caught in the blasts, both friend and foe. This caused other problems as the smoke from the explosions thickened after a while to obscure the human pilots' vision.

The automated pilots obviously didn't have this issue. However, they dealt with a very particular problem of their own as they were hacked by WCM technicians, many of whom flew as co-pilot in two-seater fighters or bombers. This allowed them to get close enough to quickly hack into the enemy fighters and either disable them or have them fire on their own men.

"Approximately thirty percent of EI-controlled fighters have been compromised," Aurora advised Nolan. *"The program they use to do it so effectively appears to be a modified version of the same program Chancellor Damyen Orlov used to capture some of his destroyers."*

"They must have been able to make a copy or covertly hack one of the stolen destroyers." The general cursed and thumped his fist on the arm of his seat. "Even when he isn't here, that bastard is a pain in my ass."

"Incoming communication from Damyen Orlov."

The general exhaled slowly through his nose and shook his head as he tried to regain his composure. "Speak of the devil. Put him on."

"Aye, Nolan." The chancellor chuckled. "I hear you're in a spot of trouble, my friend."

"Is that so, Damyen? And who would have told you this?" he asked.

"Merrick notified me," the man explained and Nolan paled slightly. "It doesn't surprise me. They've taken shots at you every time you make planetfall. I came to extend a hand."

"You have a ship in the area?" he asked.

"I have three." Damyen held up three fingers. "Three destroyers, all Maverick class. I also made contact with some of the Omegas as well and they'll send a small fleet. We should have this rounded up in no time."

"Do you think it will be enough to deal with the Dreadnaught?" the general asked.

The other man frowned. "Dreadnaught? Where did they get one of those?"

"That was something I wanted to ask you," Nolan retorted. "I was under the impression that we had destroyed the last of them last month and the rest were stuck out in space."

"You got me there." The chancellor shrugged. "A Dreadnaught, eh? That definitely has the firepower to finish what these destroyers have started."

"I am well aware of what a—"

"Why haven't you simply melted them by now?" the Russian asked. "These destroyers are grouped together and directly ahead. You should have finished this almost as soon as they appeared. Are you saving it for the Dreadnaught?"

He looked away briefly before he nodded his head slowly. "That was the plan,"

"You didn't get hacked, did you? You still have that fancy EI of the professor's onboard, don't you?"

Aurora appeared onscreen. "I am present, Chancellor Orlov."

Damyen nodded. "Well, I guess that answers that,"

"Not entirely," Nolan stated. "The WCM technicians are using a hacking program similar to the one you used to commandeer some of your ships."

"What's that?" The man sounded genuinely puzzled.

"Where did you get that program, Damyen? And is there any way they could have hacked one of your ships or systems to retrieve it?"

"I suppose it is possible, although unlikely. They couldn't get it from a ship as I delete it from the systems as soon as I execute the crew to make sure they couldn't get to it." The Russian reached into his shirt pocket. "As for where I got it—or rather whom—it was from Oswald." He produced a small circular device, one quite familiar to Nolan. "He said it was based on the one he gave you to take over the embassy. I keep it on my person at all times. There is no way to steal it from me without taking the only copy."

"Which means they backward engineered it, most likely." He sighed but a thought occurred and a small chill shivered through his body. If they had developed a hacking program similar to Damyen's, it stood to reason that they had also created a counter to it. And if it was based on the one he used to take over the embassy, how long would it take them to develop a counter to that? And if they got close enough to use it, everything would fall out of Merrick's control while he was still on board.

"Damyen, if your ships are on the way, then you need to alert the master of this development. Make sure he is aware that they could potentially have a way into the embassy," the general ordered. "I'll deal with these pests, recover my target at the Nexus Academy, and return as quickly as I can."

For once, Damyen didn't regard him with nonchalance or levity and instead, nodded with seriousness and sincerity. "Understood, Nolan. To ensure that you do, my ships will make the jump in ten seconds. They are yours to command."

"That is appreciated." The screen turned off and he focused his attention on the fight. "Are the golems ready?"

"They are being sent to the hangars, along with the last batch of Ark and Omega pilots."

"I want the Ark soldiers and Omegas in fighter and interceptors. Hold the sentries for now and send drones out as defense for the transports, even if all they are good for right now is to take the blasts instead of the transports. As for the golems, get them into bombers and destroy the rest of those shields."

Damyen's Maverick-class destroyers arrived almost as soon as Nolan finished giving his orders and wasted no time before they engaged the WCM destroyers. Although the military had a few Maverick-class destroyers of their own, they were focused on the colossus and the more agile yet more fragile Tempest-class destroyers were left to deal with their larger stolen counterparts.

More transports were deployed, but as the battle had spread across a wider area, they were no longer safe in the chaos and were now priority targets that were fired at on sight. Some were able to get close enough to fire their pods thanks to the sacrifice of the drones that accompanied them, although the ships themselves usually didn't make it. Several exploded in the sky and the Arbiter droids within were either destroyed with them or hurled into empty air. Some fired their cannons at WCM ships as they fell, while others landed on enemy ships and inflicted severe damage. Usually, the vessels spiraled out of control before both they and droid exploded.

A few of the Tempest destroyers broke away to engage the new enemy destroyers. Although they didn't have the massive and consistent firepower of the Mavericks, they did have one trick their opponents did not. They could sacrifice their shields to grant a quick and massive boost of energy to their main cannon and fire a large blast. While this sacrificed their defense and left their armor exposed, the result was so powerful, even a single blast put a considerable dent into the bigger Mavericks. There were currently four Tempests on their way to engage the enemy, which increased the destructive potential of that particular advantage.

In the distance, a small fleet of Omega destroyers, corsairs, and assault ships made their way to the fight but the WCM Dreadnaught was only a few minutes away. Should it get close enough for a direct strike on the colossus with its main cannon, that could be enough to not only turn the tide into the military's favor but potentially destroy the enormous vessel, as the battle had already weakened its shields to only twenty percent capacity.

Nolan watched the various monitors which displayed feeds from the different battles and the amount of time until the cannon was ready. It would come down to one shot and he only needed a little more time. If sacrifices needed to be made, so be it. He had more than enough expendables on board.

CHAPTER SEVENTEEN

"Do you think we'll be lucky enough to get a shower and some sleep when we get back?" Cameron asked as Wolfson brought the dropship in to hover over the landing pad in the Seattle base.

"I still kinda have adrenaline pumping," Luke replied and frowned when he glanced at Kaiden "Do you feel all right, buddy?"

"Yeah," the ace said, his voice quiet. His conversation with Flynn still weighed on him. As he didn't know if telling the others what happened would rouse them or depress them, he kept it to himself for now. "I guess I hoped it would last longer. You guys seem tired, though."

"We've been out longer," Silas reminded him and nodded at the two heavies. "Even the big guys are starting to pass out."

"What? Naw, I can definitely— Shit, I'm lying," Mack admitted and shook his head, fatigue evident in his eyes. Luke merely grumbled and nodded.

Although he wanted to take a couple of digs at the

group, Silas was right. Not only had they been out in the field much longer than his little jaunt, but they had willingly come in at the end of his and Wolfson's mission. They deserved a reprieve.

Once the door opened, the five of them exited and Wolfson followed soon after, talking to one of the crew about the damages to the ship. Although Kaiden moved purposefully to the nearby tech center currently being used as a temporary HQ, his stride was halted by a familiar greeting. "Friend Kaiden!"

He turned and Genos waved at him from halfway down the path, Jaxon behind him. With a smile, he returned the gesture and redirected his steps to the two Tsuna. "Hey, Genos, Jaxon. How did the mission go?"

"Splendid. There was impressive devastation," the engineer told him. "We retrieved the device—some kind of targeting system for a satellite cannon."

Kaiden was caught off-guard by that. "A sat-cannon? You would think they would be offline along with the warp gates once the AO…uh, Merrick took over."

"I believe that's why they wanted the device," Jaxon explained, his voice calm and serious. "If most of the other satellites and arrays are down or cannot be accessed, this device can be something of a workaround if properly recalibrated. As of right now, it is simply a powerful weapon, but Cyra has said there is considerable potential in it."

"Speaking of which," he began and shook the case in his hand. "Do you know if she's in? We found our device too."

Genos glanced at his prize. "What were you sent to retrieve?"

"Some kind of energy dampener or draining device. My guess is they wanted to mass produce it or something like that. It gives them easy access to any locked-down area." He held the case firmly in both hands. "It's better with us anyway."

A member of the outpost collided into Kaiden's back and both men fell. The man scrambled hastily to his feet and moved to help the ace up. "I'm so sorry, sir."

He held a hand up and nodded before he checked to make the case was undamaged. "It's cool, man. What's the rush?"

"The enemy colossus—I heard the military engaged it," the crewman explained.

Kaiden and the Tsuna's eyes widened in shock. "What? When?" he demanded

"Only a little while ago. There should be a feed in the main hub." He opened the door to the HQ for them and the group ran hastily inside.

The Tempests closed in on the Mavericks, who seemed aware of the potential danger of their nova cannons. They pounded an ongoing barrage into the incoming destroyers. Even if they wouldn't break through, less stability and power to the shields meant their shots wouldn't be as powerful either.

WCM bombers made runs at the new opponents and other fighters broke away to help as the destroyers had brought a small fleet of fighters with them as well. These now poured out of the bays of the vessels to assist the colossus. The WCM were not without their own aid, however, as from behind the line of destroyers, more fighters and interceptors swooped in, having been deployed from the Dreadnaught that moved slowly but inexorably closer.

However, any hope many of the military pilots felt at that moment was dulled when several large shadows appeared in the distance and gradually revealed themselves as Omega Horde ships of different varieties. The faster assault craft reached the battle only a couple of minutes after first sight and began to fire on the destroyers, while the smaller and more agile corsairs assisted in dealing with the personal fighters.

Two of the four Tempests had broken away, but the other two continued their push and finally moved within range to fire. Their captains gave the command and focused on a single target. They knew what it meant to purge their shields at this point, but they also had a plan. Their nova shot began to charge as they set their path to cross directly in front of the enemy destroyer.

The Maverick vessel did not move to dodge the incoming blast and instead, its shields focused on the impact zone of the shot. The other two destroyers did make their way to the side to avoid the fallout, and the assault droids that had joined the fray began to fly low to do the same. Unfortunately, when the two blasts were fired, they collided to create a much larger explosion that not only destroyed the front portion of the Maverick but consumed the assault ships below. The force also thrust its two companions away and destroyed their shields, and one of them actually crashed into the side of the colossus.

The main deck of the enormous vessel rattled and a large crunch of metal echoed throughout the ship.

"Status report," Nolan ordered and glanced at the row of technicians.

"We're hit, sir, but not by any blast," he explained. "One of our destroyers was thrown into our port side by a cross blast from the enemy Tempests."

The general snarled his outrage. "Damage?"

"Moderate to severe. It ripped through some of our armor on that side, sir."

He shook his head. "Get the bots there to start repairs. Those of you handling the shields, decrease the dispersal from lightly damaged areas and increase the capacity in that section to cover for the lost armor. The meeting of our shields with the destroyers will cause a blow-back that will knock them away from the ship. Get going!"

"Sir!" they shouted and hastily followed their orders. Nolan looked at the monitor. There were now only two minutes until the cannon was ready and an eta of two minutes before the Dreadnaught would be in its range of fire. They needed a diversion and he looked at Lana. "Since we pulled the sentries back, how many do we have?"

"A little over a couple of hundred at last check," she stated but began to double-check her tablet. "They weren't particularly effective."

Nolan placed a hand over his fist and nodded. "Not to take on the smaller fighter ships, but they could have another use."

The destroyer that had been knocked into the colossus was pushed off with tremendous force when the ship's shields were charged in that area. While much of the destroyer's starboard armor had been destroyed in the crash, it was still able to fly. The Tempests that had fired upon them didn't stay to celebrate their victory and tried to retreat quickly as the Mavericks resumed their positions. It appeared they were so focused on the stolen vessels that they had forgotten the Omega Horde destroyers that had not reached the battle but now approached from behind the Mavericks.

They were equipped with modified cannons and more energy to spare and launched an assault on the two Tempests as they tried to spin away. Both ships fell victim to the combined attack. They had eliminated one destroyer, three assault ships, and some corsairs, but the other Mavericks were still airborne and the four new destroyers were Tempest class themselves. Not only that, they were fresh, unlike the WCM destroyers at this point.

And the military's tactic had, unfortunately, given the Omega Horde an idea.

The four destroyers took their positions and aimed at their counterparts that were still focused on the colossus. They lined their sights up so their own nova shots would collide in the middle of the air space between the five destroyers that targeted the large vessel. They fired on orders, their collective power much stronger than what the WCM had delivered as their shields were mostly still full and so had more energy to spare. When all four collided, the resultant explosion was enormous. At least two of the military destroyers were immediately annihilated. One was almost melted in half as it had no shields remaining to absorb the blast.

Nolan took the opportunity and the sentries were sent out again. Instead of engaging the fighters, they headed farther away, followed by bombers, toward a distant shape that moved slowly closer to the colossus. The haste with which the military had completed construction of the Dreadnaught in secret to have it ready for this attack proved to be a costly error. The unfinished point defense system allowed the enemy through undetected, and with the fighter craft engaged in the battle, the large vessel was entirely vulnerable. The bombers reached the Dreadnaught first and instantly fired missiles and dropped bombs along the massive vessel, all of which were absorbed by the shield. They focused their attack on the front of the ship and particularly around the cannon.

This was when the sentries engaged. The smaller drones all coalesced into a swarm that flew directly at the large weapon, impacted against the shields, and erupted. All two hundred and seventeen sentries careened into the cannon, one after another, and eventually destroyed the shields and entered the maw of the main barrel. It wouldn't be enough to destroy it, of course, but the onslaught served its purpose.

The bombers couldn't make a run at it as the military fighters had fallen back to protect the Dreadnaught. Even if the pilots were disposable golems and flew much more recklessly than a normal pilot concerned with survival, they were low on munitions and needed to restock. But the point wasn't to simply be a suicide run to try to destroy the cannon. That would cost too many resources. No, Nolan knew that wasn't the optimal choice. He merely needed a few more precious seconds and although the attack didn't destroy the weapon, the damage did mean it had trouble charging. As the Dreadnaught broke through the cloud line and approached the colossus, it had only begun to charge its cannon and the progress was slow.

"Main cannon functional for one blast," Aurora notified Nolan. *"Would you still like a scattershot, General?"*

"The destroyers are mostly dealt with," he stated and a smile settled on his lips for the first time since the destruction of the city the previous day. "Focus fire on the Dreadnaught. Let them know that even when it is not optimal, our might is more than they can ever bear."

"Understood. Taking control of battle functions," the EI stated and a crosshair appeared on the front window of the main deck. *"Initiating cannon."* A circle formed slowly around the crosshair, met at the top, and began to expand *"Ready to fire. Increasing power."*

The general's eyes narrowed as the circle solidified to white to indicate that it had reached its peak of available power. "Fire."

The red light almost blinded anyone who looked at the shot and the echoed boom from the cannon as it fired always rattled the bones of those within. A large red beam rocketed into the front of the Dreadnaught and continued along its deadly trajectory. Smoke, fire, and red plumes surged from the side of the WCM vessel as the beam coursed through it. The ship seemed to collapse in on itself for a moment before it disintegrated in a massive fireball.

The beam traveled on and Nolan and everyone onboard watched it disappear into the distance.

The general stood, calm and satisfied, and began to step down from his seat and head out of the deck. "Sir?" one of the technicians called. "What should we do with any remaining hostiles? I'm hailed by the remaining destroyers, possibly for a surrender?"

"Deny them," he stated flatly. "Tell our men to destroy them, as well as any personal ships foolish enough to stay here. Send every remaining military ship to the waters below." He reached the exit and glanced over his shoulder as the doors opened and he stepped out. "Let the wreckage be a memorial to our triumph and their utter failure."

With that, he left the crew to their orders and all felt a small chill from the general's haunting words.

CHAPTER EIGHTEEN

"My God..." a shocked voice uttered. A few people sobbed and others fell to their knees. Kaiden turned away. The only thing left to watch from the feed was the sight of the destroyer that hosted it attacked and obliterated by the remaining enemy forces. It wasn't something he wished to see. While it wasn't something anyone did, some were either in shock from watching the destruction of the Dreadnaught or were driven by some other morbid reason—maybe watching to see the full capabilities of the enemy. All he took from it was that unless they could bring the full might of the military to bear on them at once, the colossus would not be destroyed by an aerial ambush.

A hand grasped his shoulder and he turned quickly. Cyra motioned for him to follow her. "We have a call, Kaiden," she stated. "From the professor."

"Ah, Kaiden. It's good to see you after so long." Laurie's hologram greeted them cheerily as Kaiden and Cyra walked into a room with Sasha, Wolfson, Genos, and Jaxon.

"It's good to hear from you as well, Prof," he responded. "I was worried and thought the military had dragged you off to a secret base and we'd never hear from you again."

"It's not entirely incorrect." The man sighed. "This is actually my first call to the outside world besides talking to other military or scientific officials."

"What do you require, Laurie?" Sasha asked, his arms folded.

"A good wine and a massage, really, but I assume you asked why I called?" The professor chuckled and his fatigue was very evident in the laugh. He certainly was being run into the ground, it seemed.

"Do you have any news—something positive?" Kaiden asked. "I've just seen one of the WCM's Dreadnaughts get blown out of the sky."

Laurie frowned and nodded. "Yes, I have been informed of that. I'm no great strategist, but the attacks that are based on pure might will not solve every situation, especially against that colossus of theirs. Once we discovered how to bypass their automated hacking program, they thought it would be enough to turn the tide while I and almost everyone else here simply saw it as a small step."

"You would be correct," Sasha agreed. "The AO would not be in the position they are in with a couple of simple tricks. They have might as well, maybe not as much as the military but they certainly have enough to be a menace. And the military also has to deal with the populace and is far more widely spread. My guess is that many in the higher command have grown used to all problems being a simple fix. They've grown comfortable over the decades of relative peace outside the occasional terrorist scrap."

"Please speak louder. Maybe one of them will hear you and actually understand," the other man muttered. "I've said virtually the same thing all this time while here."

"It's weird to hear that Laurie has been the voice of reason," Wolfson interjected as he moved to the corner of the room and leaned against the wall.

The professor coughed and refocused. "As much fun as it is to gossip, I really should answer your first question," he stated, his expression serious. "Although it is kind of related. I wanted to check on the missions I requested for the retrieval of the sat-marker and energy-draining device?"

"I actually have the energy drainer right here," Kaiden said and held the case up. "I didn't realize it was you who posted the mission."

"Technically, it was my request but some postmaster sent it to you, I think," Laurie said and glanced at the others. "And the sat-marker?"

"We acquired it," Jaxon said. "It is currently being studied by a team of technicians led by Cyra."

"Ah, well done." Laurie pursed his lips and focused on his assistant. "I assume I missed your report?"

She waved dismissively. "And I guess you've been busy."

He nodded. "Very much so, but I still shouldn't slack. Thank you for picking up my pieces. How goes the reconfiguration?"

"I had to get a cracker in to mod it and change the

signal." Cyra moved to stand beside Kaiden and gestured at the case, which he handed to her. "This should hopefully be much simpler. You have identified the changes to the Nexus shields, right?"

"It was more of a pain than I had thought," the professor admitted. When his gaze darted aside briefly, the ace took it to mean someone was hurt or worse in recovering that information. "Honestly, there weren't many differences from my design when all is said and done. But they can increase the potency and solidification of the shielding because there's no one inside who needs to breathe, which is convenient." He pointed to the case. "Get the device working. I'll send you the specs for the changes and when the colossus arrives, you'll be ready to infiltrate the island."

Kaiden's heartbeat quickened momentarily in excitement but a nagging concern remained. "I hope the attack didn't scare them off," he said and glanced at Sasha and Wolfson. "I'm also pissed that no one seemed to know it was happening. At least no one out there in the lobby who watched it go down."

"I didn't either," the commander replied. "None of my contacts mentioned it. Right now, the military network is rather loose with both central hubs currently offline. Before Laurie confirmed it, I thought it was the plan of a separate faction—or maybe several that came together and thought they had the arms to confront it. Maybe it was a spontaneous attack in retaliation for the destruction of the city the other day."

"Getting a Dreadnaught isn't really a spontaneous move," Wolfson pointed out and looked at the professor.

"It's hard to hide a Dreadnaught. Where the hell did that come from, Laurie?"

"It was built in secret in a nautical base off the Gulf of California," the other man revealed, "and was only completed ten days ago. It wasn't hidden so much as it was turned on immediately before the attack, used a gate to make the jump out of the base, and appeared off the coast of San Diego."

"We have gates?" Genos asked. "I was under the impression that all gates were offline once the Arbiters took over the embassy."

"There's nothing we can do about the interstellar gates at this point," Laurie said. "But the gates we have on Earth for intercontinental travel or for ships that can't make jumps can be repurposed if you have a power source and the proper connection keys." His face fell slightly and he shook his head. "Unfortunately, the base that housed many of the keys had been ransacked during the initial invasion, along with many of the gates being destroyed by the Arbiters in the last couple of months. We have a few well-guarded and are looking for more connection keys. But that's not for you to worry about right now. It was something that gave me an idea on how you can get on the colossus."

"We won't fly in?" Kaiden asked.

Laurie, Sasha, and Wolfson looked at him, frowned, and shook their heads. "Do you really think that would work?" the professor asked.

He looked away and folded his arms. "I didn't see another option unless we had a teleporter or something."

"Well, I don't have anything, but the island does have a teleporter."

Kaiden, Genos, and Jaxon stared at him. "Really now?" Genos asked. "Is it still operational?"

"It's a small teleporter meant for quick extraction and things like that and still needs connection keys, but someone is handling that," the man clarified. "As for what the AO is trying to get from this vault, intel appears to indicate it is the serum."

"The serum?" Sasha recoiled, his normally calm demeanor shaken in a moment of surprise. "Is it still even usable at this point?

"What serum?" Genos asked.

The ace looked at the Nexus faculty members. "What he said."

Laurie glanced over both shoulders to check if anyone was around him. "An enhancement serum, one designed to turn a normal man into…well, something quite far off the current evolutionary path."

"What the hell would we have something like that for?" Kaiden demanded.

"Because of what this vault really keeps secret," Wolfson said, his eyes narrowed. "The abandoned facility that was the original Academy."

"You built Nexus over the old bones of a eugenics lab?" The ace regarded them with an expression of disbelief.

"Not I!" Laurie protested. "Or any of us. Wolfson here is the oldest and he was a child when it was originally built."

"It wasn't exactly a eugenics lab, although in terms of what it tried to accomplish, it wasn't much better either," the commander admitted. "Many of these devices were considered too important to destroy for one reason or another. Everyone felt it was better to hide them beneath a military Academy where there is constant protection and an unassuming façade to go along with that."

"It still seems a dangerous idea," Genos pointed out. "Was there no other place they could hide these devices and weapons?"

"I've brought that up to the board before," Wolfson stated, his expression grim. "The other plan was to put it on Terra."

The Tsuna engineer nodded and looked a little sheepish. "I see. Then they would have it by now."

"Presumably, but maybe they wouldn't have simply destroyed Terra if they were trying to retrieve it," Laurie suggested. "Who knows?"

Kaiden shrugged "I guess it's worked well so far. Do you think they'll finally break in this time?"

The professor's hologram raised a hand and several holoscreens appeared to display footage of Arbiter bots and Ark soldiers moving through various tunnels. "One of the few things I have been able to maintain is a connection to the cameras in the tunnels leading below the island," he explained. The monitor on the top right showed a soldier pointing his pistol at the screen and he fired before it went black. "Unfortunately, they have an easy solution to that." The screens vanished but a larger one appeared to display only the static image of a massive metal door. "They are at the final gate. It requires the right codes, personnel, and quite a few other necessities to open. I highly doubt they have any of these as they need at least four of ten specified people and several are dead, I'm here, and two are in that room with you."

Kaiden pointed to Wolfson and Sasha, who simply nodded.

"And the codes change daily. Since I don't have my personal computer, I'm not even aware of what they are. Based on that, I'm sure they will attempt the brute force route."

"That looks damn strong," Kaiden noted. "Do they even have something that can get through it? It's not like they can have the colossus blast it down...can they?"

"I'm sure they would have tried that by now if they could," the commander replied. "They have been wearing it down with several different cannons, explosives, acids, and many other things. My guess is they are bringing the device that will finally let them through."

"Which will be the first part of your mission," Laurie explained. "You will infiltrate the island and follow them to the old Academy. Destroy or recover whatever they are trying to take, then use the teleporter to get onto their ship. Once I have the connection keys, I will set them up—or Cyra or someone of exceptional skill will in my place."

"I have a list if you'd like," she offered.

"Hold on a second—how do we get in there?" the ace asked. "Simply follow them? If they use this big tunnel, I think we'll be seen right away. I don't mind fighting through, but we won't be able to keep our arrival a secret."

"I have no issue with fighting either," Jaxon agreed. "However, assuming they are able to get in, they may simply hurry to retrieve this serum and retreat. Or they could lay in wait to trap us. It could lead to any number of complications."

"You'll use the express route," the professor told them. "The tunnel may be the primary route, but there is a secret passage located in the main building. It will require the chancellor codes to access, but I assume you won't have a problem getting those now, will you?" He looked at Sasha as he finished the question.

"Those codes change as well, but I still have emergency codes that can be used to access the chancellor's computer if it is still active."

"It would be more convenient and practical for them to keep it if they still want to run all the systems from a central station," Wolfson pointed out.

"Then we have a more practical way in," Jaxon agreed.

"So now, it all depends on the guys going to get the keys, then?" Kaiden asked and nodded. "Will they be back soon?"

"I'm sure she will. She said it wouldn't take her long," Cyra interjected.

"Only one person?" He frowned as he considered this. "What, will she pick it up from someone?"

"Kind of." She shrugged and rubbed the back of her neck. "See, this teleporter is old and uses older keys that are hard to find, even without all the stuff that has been going on. We tracked a pair to some Vice Ghouls out east. They run droid construction and tech cracking, things like that."

"Vice Ghouls? Those guys aren't exactly friendly when it comes to people messing with their business," the ace muttered. "She must be exceptional if she was willing to take them on alone."

"Well, you have seen her work," she responded.

He gave her a confused look and she gestured around them as if to ask if he'd noticed that someone was missing. The truth struck him and he almost felt weak at the shock it brought.

CHAPTER NINETEEN

Chiyo had made her way inside the main building at the center of the stronghold and tried to locate the leader's office as quickly as possible. Although the premises were empty, she knew she was on the cams. Hopefully, her change of armor would fool them for long enough to not raise suspicion if anyone even manned the security systems at all.

She finally located the target destination and began her search for the blue micro-vault Laurie's informant had described, although he had mentioned this information was two weeks old. It was a detail she now regretted not taking more seriously. In her eagerness, she could have put herself in danger for nothing.

Although the sound of the battle that raged outside made her feel that she would at least assist in pushing this violent gang out of the area—rather violently too.

"Uh, madame? On your left." Kaitō's avatar turned to the side and nodded. She glanced in that direction and noticed the vault partially obscured by a cloth beside the desk.

Quickly, she crossed the room and removed an auto-pick to work the lock. "Much appreciated, Kaitō,"

"Of course."

Chiyo knelt and set to work. "How are things going out there?"

"I suppose I would say splendid, given what we are trying to accomplish. We have lost eight Raiders and nine Assassin droids but on the plus side, they are not military units so they shouldn't cost us anything."

"Except the marketeers the ghouls stole the droids from might come calling...if they were left alive." She focused, continued her efforts on the lock, and allowed herself a small smile at a couple of promising pops. "Well done. I'll be out in a—" A loud, frenzied scream was followed by several others, undoubtedly from the Vice Ghouls. Under the circumstances, it wasn't too unexpected, but if they had simply been fighting up till now, why did they suddenly sound so frightened?

"Miss Chiyo, there are—" Kaitō's avatar vanished for a brief second before it reappeared. *"I lost connection to my droid...reestablishing."*

"What is going on, Kaitō?!" she asked as the vault finally unlocked. Several small cases and containers lay within and she simply snatched all of them and placed them in the storage compartment on her left leg. She rushed from the room and raced through to exit the building but stopped in shock as she viewed the scene in front of her.

Large, gaunt droids—all black with white eyes—lumbered through the field. They hacked and slashed at anything in their path with long blades on their arms that glowed a burning red. The Ghouls were shoved to the ground and their skin shredded as the demented fiends touched or clawed at them. The other droids attempted to fire on these terrifying new arrivals, but their efforts seemed futile. Most simply ignored the damage and stood again or continued to attack. They either tore the other mechanicals apart or thrust their hands into their chests to deliver a surge of energy and overload them so they exploded.

Chiyo looked hastily at the gate. Four of the dark droids covered the distance between it and the armory and wreaked destruction on fleeing Ghouls along the way. It seemed she wouldn't escape the same way she had snuck in. She followed a cautious but hasty route toward a small airfield a little farther away with several rusted hangars. Hopefully, there was something there she could use.

"Madame, I've reestablished connection to a new droid host. I will join you momentarily," Kaitō promised.

"What are these? I've never seen anything like them," she asked as she skirted the massacre as inconspicuously as she could and chose the closest hangar as her destination.

"They are Reapers, madame, a model of droid long obsolete. All were thought to be destroyed along with their schematics," the EI explained. *"There is something wrong with their programming and OS. They always malfunction when it comes to distinguishing friend from foe and they are very difficult to destroy."*

Two Vice Ghouls with shotguns successfully felled a Reaper and continued to fire at point-blank range while it struggled to stand. It popped its blades, spun them while still in a seated position, and sliced through its attackers. When the blades slowed, a number of holes were visible in its chassis but it continued to move. "I can see that."

"I will join you as soon as I am able—" A loud crash was immediately followed by static, and Kaitō went silent.

"Kaitō? Kaitō! Are you all right?" Chiyo cried, hurried to the back of the hangar, and yanked the door open.

"I am here, miss Chiyo." The EI reappeared in the display. *"I'm sorry I worried you. I was attacked by a Reaper and had to separate from the droid once again before a surge could shut me down."*

"It's all right, Kaitō. I'm merely glad you're safe," she said calmly as she entered the structure and looked around her. A crew shuttle stood in the far corner and she raced toward it. "I'll need your help to get this shuttle running."

"Understood. I'll get it unlocked."

The door on the back of the shuttle slid open and she scrambled in, and it closed behind her. She pushed quickly to the front and began to power it up, but the screen asked for clearance to activate flight controls. "Hack the system and get us airborne, Kaitō."

The fox avatar nodded and disappeared from the display. She began to activate everything else needed for takeoff when she heard a loud thud behind her. The infiltrator turned as the door to the shuttle was ripped apart and her breath hitched as she took her submachine gun out. "What does it look like, Kaitō?"

"This ship is not in good shape, madame. I don't think—"

The door finally gave and Chiyo fired as soon as she had a clear shot.

The Reaper surged forward and while the laser fire from the submachine gun inflicted visible damage, it didn't stop the terrifying machine. It continued to shamble toward her, almost as if it was toying with its prey before the feast.

"Chiyo, I cannot hack into it. You must get away," Kaitō shouted.

The gun overheated and the infiltrator recoiled as the Reaper's blade swiped overhead. She vented her submachine gun and holstered it, drew her pistol, and pushed deeper into the cockpit.

"Madame, run now!" Kaitō yelled.

The Reaper tilted its head as it continued to advance. It emitted a hiss, followed by a series of high-pitched shrieks with an electric drone woven through them. The mechanical attacked and Chiyo fired at the cockpit window behind her and flung herself through the aperture. She landed in the hangar but before she could find her feet, two more Reapers appeared in the entrance. They saw her immediately and began to advance.

"Kaitō, are you still connected to the ship?" she asked and backed away as she held her pistol ready.

"I am, madame, but I do not think we should still try to use it while—"

"Activate the thrusters and aim at the droids," she ordered and prepared to fire as the Reapers on the ground began to run toward her. The mechanical that had attacked her first tried to jump out the door but the craft took off and it fell inside. The shuttle powered into the two oncoming enemies and pinned them to the front before it burst out of the doors of the hangar and careened into a tower at the edge of the camp.

The infiltrator steadied herself, took a deep breath as

she put her pistol away, and drew her SMG and closed the vent. "How many droids do we have left, Kaitō?"

"Our forces have been mostly decimated, madame. We have only four Assassin droids, two Havoc droids, and a handful of Troop droids," the EI replied.

"Are you able to identify how many of those Reapers there are?" she asked.

"I believe there are fifteen remaining. The Vice Ghouls and droids combined were able to eliminate about six of them, along with the three you destroyed now."

"There were less than thirty of them? And they've done this much damage?" She was aghast but put it out of her mind as she moved to leave through the back entrance of the hangar she had originally entered through. "Are the Vice Ghouls still around?"

"Allow me to access the thermals of your helmet for a moment."

"Go ahead." She moved her head from side to side and kept her eyes closed once Kaitō activated the thermals. A soft beep let her know he was finished.

"I count twenty-one remaining people within this settlement. Most are headed toward the main gate. Somewhat fortunately, they are distracting the majority of the Reapers. However, the crash of the shuttle was surely noticed. I picked up at least three headed in this direction."

"Is there no way to hack them? Even to shut them down?" she asked and hurried across the lot in search of another shuttle.

"Not with Reapers, unfortunately. Their defect stems from their original purpose, which was to be unhackable droids. The

cost of this was the failure of their ally process. They cannot be hacked or commanded."

The infiltrator frowned. It seemed like an interesting challenge and probably a little ahead of its time for such a massive failure. Of course, she realized it was probably something she needed to research much later when said droids weren't coming in search of her.

"If we cannot find a ship to get us out of here, I'll find another exit and call for evac once we get away." She hesitated and glanced at the camp. That would leave the Reapers roaming the area and how long would it take before they reached a populated town or city? She could alert the military once she escaped, but that would give them far too much time to scatter if they did respond and attempt to wipe them out.

"Kaitō, is there a supply of explosives or power units in the camp?"

"I saw some kind of munitions room in the main building when you retrieved the chips, madame. Why?"

"Use the remaining droids to lure the Reapers there," she stated and began to head back.

"Madame, I'm not sure that will work. These Reapers are more durable than guardian droids. Even a massive explosion isn't guaranteed to destroy them all."

"We can't simply leave them to go out and attack innocents once they've left the base," she stated and pushed into a jog. "Besides, you said they were already after me."

"They could simply be investigating, Chiyo. I admire your concern, but those chips are more important, as well as your life. They can be dealt with at another—on your left!"

She rolled to the side seconds to avoid a sizzle and whoosh of air above her. On one knee, she aimed her SMG as the Reaper retracted its blade and its claws crackled with electricity. How had it snuck up on her? It was over seven feet tall, and she had to fight back the instinctive surge of panic. She fired and the droid raised one arm to shield its head against the barrage of shots. It advanced and brandished its opposite arm with its blade unsheathed, quickly heating up.

Chiyo scrambled to her feet and skipped back hastily as she retrieved a nano grenade from her belt. She pressed the switch and lobbed it at the Reaper when her weapon overheated and she opened the vent. The grenade erupted and thousands of small silver nanos covered the droid. They weren't the overwriting model, however. The mechanical attempted to brush them off and even placed its electrified claw on itself in an attempt to electrocute them. Instead, they simply began to glow as they drained its energy. It took several steps closer to her, the blade began to still, and the red glow disappeared. It hobbled a few steps and collapsed to its knees before its head lowered and it powered down.

That was one more disabled but unfortunately, it was the only nano grenade she had so she had to rely on her original plan. "Kaitō, did you get those droids back to the base?"

"We lost another Havoc droid. I am trying to bring them together, however— Chiyo, more are coming."

A thud against the wall of the hangar she crouched behind was the only warning before a blade thrust through the metal and began to slice a hole. She sprinted away down the alley between two hangars but heard the

Reaper's metal legs pound behind her. Without slowing, she shut the vent on her SMG and twisted to fire but had barely enough time to react to the Reaper's blade being launched at her. She was able to duck under it, but the side of the blade knocked against her shoulder and she lost her balance, tripped, and tumbled into the center of the hangar area. Her attacker surged forward and drove its electric claws into the ground as she rolled away, but the shocks still reached her. She bit her lip as she forced herself farther away from the electrified area.

She stood and her disguise failed, shorted out by the electricity. The pursuing Reaper was still behind her and another looked down from where it perched on the edge of the second hangar. There was no way she could outrun them so she would have to think of a plan to either subdue or escape these bots.

Blasts shattered the momentary silence and Chiyo raised her arms over her helmet and uttered a surprised gasp. Two shuttles outfitted with cannons swept in. The doors opened and a dozen droids dropped out in blue armor. They turned to the recovering Reapers as their arms transformed into cannons and fired in unison at the one on the ground. Their combined blast was enough to destroy it and the other leapt from above with its blades at the ready.

The blue droids moved aside as it landed and lashed out. They fired wiring from their palms to bind the Reaper's arms and yanked these to the sides. The mechanical's arms began to snap and groan before they were yanked out of their sockets. It staggered as several droids aimed their cannons and fired as one.

Chiyo was surprised and relieved, but a new concern took hold. Who were these droids' creators? She watched one of the shuttles bank toward the gate as the other began to make a landing and noted a familiar symbol along the side of the ship.

A blue circle—or, as they preferred, an Azure Halo.

CHAPTER TWENTY

Nolan walked into his private quarters and instructed Aurora to shut the windows and activate the glow strips as he removed his jacket and shirt and tossed them aside. He walked over to his alcohol cabinet, removed a bottle of wine, and looked at it before he replaced it in favor of a bottle of vodka Damyen had gifted him some time before.

He sat in his comfortable chair and sighed, opened the bottle, and took a sip from it.

"It doesn't take you too long to unwind, does it, General?" He almost spat the alcohol out but managed to yank the pistol from the underside of his desk and aim it at the corner where he had heard the voice. Dario stepped out of the shadows and held his hands up. The dim white light illuminated the sinister smile on his face.

"Dario?" he responded but didn't replace his sidearm. "When did you arrive?"

"I've been here for a while, General," he replied and lowered his hands. Nolan didn't like the way he used his title. It was obviously mocking. "Ever since you departed, actually. It's been rather amusing to watch you work all this time."

"Merrick sent you?" he asked. His visitor simply nodded and Nolan's gun hand trembled slightly as he asked his next question. "To kill me?"

"Why would he want that?" the assassin asked and walked to the side as if to circle him. "You've been quite useful to him and shown yourself to be a capable warrior and very loyal…at least formerly."

"What are you implying?" He sneered. "I have followed the master's orders to the letter."

The other man chuckled and nodded. "Certainly, I suppose there was no explicit order to not destroy an entire city in a tantrum—although that might be in conflict with the order to head directly to Nexus and retrieve the serum. And to not draw attention to yourself." The general frowned when the man chortled quietly. "I thought that was a silly order myself, considering." He gestured around the room to indicate the vastness of the ship. "And yet, if there was any other way to be more unsubtle than flying the largest craft in the world, you certainly found a way to do it."

Nolan sucked a breath in through his nose and lowered his weapon only slightly. "You've reported to Merrick?"

"On occasion. There wasn't too much to report until the last couple of days. You've done well. You picked the bomb up, assisted in fights with the golems, and checked held territories on your way to the Academy. A solid A so far, General."

"You keep dancing around my action to use the cannon

to destroy that city the other day," he stated and his gaze followed the other man, who continued to pace slowly around him.

"I wanted to see if you would simply say it was a preliminary attack or something and make it sound nobler than I did." Dario stopped in his tracks and ran a hand through his hair. The gauntlet on the hand lit up. "Or were you simply having a little fun?"

The general looked at his gun. He knew what that gauntlet indicated and he glanced furtively around him for any signs of the man's nanos. Could they already be on him? Inside? He wondered if he should point the gun at Dario or himself in this situation.

"No answer, my friend?" his visitor asked.

He lowered his gun fully and looked at the assassin. "What is your game, Dario? If you've simply been sent here to spy on me, what is the point in showing yourself? Have you become bored?"

The other man snapped his fingers and nodded as he made his way to the bed. "There's something of a kindred spirit in you, I imagine," he said thoughtfully as he sat. "That battle, this attack by the destroyers…it was exhilarating, but I can't say I enjoy sitting around with my life in the hands of others."

"You could have told me you were here," Nolan muttered. "I'm sure I could have found a spare fighter for you. That way, you could go off and die on your own terms."

Dario laughed as he laid back on the bed. "Much appreciated, but I'm not all that great a pilot. My ship is mostly flown by my EI, you see."

The general tossed his gun onto the table and picked the bottle of vodka up. "I suppose that's understandable. So, will you give me a straight answer?" He took a sip and noticed the man look at him so offered the bottle. The Italian declined.

"I'm more of a wine and fine liquor man myself," he stated and waved his hand as the gauntlet's lights faded. Nolan breathed an inward sigh of relief that he tried not to show. "As for why I showed myself, I wanted a moment to make an offer."

"What offer? he asked, intrigued.

The assassin sat and leaned against one of the poles on the frame of the bed. "You have to realize that we will be attacked once we make our way into the Academy."

"I don't see why you think that is certain," he retorted. "Our last visits could even be considered boring. In fact, we are at our strongest at the Academy as we have the might of both this vessel and the droids occupying the island."

"The…rebels? Resistance? Whatever, same difference. They haven't simply hidden all this time. All over the world, both the military and escaped students of the Ark Academies have fought back and we are losing ground." The man leaned closer. "I've been told there have been a number of attacks and skirmishes with the rebels, especially in the last few days. In fact, a couple of little gadgets Merrick wanted were taken before he could acquire them."

"And what does all this have to do with my objective? It sounds like either your or Damyen's responsibility."

"Because the ones who have recovered the items of

interest were Nexus students. And from what I've heard, they didn't fly WCM colors."

The general narrowed his eyes. "And? I don't see what is so important about this. We've known their actions up till now. I'm more confused as to why we haven't been given the go-ahead to pursue them into Seattle."

Dario chuckled. "Given how many military weapons developers are in Washington and military personnel have been stationed in the area since our initial invasion, even I would think that's a gamble, at this point. It would probably make for a good show, though." He waved the thought away. "It doesn't matter. What I am trying to get at is that they are obviously working independently to the military. They have their own agenda and I'm not sure how much the WCM is involved. You know, I've wondered if they are still the World Council Military now that the World Council is gone."

"Focus, Dario." Nolan snapped, although he did feel a sharp stab of fear that he might have pressed his luck.

His visitor, however, paid the rebuke no mind. "Right, right. Anyway, I want to come out of the shadows now. It's been so long since I've had the opportunity to apply my profession. I'll act as your second-in-command. Does that sound all right?"

The general eyed him warily. "You work alone, Dario. What do you know about leading a team?"

The assassin shook his head. "You can handle the logistics and such. I only want access to the bots." He launched himself off the bed and landed next to Nolan's chair, which made the general almost fall. "And I have a great idea to start with. You know that base outside the island?"

"Let's get to it, boyo!" Wolfson shouted and pounded on the door. "Kaiden, are you ready?"

"Yeah," he replied weakly and stepped out in a spare set of camouflage medium armor taken from the military armory. "I can't make contact with Desmond or Zena. Ah, well."

"What's wrong with you?" the older man asked as he simply strolled past.

He looked back but continued his slow walk. "What? Ah, nothing. I thought about Chiyo—why would they send her alone on a mission like that?"

"She asked for it. I was in the room the same as you when they told us," the head officer replied and pushed him forward. "You're worried about her, eh? Now you have an idea how she felt whenever you ran off on a lone gig."

The ace shook his head, pushed the door open, and walked onto the outpost grounds. "That isn't the same. She's a technician—"

"An infiltrator. This is her thing. Do you really want her to come back and the thing she hears is that you thought she couldn't handle herself?"

That made him stop and he rubbed the back of his neck sheepishly. "Naw, you're right. It would be a dick thing to do. She's got this."

Wolfson smiled and nodded. "Damn straight." A drop-ship flew overhead and into the landing zone. "Hey, is that my ship?"

Kaiden nodded. "It looks like Haldt is back." He waved for Wolfson to follow as he ran over. Most of the other troops filed out of the craft before the man stepped out behind them. He saluted Wolfson and removed his helmet. "I haven't had the chance to buff out any scratches yet, sir."

"That's fine, soldier." The large man chuckled and placed a hand on the ship's hull. "She's about to see more action anyway."

Haldt looked from one man to the other. "Where are you off to?"

"We're going to see some old friends," the ace replied and strode up the ramp. "To see if we can't get extra guns for the assault on the island."

"Is that right? Do you want help?" the officer asked.

Wolfson placed a hand on his shoulder. "It's appreciated, but you've done more than your fair of running around, haven't ye? Go and get replenished."

The other man simply unclipped his canteen from his belt and downed the contents. "Refreshing," he stated, stowed it, and saluted. "Replenished and ready to go."

The head officer chuckled and looked at Kaiden, who shrugged. "It couldn't hurt. Hopefully, the mission won't be too rocky anyway."

"Good point," Wolfson agreed and headed into the ship. "If you feel like coming, let's go, Haldt."

"Of course, sir." He ran up and replaced his helmet.

"But I'm driving," the large man shouted as the ramp ascended and the dropship began to take off.

CHAPTER TWENTY-ONE

"Thank you." The small child took the candy gratefully and ran to meet up with his mother. Izzy waved to him as they boarded the carrier to take them to Seattle and Amber came down the hill after helping two elderly passengers board as well.

"I'm glad the caravan could finally make it out," she said as she joined her friend. "It's all because you and the other scouts found enough civilians that they couldn't simply ignore them anymore."

"That and the fact that the colossus will be here soon," the scout said and shook her head. "They kept saying that with mercs and droids out in the wild they were technically safer here. Many of us doubted that but they certainly can't say that when that big beast returns."

Amber nodded and gazed at the horizon. "Will you stay?"

"Of course." Izzy's voice filled with a fierce determination. "This will be the one. Everything is lining up for a big push," She leaned closer to whisper into her friend's ear.

"Most of the military higher-ups are still trying to stall and focus on getting the embassy back and all that. But I've heard that many former soldiers and Nexus students have been approached to join us. The military has no sway over them."

"Where did you hear this?" Amber asked. "And where will they come from?"

"I heard it from Silas before he was sent on another mission. It's the work of Sasha, Wolfson, and all the teachers who still have connections to the military. Hell, many of the students themselves reached out when they heard what had happened and are working in the Seattle area or running around the world to get supplies in order. Everyone is doing their part in all this."

"That's certainly comforting," Amber agreed and glanced at her stim gun. "I don't lie to myself and say our victory is guaranteed but I do have hope that we can rescue everyone who was taken during the invasion. We will see our friends again." She turned to Izzy with a serious gaze and a fist held to her chest. "Right?"

She smiled. "Damn right." Instead of a smile or nod from her friend, her eyes widened and she grasped Izzy's shoulder and threw them both down as an explosion detonated behind them to scatter crates and tables and destroy the eastern walls of the outpost.

The two friends turned quickly as dozens of Arbiter bots advanced into the base. Alarms activated as both military and Nexus resistance members engaged the invaders, many not even wearing armor. The droids simply blasted or slashed their way through the defense and carved through the field.

Izzy stood and drew her pistol. "Charging a shot," she exclaimed as she held the trigger and energy built within the weapon. A mechanical turned toward her and she fired, the blast enough to destroy the bot's shields but leave it mostly undamaged. As she charged another shot, Amber replaced her stim-gun and drew her sidearm to pepper the bot with several kinetic rounds before it attempted to simply leap at them to close the distance.

The scout darted beneath it as it descended and delivered her second charged round directly into its chest. It emitted an electric whine as she rolled out of the way and it exploded as it landed to knock Amber off her feet.

She helped the medic to stand, who grimaced from the pain in her leg as they began to move to the south. "To the bunker," Izzy shouted. Amber nodded, retrieved her stim-gun with her other hand, and used it to heal the damage to her leg. Thankfully, it did what was needed, and she was able to push into a full sprint. Something caught her eye, however. While the droids killed many of the soldiers they engaged, some were simply tasered or knocked out with blows to the head, many of whom she recognized. They were taking Nexus students again.

Angry now, she raised her pistol but her friend forced it down. "Amber, we don't have the weapons to fight. Get to the bunker."

"They are taking them again, Izzy!" she cried frantically. "I don't want to see—gah!" she uttered a pained cry as electricity coursed through her and she collapsed onto the field.

"Amber!" her friend shouted and fired at something behind her before several small spikes struck her. She convulsed and fell and her eyes closed on impact. Amber fought the urge to succumb to unconsciousness as an Arbiter droid walked passed her, grasped Izzy by the ankle, and dragged her away. The battle medic rolled onto her back and gasped as a swarm of large drones flew in. Several swooped down to snatch bodies given to them by the droids and haul them away.

A mechanical stopped beside her and she held her breath as its artificial eyes analyzed her. It grasped the collar of her jacket before a force hammer pounded into its chest and knocked it away.

"Get her to the shelter," the military vanguard ordered and two other workers helped her up and virtually carried her. A group of soldiers ran past them to join the vanguard, who activated a shield and attacked the droid to finish it off.

"Izzy," she whispered, her voice despondent as the drones returned for more victims.

"Do you still have nothing, Kaiden?" Wolfson asked and turned to look into the bay of the ship.

The ace shook his head. "Nothing so far. Our best hope is that those reinforcements Sasha talked about come through. I've tried every channel and link they gave me to contact them. Nothing doing."

"You've worked with these gangs before, right?" Haldt asked. "If you trust them enough to help us, I would imagine they've shown grit."

"That's the nicer way to put it," he agreed. "Better than

bullishness, anyway. But they are good fighters and they have numbers, although a little less after the raid last year. I hoped they'd been able to weather the invasion but they are located in San Diego, and the Omegas have a large presence there...as we learned."

"You should have come up with this plan yesterday," Wolfson retorted. "It would have saved time."

"I didn't realize how close we were to finally taking on the colossus, and I guess I expected those reinforcements you and Sasha keep mentioning to make the big difference."

The head officer nodded. "We're calling in every favor we have and looked for any spirit willing to take up a weapon and help us get the Academy back and take it to the Arbiters. It's been something of a challenge, but they'll be ready. Still, if you have more to offer who are crazy enough to join us, we'll certainly take them."

"I guess we'll see if they are still willing to work with us despite everything," Kaiden muttered in response. "Part of the reason they joined us in the raid was to prevent something like this from happening in the first place."

Haldt looked at Wolfson, then back at the other man. "Maybe bring that up if we see them."

The two other men laughed, but the ship rocked suddenly as sounds of battle roared in the distance. "What the hell was that?" the ace asked and scrambled into the cockpit.

They came over a ridge and gazed below at what was the Fire Riders' and Skyway Kings' stronghold. A black-and-red assault ship fired a relentless barrage as a couple of dozen fighters engaged in an airborne battle. The trio could see a skirmish taking place in front of the base. The Fire Riders and Kings fired at an approaching enemy in dark armor.

"The Omegas." Wolfson growled his frustration.

"What the hell did the Riders and Kings do to get their attention?" Kaiden wondered.

"You said they helped you destroy one of the AO's bases, right?" Haldt pointed out and leaned forward in his seat. "Well, the Omegas work for the AO now so this might be retaliation."

He shook his head as he turned to return to the bay. "They took their sweet time if that's the case." Quickly, he found his helmet and put it on, removed Sire and Debonair from the case he stored them in, and holstered them. "Wolfson, get low so I can bail out."

"Do you have shocks in that suit?" the head officer asked.

"This is a basic set of medium armor and has no mods other than the HUD and shields," he explained as Haldt stepped out of the cockpit.

"Pah. You should have waited until your armor was fixed," Wolfson muttered.

"Then we wouldn't be here to help," he protested. Haldt knocked the back of his hand against the ace's shoulder.

"I thought you said these guys were good fighters." He stretched up into the overhead compartments and withdrew two large white cases. "But they need you to save them?"

"Oh no, they are good," he promised. "I'll simply get this done faster."

The man chuckled as he unlocked the boxes. "I like that

attitude." The tops popped up to reveal a set of jets inside. "You can use these, right?"

He nodded emphatically. "Oh yeah,"

"Good. Put it on and let's go," Haldt ordered as he picked the other case up to equip his jet.

Kaiden looked at it. "Chief, I don't think I ever took a talent to know how to use one of these."

"Admittedly, it doesn't come up often," the EI stated.

"You know how these work, right?"

His orb bobbed up and down. *"Well sure, but I'll only feed you the information. You still gotta work it."*

"That's fine." He removed the jet from the case and Chief displayed instructions on how to equip it. "I've done a damn fine job keeping us alive so far."

CHAPTER TWENTY-TWO

The ramp dropped as Wolfson hovered over the center of the fight. "You two hurry and get your asses out!" he yelled. "I have the cannons warmed and ready and you're cutting into my time."

"It's good to know you care, sir," Haldt retorted and looked at Kaiden. "Are you ready?"

He nodded and held his rifle up. "Let's go. Remember, bright red and blue are on our side."

"I think at this point, they will be grateful to not have someone shooting at them." With that, the officer leapt off the ramp and fell about two hundred yards before his jetpack activated. He began to sail over the battlefield and lay down kinetic machine gun rounds from above as he flew to the gangs' side of the fight.

"Ready, Chief?" the ace asked as he released the rail.

"I ain't the one jumping," the EI replied. *"After you, buddy."*

"Right." He held his gun to his chest, ready to jump, but before he could, Wolfson yelled "Shit!" and banked the dropship. The sharp turn hurled him off the ramp and he spiraled toward the ground below.

"Goddammit, Wolfson!" he yelled into the comms as he tried to right himself.

"I told you to move! I was getting shot at!" the man retorted as the dropship spun to avoid fire from an Omega interceptor.

"He'd better not die. We still need him to take us back," Kaiden griped as he finally managed to twist to face in the right direction but noticed the ground coming up quickly. "All right, Chief, what do I press?"

"The purple button, I think," Chief told him and his eye narrowed quizzically.

"You think?" he demanded. "I thought you said you knew how to work this. And I don't see a purple button."

"Oh, that might be an issue."

"Chief!" he yelled and tried not to panic as the earth seemed to accelerate toward him. As he looked for said purple button, his jet activated on its own and his descent stopped and he began to move forward. "What the hell?"

Chief didn't share his shock. In fact, he made a gurgling sound some would describe as laughter. *"Come on, partner. Did you really think I couldn't control this? It's top-of-the-line, not one of the junkers the Kings take so much pride in."*

"Oh, you dick!" Kaiden was about to expand on his opinion when he noticed a mech about fifty yards away, the jock's cover partially shattered. "We'll talk about this later. For now, get me close to that mech."

"On it," the EI acknowledged. The jets whipped him around as he charged a shot and he waited until he was close enough for the jock to see him coming. The

lumbering arms of his target weren't fast enough to fire first or block his shot and it streaked through the damage in the jock's canopy. The mech stalled and fell in the blast of green energy and red mist.

"Heh, nice," he said smugly. "Let's look for Zena or Desmond. Find a relatively safe place to land so I can get this off me."

"Uh, Kai—to your left," Chief said as a small arrow formed and pointed in the direction in his HUD.

One of the Skyway Kings' jet jockeys flew beside him and pointed to his helmet to indicate that he tried to establish a commlink. "Go ahead, Chief."

"Who the hell are you?" he asked once they could communicate. "Nice pack, by the way."

"Appreciate it, but I only borrowed it for the moment." He looked down and fired at an Omega who ran below and prepared to fire a cannon. "The name is Kaiden Jericho. I worked with you guys not too long ago. I'm looking for Desmond or Zena. Have you seen them?"

The jockey nodded and made an okay sign. "They're in the base. Desmond took a fairly big hit and they are patching him up."

Kaiden responded with the same gesture. "All right. I'll go take a look. If you see another guy with a pack like mine and white armor, don't shoot him. He's with me."

"At this point, as long as you aren't firing at us, we're cool." With that, he broke off and the ace headed toward the main building.

He contacted Haldt. "Hey, I have the leaders' location and I'll go have a talk."

"Understood. I'll help out where I can, but we need to

do something about that assault ship," his teammate replied. "Even if we drive all the ground and air troops back, I don't see anything here with enough power to destroy that. Maybe a concentrated attack by the gangs' ships might work, but that relies on them defeating the Omegas ships and there being enough left for an attack."

"I'll think of something after I talk with the leaders and get back to you soon," he promised.

"Roger," the man acknowledged as a large explosion sounded over his comm. The ace looked at the field as Haldt flew through it and tossed a couple more thermals.

"I wonder if this is him cutting loose or if it's normal," Chief said.

"He's a man after my own heart if the latter." Kaiden finally landed in front of the base and a couple of guards aimed their guns at him. He held a hand up as he removed his helmet. "Tell Desmond and Zena it's Kaiden. I wanted to talk."

The men lowered their weapons slightly. "I remember you," one said. "We're a little busy here if you hadn't noticed."

"Did they send for you?" the other asked. "We're grateful for the help, but is it only you?"

"Nonsense, there's three of us," he responded. The two guards exchanged a disbelieving glance and one rolled his eyes. "Trust me, it's more than enough. Can you take me to them already?"

The first man nodded. "Head in. They are in the lobby. Desmond wanted to get patched and go back out. I think Zena is trying to make him stay."

"It's funny to think she cares so much now," his teammate commented. "Only a couple of years ago, they were rival leaders at each other's throats."

"We would have been too, stupid," the first guard replied and pointed to his red armor and the other's blue armor.

He walked past them and into the building as the guard responded with a succinct, "Good point."

"Hey, Zena! Desmond! Are you there?" Kaiden shouted and drew the attention of several other gang members in the building as he walked in.

"Who is looking and why aren't you fighting?" Desmond shouted in response. Footsteps approached from the western hallway but no one had appeared as yet.

"Take it easy or the gel won't set," Zena ordered. She finally stepped into view, pushing against a taller man in blue.

"We need to get a crate of ultrafast setting gel when we are done with this," Desmond muttered and glanced up to see Kaiden. "Well, I'll be damned. Zena was just saying we should give you a call."

He extended his hand as the woman turned to see the ace as well and shook both their hands and nodded. "I tried to call you. How long have you been under attack?"

"We've only been fighting for about forty minutes," Desmond explained, "but just got back from a different gig. The bastard Omegas jammed our comms. They've tried to take our base over the last few weeks. They were already here in force when we got back."

"I guess they thought this would be easy pickings," Zena muttered. "They want our supplies and the fort but thought we would simply roll over when they brought real firepower instead of only a few armored shitheads with big guns. My guess is they've learned that was a painful miscalculation."

"I'm glad to see you can still give as good as you take." A blast rattled the area and a few of the remaining windows broke from the force. "I wanted some help but it looks like you need it first. Let's get these guys off your lawn."

"I'll be right behind y—ugh." Desmond stepped back a bit warily. "This damn gel is making me woozy."

"That would be the blood loss, idiot," Zena snapped. Kaiden finally noticed the long trail of dried blood on the armor of the Skyway Kings' leader. There was a large patch around his left shoulder, cuts along his face, and another trail from his right ribcage to his leg.

"What happened?" he asked and checked his supplies to see if he had anything to help.

"I was shot by a sniper in the shoulder. The armor took most of it but it was a ballistic round—small but still an annoying little bastard," Desmond stated. "Then a gut strike by a plasma blade. I killed both of them for their trouble, but things got a little dark."

"His men brought him back. They stitched him up and put some healing gel on. Not the really good stuff, unfortunately, and the fool thinks he's okay to go back out there like this." Zena sighed.

The ace shook his head. "It looks to me like you may be all right on that front. You still gotta fight hard, but the bigger problem is that ship."

"No kidding." Desmond groaned as another rumble shook the fort. "Those are probably from it firing on this building to batter the shields. Either they are trying to scare us or they've taken the position that if they can't have our stuff, we can't either."

"It's better that they focus on us rather than fire at the grunts," she pointed out. "We don't have any big cannons or anything like that to destroy it. We were hoping to maybe make a run with explosives using the jockeys but it's too hot right now. Even the craziest jockeys won't fly through a battlefield carrying armfuls of explosives with all this fighting and them exposed."

"Do you think you have enough explosives to blow a hole in its hull?" he asked.

Desmond shook his head. "Probably not, but we've seen troops drop out of it so thought we could blow up the underside where they've come from and get in to plant more."

"So you can get inside the ship?" he asked as a thought crossed his mind and he tapped the strap of his jetpack. "Or, rather, maybe I can?"

CHAPTER TWENTY-THREE

Wolfson was pursued by three enemy fighters after he'd eliminated the Interceptor that had attacked him and two other Omega ships and he assumed he had their full attention by now. Or they simply wanted to beef up their kill tally and his dropship was a bigger and more appealing target than the Skyways' smaller, faster ships. If so, it meant they were probably rather pissed at how agile his modified ship was.

The head officer grinned as he flipped a switch on his console to focus his remaining shields on the front of the ship as he spun it in place to face the three pursuers. He fired his cannons and caught two of them off guard to destroy them with little effort and clipped the third. It was able to break away but one of the Skyway fighters streaked in to deliver the final strike.

He shook his head and sighed as he pressed the shield switch again to cover the whole ship. "Pah. I'll still count it."

"Hey, Wolfson, are you free?" Kaiden asked and his

voice crackled over the comm—that would need to be repaired once they returned.

"I still have a good number of targets, boyo, unless you have something more interesting." He lowered his drop-ship a little to offer air support for the gang members who fought on the ground.

"It's more of a taxi service but still appealing."

Wolfson chuckled as he fired at a group of Arbiter bots and Omega troops on the ground. "Will you pay me?"

"I need you to take me close to that big ship," the ace explained. "I have explosives we're gonna use to blast through the bottom. I'll infiltrate and take it over."

His gaze moved to the assault ship and he realized how lucky the unintended warning had been when a couple of the mounted turrets swung toward him and opened fire. He rolled his ship and forced it up while he punched it to gain distance. "Do you think you can take on the entire crew of an assault ship?"

"Have I ever given you reason to doubt me?" the younger man retorted. He had to admit, everyone knew Kaiden's specialty was destruction, but this sounded almost like a plan, which gave him pause. "Besides, from what Zena and Desmond have told me, there really aren't that many people on board. Most have been deployed onto the battlefield. At worst, I'll fight a skeleton crew and maybe a handful of spare droids."

The head officer pulled his craft up and spun to make a run at the assault vessel. He fired the two missiles he kept at the front of the ship for emergencies but they merely impacted with its shield to create a large red glimmer but no damage. More turrets began to fire at him and his own shields fell as he sped away. It didn't look like he had the firepower to destroy it, which was something of a disappointment. He had kind of hoped to show the younger soldier up.

"I don't hear a reply, Wolfson," Kaiden badgered. "Come on. I'll buy you dinner."

He sighed, although his smile was broad. "Fine, fine. Where are ya, boyo?"

"At the entrance of the big-ass building. There's a landing pad a few yards down and to the left. Open the bay and I'll get in and we can go."

"I'm on my way." Wolfson activated the jets, hurtled across the battlefield in a little over a minute, and fired a few shots at the enemy along the way. He saw the pad and circled to lower the back ramp while he hovered the craft above the landing zone. A glance over his shoulder confirmed that Kaiden scrambled on board with a large sack. The younger man pointed up and the pilot nodded as he retracted the ramp and elevated sharply again.

"What's with the bag?" he asked as the ace walked into the cockpit.

"It's the explosives," he replied and withdrew a gray box about a foot-and-a-quarter long to show him.

"That's not exactly the correct storage for high-grade explosives," the head officer noted jokingly.

Kaiden put the explosives in the bag and tossed it over his shoulder. "Oh, I'm aware of that. Why do you think I asked you to carry my happy ass over there instead of simply jetting in myself?"

"So I'm your nanny, then?" he asked as they closed in on the assault ship.

"Taxi," his companion clarified as he opened the side door of the ship. "Keep the tab running." Wolfson twisted the ship to its side as the other man dove out. His jet activated as he flew to the underside of the assault ship and the large vessel flew away but delivered a few shots at the target to annoy those inside.

"Do you see the door, Chief? the ace asked. He wanted to breach quickly before too many of the other soldiers saw him.

"Yeah, hold on." He drifted to the left and located the drop door of the assault but scowled when he saw a hard cover over it.

"I guess they thought it was a weak point too."

"It's fairly standard on ships with a hatch on the bottom but it still won't be enough to stop us from getting inside. Five should be enough."

He hovered under it, retrieved the explosives from the sack, and stuck five onto the cover. "We have five left. What should we do with them?"

"I'm sure you'll come up with something." After they were securely in place, Chief guided him far enough away from the impending explosion. "*Should I start a countdown?"*

Kaiden drew Debonair and aimed at one of the charges. "Nah, I got this." He fired and they detonated with sufficient force to destroy the door and thrust him back a few more feet even at a safe distance.

"Damn, those things pack a punch." The ace righted himself as laser fire from below indicated that Omega mercs who hadn't noticed him before sure as hell had now. "Let's get going, Chief," he shouted and held the bag with the remaining explosives close when everything in his mind and body screamed for him to hurl them away before they were hit. Chief controlled the jets and flew into the underside of the ship to land inside a small room and to the side of the entrance as more shots streaked through the hole and into the ceiling.

Kaiden removed the jets and set them aside as he turned to a heavy door that barred their way out of the room. "I assume that's locked."

"Yeah. It shouldn't be a problem for me, though." Chief had already begun to take control of the terminal. *"Although I pick up a dozen energy signatures, both droid and armor shielding. You can expect a warm welcome by Omega standards."*

"How nice of them," he muttered sarcastically as he placed the bag on the ground and fished out one of the explosives. "I probably shouldn't run around with these but can only fit one into the storage compartment on my armor."

"I told you a few times that you should have sprung for the armored backpack for instances like this. Oh, more are coming. I have about twenty-two door-greeters now."

"Shut it," Kaiden snarked, placed the explosive into the compartment on his leg, and held the sack up. "Our plan wasn't to blow the ship up but I still have a use for these. Crack the door a little, would you?"

"Fire as soon as this little bitch opens the door," one of the mercs ordered, his shotgun ready as a green light flashed above the doorway. A hiss of escaped air was followed by a heavy clunk as the bars unlatched. "Got it?"

The other troops nodded and the droids merely aimed their blasters at the barrier and stood unmoving. It began to open slowly. A flash of brown peeked out and lurched toward the first soldier in the group. They all fired at once and the sound masked a click when the door locked again.

Even with the sound dampeners in his helmet activated, the explosion was loud and the force it unleashed shook the entire compartment. When it steadied, all Kaiden heard was crackling and thuds from metal falling to the floor. He paused for a moment, knocked on the door, and listened for a response. Nothing other than the sound of falling debris from the destruction could be heard.

"Do you think they're dead?" he asked jokingly.

"Even with all the medical advances in the world, I don't think we've come up with anything that can take remaining pieces and turn them into a proper human," Chief responded and turned a sickly green. *"If you need me to say it, kills confirmed. Also, you will have a hell of a cleaning bill walking through there."*

With a grin, he released the lock and opened the door. "Do you really think there's that much—" He stepped out, gaped at the damage, and almost slipped on something that was totally unrecognizable. When they returned to the base, he'd have to apologize to some poor bastard responsible for the upkeep of the military armor who would definitely not be impressed by the gunk he'd accumulate. He grimaced. The situation was not helped at all by the gross remains that dropped off the ceiling, and he decided to ignore it all and push through as quickly as possible.

Besides, he had a whole ship to negotiate, and if there were more stubborn troops in there, this was really only the start of it all.

CHAPTER TWENTY-FOUR

Haldt landed in the middle of a group of Omega soldiers and the surprise of his sudden appearance blindsided them. He held his hands up and two pistols emerged from his gauntlets and settled smoothly into his palms. The four troops hadn't fully recovered when he fired, although one managed to duck under the strike that caught his buddy. The officer delivered two point-blank shots into the trooper's chest before he swept another off his feet and finished with rapid shots at the fourth.

The grounded man tried to retaliate from his prone position but he simply kicked the gun away and finished him with three precise shots to the head. He had to admit, although he loathed how things had become, being out in the field in real combat was exhilarating compared to his days as a security officer.

A droid tried to sneak up on him and he glanced over his shoulder as it crouched in preparation for an attack. He turned to face it and as it leapt toward him, he activated his jets, soared up and over it, and fired as he descended. The mechanical uttered a metallic screech as it fell beneath the hail of laser fire. Haldt landed gently on top of its corpse and smiled. It definitely was good to be back.

"Hey, Haldt!" Wolfson called over the comms. "How is it going out there for ya?"

The officer looked at the carcasses and shrugged as he replaced his pistols in his gauntlets. "Well enough, sir. How about you?"

"My ship has taken its licks but given them back three times as hard," he replied and followed it with a proud laugh. "There still seems to be a good number of these bastards but keep it up. Kaiden is taking care of the assault ship."

"On his own?" Haldt asked as he removed his machine gun pack and closed the vent. "Should I go and assist, sir?"

"Nah. The boy seems sure he can take it on his own. I didn't contact you so you could babysit," the head officer assured him. "I felt like starting a bet—maybe a hundred credits?"

"What's the wager?" he asked and frowned at the top half of a droid that crawled along the field using its arms. He felled with a quick burst from his weapon.

"How long it will take him to take control of the ship," Wolfson stated. "I'll let you take the first guess."

"I haven't interacted with him as much as you have, sir," he replied and returned to the skies once he realized most of the action was farther away. "But the few times I have seen him in action were certainly impressive and you think quite highly of him. I'll go against my better judgment and make it ludicrously low. A half-hour."

The older man chuckled. "In most situations, I would

think you were right and that was ludicrous." Haldt sensed a qualifier and simply waited. "But I know the boy. If this was only a search and destroy mission, I would say ten, but given that he's trying to take it over, I'll have to adjust. Let's say…twenty minutes."

"And four and five," Kaiden tallied his strikes as two more droids fell to Sire's blasts. It appeared that they had already sent the majority of the forces on this ship to confront him at the door and he had more difficulty navigating the vessel than dealing with the security.

"Chief, you should have maps and layouts of these ships, right?" he asked as he stepped around the corner and quickly destroyed an overhead turret. "Can't you direct me to the main bridge?"

"I did. I said go west," the EI retorted. *"I don't know what type of model this is. Either its one that isn't widely known or they built it themselves. I don't have any layout for it. Keep walking."*

"Says the guy with no legs," he muttered and vented Sire as he continued. "You've not picked up more enemies, at least?"

"None close by that I can see. They might all be waiting for you on the bridge for a last stand or something," Chief responded. *"They also may not have a huge crew. Assault ships like these have special EIs that run all everything. For merc companies like the Omegas, it means fewer crew members to bother with and more troops to replace them."*

"It seems kind of risky given that an EI can fail or get

hacked. Most military vessels use EI and still have a full support crew," he pointed out.

"These are mercenaries. Most of their members are killers, not engineers, and the techies they do have focus on making killer droids. Besides, risk is basically a part of the lifestyle."

"Even back in my Deadeye days, I knew you needed a full outfit. Nothing but gun nuts is asking to be hobbled by a good hacker. Ah, well. If they want to make this easy for me, I guess I shouldn't complain too much." A sudden flash at the right of his visor didn't blind him but it almost obscured his vision. "Whoa—what the hell was that, Chief?"

"A power spike. You're still in tech readout."

Kaiden increased his pace, closed Sire's vent, and held the weapon to his chest. "Shit. You don't think they are trying to blow the ship, do you?"

"It's not that big and it's dying quite quickly, in fact. I think it's a droid or something that turned on and used mods to obscure its energy." Chief's eye narrowed as the ace ran in the direction from which the flash had come. *"Are you going to engage it?"*

"Better that than the reverse," he replied.

"Fair enough, but be careful. I don't know what it's packing but that spike was enough to know that it needed enormous power to use it."

"Don't worry. I know to be on guard at this point." The ace reached the area where he estimated the flash had originated and hesitated at a double door that blocked his path. The terminal indicated that they were unlocked, which made a nice change of pace. "I'm prepared for anything at this point."

He raised his hand toward the terminal but fell back instinctively when a loud boom from behind the barrier provided a split-second warning. The doors launched from their hinges and both them and a large energy beam careened into the wall behind him. "What the hell is that?"

"What you should have been prepared for," Chief replied. "And it looks like I was half-right. That's not a droid, but it is droid-like."

Kaiden regained his feet and entered the room with his gun held ready and stared at a tall, metallic being with a skull-like black helmet, glowing white eyes, and a sleek frame in black-and-red. "That's not a droid."

"It's a guy in power armor. The name is redundant, but this was the prototype to modern armor," the EI explained. *"You don't see that too often nowadays. It's somewhere between a heavy and a mech jockey—a bitch to maintain but powerful."*

"Does it have any weak points?" He held Sire's trigger as he studied his adversary.

Chief simply nodded. *"Shoot it and keep shooting."*

"That's helpful, Chief."

"What the hell are you doing on my ship? Are you a Fire Rider or King?" the man in the suit asked, his voice masked by a metallic speaker. Before Kaiden could answer, the challenger stepped forward. "It doesn't matter either way. I'll rip your arms and legs off."

"I need to start keeping a record of these threats," he said aloud and aimed Sire at the slowly advancing attacker. "I'm fairly sure that's at least the tenth time someone has said that to me specifically." He fired and the blast struck perfectly. It masked the man—the captain, obviously, since he'd called it his ship—in smoke while sparks erupted when the blast also impacted with several other machines around him.

The ace smiled for a moment before the captain spoke again. "Is that so? Well, I'll make sure it's the last time you hear it." The familiar hum of charging energy accompanied a red glow in the armor's cannon arm as the smoke cleared. The man looked mostly undamaged. "Or anything, for that matter."

"I said keep shooting!" Chief yelled as the captain prepared to fire. *"Get down!"*

Haldt hauled a Fire Rider to his feet and supported him until another stepped in to help him back to base to attend to the wound in his stomach—if he would even make it. The officer tried to take flight again but as he ascended, his pack ruptured when a sniper shot damaged it. He landed on his feet and while the shocks in the armor dispersed the force of impact, he wondered if he had maybe been too cocky thus far.

"Look out!" He spun in response to the warning. Omega fighters had broken away from the dogfight above and swooped down for a run along the battlefield. Given that they hadn't done so before, it was very likely that Wolfson had given them the idea.

The officer began to run, along with many of the other gang members. The attackers had already opened fire and he realized that he wouldn't make it. One of the Skyway Kings held a shielding device and pounded it into the ground. Haldt dove inside and it enclosed him and several others as blasts erupted all around them. Three shots drilled into the shield and that was almost enough to destroy it.

The constant changes in the tide of battle was something he didn't miss when out of the action. Now, they were on the defensive.

CHAPTER TWENTY-FIVE

Wolfson peered at the battle below, where the members of the Riders and Kings moved back along the field. "Haldt, are you still there?"

"Barely, sir," the officer replied and had to yell to be heard above the loud blasts around him. "Is everything all right?"

"I'm fine. What the hell is going on down there?"

"We're being pushed back," the man explained and the clamor of gunfire all but drowned him out. "I don't know if the enemy has rallied or brought in another group of troops. They've gotten their shit together, either way, and are coming in hard."

A squad of Omegas approached and Haldt and two Fire Riders fired at them but managed to only eliminate two of the six as they returned fire. One of the Riders took a thermal out and activated it but was shot and dropped the grenade. The officer scooped it up quickly and lobbed it at the enemy group, who scattered as it exploded.

The head officer grimaced as he prepared to change direction and banked toward the battlefield. "The gangs were in a bind when we arrived. I guess there's only so much two or three guys can do at the moment. Kaiden should finish at any minute now. I'll come around and—" The ship rattled under a volley and the small number of shields remaining was reduced to the bare minimum. "Son of a bitch!"

"Sir?" Haldt called in alarm before there was another explosion and the commlink was disconnected.

"Shit, Haldt!" Wolfson yelled and backed the ship hastily as he glanced at the monitor to see two Omega fighters in pursuit. "You're determined bastards, aren't ya?" He growled and accelerated to put some distance between them and his ship before he opened his comm directory, selected Kaiden's name, and waited for it to connect. It did but the only response was more blasts and the pounding of metal. "Kaiden! Where are you and what's going on?"

"I'm working," the ace yelled and darted into cover behind a metal pillar as he tossed two shock grenades while he charged another shot. They exploded and coated the captain in an electric web, but it did little more than slow the suit for a second before the armor simply dispersed it. "This damn thing is hacked!" He spun around the pillar and fired and this time, the power-suited captain did attempt to dodge. However, the suit made him powerful, not agile, and the shot struck home. After the discharge, cracks and melted pieces of metal on the chest and arms of the suit were visible. There weren't many but better than the nothing he had achieved so far. "All right. I'm finally starting to get through the bastard."

"Don't get—" Chief began, only to be interrupted by the Omega's distorted yelling.

"Don't get cocky!"

"The bastard stole my line." The EI's eye narrowed and he turned an angry red.

The captain's shoulder pads opened to reveal several tiny missiles within, all trained on Kaiden. "Oh, bullshit," he muttered and pushed into a sprint once again. They fired as he retrieved another shock grenade, held the switch for a moment to let it cook, and flung it back as the missiles approached in a tight group. The shock grenade detonated and caught most of them. They fell but the blast didn't stop them from exploding, however, and although the resultant force annihilated the remainder, the blast from all the small missiles combined was enough to catapult the ace across the room and deplete his remaining shields.

He fell into a group of crates, knocked some over, and kicked one aside that almost fell on top of him.

"So, any plans yet?" Chief asked.

"I've been busy!" he shouted, as the captain threw a metal crate across the room. He rolled out of the way as it toppled those stacked behind him. "What about you?"

"Yeah, because you've taken my advice to heart through all this." The EI rolled his eye.

"Your advice was to shoot and keep shooting," he

snapped and cursed when another battery of missiles rocketed toward him. "He won't let up, will he?" he muttered, charged a shot quickly, and fired to destroy a few missiles that exploded and took the rest with them, far enough away this time that he was only forced back a few steps. It made no real difference as he didn't want to stay where he was anyway.

"It's been an effective strategy."

"I'm running out of cover strong enough to protect me from his attacks," the ace pointed out. "And I've not done enough damage to outlast him. It's power armor, right? It has to have some kind of system for you to hack like the heavies use to move their big asses."

"I've tried. Something is blocking me. I've observed the suit while you've been tussling."

"Did you notice anything interesting?" he asked and charged one last shot that he fired at the captain while on the move. The blast was enough to force his adversary away. The man twisted the upper half of his body and Chief highlighted a large area on his back.

"The power unit is on the front of the armor. This is probably a back-up unit, but it also probably houses whatever is keeping me out of its systems. If you can get through it, I shouldn't have a problem."

"You come on to my ship, kill my men, and then try to take me on?" the captain yelled as he charged a blast of his own. "I'll turn you to dust."

"I don't think this guy will let up anytime soon so it would be better to go with a plan that might end this quickly, even if it is only a hunch." Kaiden vented Sire and raced toward the protection of another pillar. "How well-armored is that container?"

"Quite well and it has a personal barrier as well. It's obviously important to be double-wrapped like that," the EI advised. *"He's not fast, obviously, but you'll have to get around him to take shots at the pack."*

"That's starting from square one, at this point. I have a different plan." He shut Sire's vent and sprinted across the room as the captain fired repeated small blasts from his cannon. "The front is exposed now. How fragile are the eye holes?"

"If you can make the shot, go for it."

"Got it. Okay, it's time to invade his personal space." The ace fired a couple of half-charged shots at the captain and ended his onslaught abruptly to disorient him briefly. He held the trigger charging the gun as he closed in and drew Debonair in his other hand when his adversary released a blade from his other gauntlet. The Omega moved his arm to strike and Kaiden held Sire up and fired when he was only a few yards away. The recoil from firing a shot with only one arm put his aim slightly off-center but at that range, it didn't matter.

The captain saw what he intended but he was too close to leap out of the way. Instead, he swiped the blade in front of him, caught the shot, and caused it to erupt. The discharge of energy blew up the containers and any parts around them and Kaiden rushed forward and dropped Sire to hold Debonair in both hands. Without slowing, he fired directly into the eyes of the suit's helmet.

Sparks resulted when the shots hit and the captain roared and cursed while he swiped madly with his blade and fired recklessly. The ace rolled easily through the attacks and opened the compartment on his legs when he faced the back of the power armor. He removed the explosive he had stored and slapped it on the back container before he flung himself aside.

"That'll do it," Chief chirped. *"No countdown?"*

"I got it," he replied and aimed with Debonair. "And send Wolfson a message, would ya?" He gave chief the message as he fired. The explosion careened the suit away and hurled it to the ground as the container was ripped apart.

Wolfson had been able to shake one of the pursuers—or, rather, they were intercepted by one of the remaining Skyway Kings fighters—but the other wouldn't budge. He had been able to avoid its attacks but couldn't find the right time to change positions and eliminate it. Finally, he decided he'd had enough, activated the vessel's auto-pilot, and walked into the bay to open a chest and withdraw the cannon inside. He marched to the back of the ship and lowered the ramp manually.

The Omega fighter was almost in position for another assault when the head officer held the cannon, which rattled as the energy collected in the barrel. "Smile, you son of a bitch!" he shouted as he fired. The blast made him skid back a few feet as it rocketed out and connected head-on with the fighter. What remained of the ship plummeted as he tossed the cannon aside and closed the ramp. It was such an easy fix. Maybe he should simply install the cannon on the back of the ship when he had free time.

When he returned to the cockpit, he noticed a blinking message on the monitor from Kaiden.

I'll have this wrapped up soon. Don't die in the meantime.

He glanced at the clock. It had been twelve minutes since he had made the bet with Haldt. "You're cutting it close there, boyo."

CHAPTER TWENTY-SIX

"S*o, that got him, right?*" Chief asked and his eye narrowed.

"Can't you tell?" Kaiden asked and approached the captain cautiously while he held his last shock grenade in readiness. It hadn't done much before, but with electricity sparking out of the back of the armor, it might actually affect him now—or maybe power him up as he now had a direct line to his back-up power unit. He stowed the grenade and simply aimed Debonair at him. "Are you still blocked? Can you hack him now?"

Chief nodded. "*Yeah, I can get through. Give me a minute.*" With that, the avatar vanished.

The ace relaxed slightly but tensed again almost immediately when the captain groaned and one of his arms thumped on the floor. It was followed quickly by the other and he forced himself to stand. At this point, it wasn't clear if the power armor was that strong or the captain that tenacious.

"You...haven't won here!" his adversary bellowed and

pushed himself up in one thrust before he turned toward Kaiden. He held his blade in front, pointed at the ace, as he marched forward. "I'll slice you from your groin to your gullet, you sorry little piece of shit."

"Chief?" he called and fired several shots from Debonair. They struck the armor, did minor damage, and didn't slow the man at all. While he wasn't exactly running, it seemed logical that he would remember that he had a cannon at some point. Either that or he really wanted to carve him up instead.

With another roar, the captain suddenly surged into the attack and drew his arm back for a vicious forward thrust. "Chief!" Kaiden yelled as he ducked and flung himself to the left to roll out of his path. He spun as he tried to regain his feet to prepare for another assault, but the armor froze in mid-thrust. The ace observed it closely as he stood. There was no movement at all and he couldn't hear the captain—if he was saying anything, of course, but he imagined a string of angry and confused curses, at least.

"I activated the emergency locks. They're usually used when the armor is in for repairs or has sustained enough damage and they wanna keep parts from falling off. If activated when it's mostly intact, it simply locks it down," Chief explained. *"Get ready. I'm gonna eject him."*

"Eject?" A hiss of air issued from the armor and Kaiden instinctively readied his gun. Rather than move again, what remained of the back of the suit unfolded to the sides. A man with a bald head and disheveled black-and-red beard fell out dressed in a black jumpsuit. He grunted as he scrambled to his feet and tried to get back into the armor, his feet still locked into the boots. As he struggled and fell again, the ace walked up to him and noticed burns around his eyes.

The captain rolled his head and glared as best he could through his damaged eyes. "Come any closer and I'll throttle ya," he threatened.

He paced back slowly and out of the man's arm range and held Debonair trained on him. "I promise not to get too close. My trigger finger has a mind of its own, though."

There was a brief moment of concern on the man's face, but it quickly changed to consternation. "Why are you here? I can tell you aren't one of the Riders or Kings. You're too trained for that."

"I'm a mutual friend, and as for why I'm here...well, you can actually help me with that." He flipped his weapon and whipped it against the captain's head to render him unconscious.

"Go ahead and let him loose, Chief," he ordered. When the boots were unlocked, he hauled the man fully out of the suit before he stepped up to it himself. "This is still operational, right, Chief?"

"Indeed it is." The EI nodded and returned to the HUD. *"I'm guessing you like the look of it?"*

He smiled as he studied the armor speculatively. "I wonder how it will look on me."

When the captain awoke and heard thumping, he initially thought it was only his head until something shuddered under his legs and back. He sat, opened his eyes as much as they could, and grinned when he focused on his power armor. The idiot must have left him to go off and sabotage the ship without taking the time to completely destroy the suit. This was his golden opportunity, and he'd make sure to finish the invader this time.

But as he moved to stand, the armor looked at him and he froze. That had to be a trick of the light, right? When one of the arms moved and the blade in the gauntlet emerged, he knew it was no trick.

"I said you were gonna help me," the soldier's voice boomed out of the helmet. "If you need convincing...well, I have time and we're the only ones here, right?"

The captain paled.

Haldt helped a King into the base, followed by several others while a group stayed behind to guard the entry. Another man in bloody, heavy armor came over to assist and helped him to place the injured man on a cot.

"I appreciate it," the officer said and rolled his shoulders to ease the stiffness.

"I should say that to you," the King member said and extended his hand. "My name is Desmond. I'm the leader of this chapter of the Skyway Kings. I haven't seen you around—are you with Kaiden?"

He shook his hand. "Arsenio Haldt. I'm an officer in Nexus Security under Head Officer Wolfson. I'm glad to be of assistance."

"You seem to have done more than that." The large man chuckled, his arms loose at his sides. "I had a couple of reports from the boys saying there was some new guy flying around with jets. They said they wanted a set when this was over."

"Considering that's what you're known for, I'll take the compliment." Haldt pressed the button to unclip the jets from his armor. "Unfortunately, I took a hit or I'd be glad to spare mine."

"We can still use it," Desmond assured him. "We're used to working with scraps." Shouts and laser fire outside caught his attention and a couple of errant blasts thumped into the walls at the entrance. "Are they all the way back here?" he asked.

The officer drew his machine gun. "Only some but the rest are on their way. We can hold the building until Kaiden is done."

"He's taking his sweet time, isn't he?" the other man muttered. "Zena, you gonna join us?"

She walked over, flanked by a squad of reds and blues, and tossed him a shotgun as she readied her own. "I'd rather take it to them than sit here and wait for them to come knocking."

"Damn straight." Desmond activated his weapon and picked his helmet up from a nearby table. "All jockeys, if you have your jets fixed and you aren't dying, head into the sky and assist the fighters. We'll hold the rest down here."

Three men nodded and jogged up the stairs to the roof. Haldt was impressed. For a non-military outfit, they seemed to respect the chain of command quite well.

"Are you with Kaiden?" Zena asked and stepped beside him. "Do you know how he's doing? We haven't had another volley from the ship since he got in there."

"I haven't had contact. Wolfson has but hasn't reported

anything to me." He glanced at the time in his HUD. "Seventeen minutes. It looks like I might win the bet."

"Bet?" she asked, but he waved her off.

"Nothing important. We'd better get out there and finish this, right?" Haldt turned and strode to the doors and Desmond, Zena, and the squad of riders followed. They hollered and whooped as they pushed out to engage the advancing Omegas.

Wolfson cruised around the airspace of the assault ship. Kaiden hadn't responded and while he had been in the middle of a fight earlier, he had no idea if that was ongoing. That might be why or maybe his helmet and commlink were destroyed. There was only one other option but that was one he didn't want to think about.

The assault ship's turrets began to turn, as did the ship, and it slowly began to fly closer to the field. The head officer's heart stopped for a moment while his mind protested the possibility that his worst fears were realized.

"Omegas!" a voice called and echoed across the field from the ship's speakers. "Put your weapons down and surrender." Wolfson's heart began to move again and a smile settled on his face.

"If you need more convincing…" An odd rustling issued from the speakers for a moment before another voice spoke. "This is Captain Lokleer. End it, lads. We've lost."

Haldt and the others exited the fort and immediately stopped when Omega troops dropped their weapons and held their hands up. Deactivated droids lay sprawled around them. The enemy ship approached and prepared to land in front of the fort. The officer checked his time again —nineteen minutes. He sighed and accepted that he had to give it to his boss, but given the circumstances, he wasn't too upset.

Wolfson landed his vessel and noticed that the five remaining Omega fighters had also landed. As he alighted, the pilots were shepherded away by Riders and it was interesting that they didn't make a run for it. Perhaps there was some honor in them, after all. A ramp descended from the underside of the assault ship and weapons were drawn when someone in bronze armor stepped off with another man over his shoulders. Without ceremony, the figure simply dropped the man—who had burnt eyes and a beard —into the dirt.

The visor on the armor flipped up to reveal a grinning Kaiden. Weapons lowered as Wolfson walked over and clapped him on the shoulder.

"Nice work, Kaiden," he said cheerfully. "You had me sweating there for a while."

The ace returned the gesture but his slap had a little more force than he was used to thanks to the armor. "You should know I do good work by now, Wolfson." He pointed to his chest. "What do you think? Spoils of war."

"Some old power armor, eh?" The large man stroked his

beard as he studied the suit thoughtfully. “It needs repair obviously, and a paint job, but I think it suits you.”

He nodded and brandished the blade. “I think so too. And it’ll make storming the Academy a hell of a lot more interesting.”

CHAPTER TWENTY-SEVEN

"I'm bringing her in," the Azure Halo pilot shouted to Chiyo and the Halo leaders as they flew into their Seattle outpost. "I'm only waiting for confirmation."

"And to be sure, they won't shoot us down, right?" Fritz asked as he glanced at the infiltrator.

"And to repeat myself, I've already called in and explained the situation," she replied and double-checked the box she had slipped the teleporter keys into before she placed it inside the case next to her helmet and guns.

"Fritz is a little skittish around military types," Kit explained and chuckled. "I think he used to be in the military, was dishonorably discharged, and has held a grudge since."

"Honorably discharged," he snapped. "But I didn't have many good experiences. Why do I bother telling you my backstory if you don't get it right?"

She shrugged and leaned back with her hands behind her head. "I don't know—you like hearing yourself talk?

For such a bad experience, you seem to mention it every other month or so."

"I have clearance," the pilot stated. "Heading to the landing zone."

"Understood." Chiyo closed her case and prepared to grab the handle before Kit stopped her.

"Let Fritz take it. He likes to be a gentleman." He looked like he wanted to protest but he also quickly realized how that would make him look so he simply rolled his eyes and nodded.

"I appreciate it but I can carry my own gear," she responded. "I need to take the contents to my superiors. Besides, how can I ask for favors after you saved me?"

"Ah, that was only happenstance and really, you helped out as much as we did," Kit pointed out. "Those Ghouls were too close to our turf. We had planned to take them out for a few months, but with everything going to hell in the area thanks to the Omega Horde suddenly coming in, we had to push our plans back."

"We were kinda worried we didn't have enough droids to take them on or enough intel to know what they had up their sleeves, but they started taking our supplies and some of our trading partners and became a hassle," Fritz added. "They aren't the type to simply talk business matters like that though, so our response had to be rougher than we like. Imagine our surprise when we got there and most of them had fled or were dead. It saved us a hell of a lot of time."

Chiyo smiled as the ship landed and picked her case up. "It's appreciated, either way. I hope we can come to some kind of agreement for your further assistance."

Kit and Fritz both stood when the back ramp began to open. "Hey, if these AO guys are the ones who call the shots and the Omegas are with them, it's better to be rid of them now than potentially be swallowed into their little coalition," the woman reasoned

"I think it's more about general world domination," he countered. "Janis has tried his damnedest to find out more about these guys ever since the raid on that factory we helped with, but besides that maniac leader's doomsday announcements, he hasn't been able to turn up much."

"Unfortunately, that has been the same for us and the military as far as I know," Chiyo stated and they walked down the ramp. "For now, our focus is their main vessel and reclaiming our Academy."

"Is that a pride thing?" Fritz asked.

"In some respects, but that colossus would be an asset once we push to reclaim the embassy and many of our comrades and possibly other innocents are stowed onboard," she explained as they walked toward the central building. "And it appears that their leader wants something within the Academy rather desperately. We'd rather stop him from getting to it."

Kit nodded as the infiltrator pulled the door open. "Fair enou—whoa. What's going on in here?" Dozens of men and women, both military and resistance alike, ran through the lobby to different parts of the building and yelled orders hastily or tried to talk to others.

Janis scratched his chin. "Is this normal?"

Chiyo shook her head. "Something must have happened or is about to happen." She headed to the stairs and motioned urgently for them to follow. "Hurry. We need to see Sasha."

She was not the only one who wanted to see the chancellor. When they arrived on the floor where his office was, the area was almost as packed with people as the lobby had been. Chiyo and the two Halos pushed through and she explained at high volume that she had an important package to deliver. Despite her efforts, her voice was virtually drowned out by the noise.

"Everyone, I know of the attack!" Sasha shouted at the crowd from the door to his office. "The military does as well. They are preparing a response."

"A response?" one of the mob bellowed. "Aren't they going to attack? They have no choice now. The colossus is back."

"It seems we were a little late," the infiltrator muttered, currently stuck several yards away from the commander.

"What about us?" another asked. "We have to engage, right? That's what we've done all this prep and recon for. This is our chance."

Sasha pursed his lips but nodded. "I agree, and plans are coming together quickly. But we cannot be reckless about it. We do not have the luxury of failure."

Although this did little to quell the crowd, most had to agree with the fact even though they didn't like it. She finally found a place to push through to the front and waved at the chancellor. "Sasha!"

He glanced at her and nodded. "For now, get back to work and prepare for battle. I will give you our plans soon, you have my word." Some in the crowd agreed audibly while others simply nodded or began to talk amongst themselves. Finally, however, they began to leave and the crowd filtered out slowly as Chiyo and the Halos hurried into the office at Sasha's urging. He shut the door and exhaled a long sigh. "It's good to see you made it back safely, Chiyo, and with some old allies," he said, his way of greeting the Halos as he walked over to a chair. "May I see the keys?"

"Of course, sir." She accessed her case, removed the box, and handed it to the chancellor who opened it and nodded appreciatively. "I didn't have the tools available to check them but they appear to be in working condition."

"They do seem to be in good shape given the circumstances and being in the hands of Ghouls. How they acquired them is beyond me."

Fritz coughed into his hand and Kit shook her head at him. "That might have been our fault in a way," she admitted. "We had actually received them from a dealer and had them stored in a bunker away from our base as we couldn't work out what they were for. We assumed they were junk but maybe some kind of collector's piece that would appeal to a potential buyer. Ghouls raided the bunker some time ago. I guess they knew they had something important since they kept it in a special vault, according to Chiyo."

"I do not think they knew any more than you did. But they frequent the underground and black markets much more than the Halos do so perhaps they saw the potential of trying to trade it there or at least finding someone who did know," Chiyo suggested.

"In any case, getting them to function properly is up to Laurie and Cyra but they both seem confident that they should be able to work even now. I'll have her take a look soon." The commander closed the box and placed it on his desk. "Now on to you two. It's quite fortunate that you appeared at this hour."

"Yeah, we've already been through the how do you do's," Fritz replied and earned an elbow in the ribs from his teammate. "Ow—look, there's no need to bore the man with pleasantries. From what I heard, they are about to go to war so we should probably get to it, right?"

"Technically, we've been at war," Sasha corrected. "We are about to go to battle. I understand you may be willing to lend your aid?"

The two nodded and Kit approached him. "We have permission from Janis to negotiate but in reality, we're well aware that if these guys take over, the way the world currently works will change, and that's not good for us. I'm not saying it's a perfect world by a long shot, but it is good for our skills and business. We want to see it stick around."

"That is quite magnanimous of you," the commander replied in a dry tone. "Any help you can supply would be quite valuable. I hope you were able to make a nice profit from the raid last year?"

"Oh yeah, a good sum of creds, but the big haul was backward engineering those mechanicals," Fritz said with a smile. "We hired more techies and engineers. But we've beefed up our droids. Your infiltrator can attest to their quality."

Chiyo nodded. "They are quite impressive."

He frowned. "I'm assuming that's a dry way of saying they can eliminate a Reaper unit and save my life with ease." This earned another shot in the ribs from Kit. "Dammit, ow! You know formality isn't my thing."

"Simple manners aren't either. Of course I know, but it doesn't stop it from pissing me off," she retorted.

The man rubbed his side. "You were more forgiving of Kaiden when he stole your bike."

She shrugged. "He eventually got me a new one." She turned her attention to the chancellor again. "Speaking of, where is Kaiden?"

"Ironically, off trying to get the Fire Riders and Skyway Kings to join us once again," Sasha explained.

"Oh? Getting the whole band back together for another suicide run gambit. He must think he has loaded dice." Fritz chuckled.

The commander looked at Chiyo. "You should contact him, Chiyo. He was quite worried when he heard of your mission."

She smiled and shook her head. "Worried about me? After all the things he's put us through with his recklessness?"

Sasha nodded and slipped a hand into his coat pocket. "Yes, the irony was not lost on any of us present at the time." He removed an EI device and slid it toward her as a message appeared in her ocular lenses. "As you must have heard, there was an attack on the outpost that overlooks the Academy. They were attacked in force by Arbiter droids and some were carried away. They had to abandon the base for now."

Her heart skipped a beat. "What about Amber and Lizzy? Dr. Soni? They were stationed there, weren't they?"

He nodded. "They were. That message I sent you is from Amber. You should read it and show it to Kaiden." His clasped hands tightened. "Things have become much grimmer now."

CHAPTER TWENTY-EIGHT

"Izzy was kidnapped?" Kaiden asked and Chiyo nodded grimly in his HUD display.

"She was taken during the attack on the outpost. Amber and her mother are all right and the civilians were able to evacuate fairly quickly, given the chaos. However, they lost a large number of military personnel and many students stationed there were taken, along with others."

He sighed and balled his fists, although a thought occurred to him at her last words. "What others, specifically?"

"Pardon?"

"You said others were taken besides Nexus students. Were they all military?"

She looked down to read from a tablet or another device. "Some are merely listed as missing currently and thought taken. There are some soldiers among them, but also police, medics, and other non-military personnel."

"Are they all from Ark Academies?" he asked and ran a hand through his hair. "Or have strong EI connections?"

"From the looks of it, yes. All were former graduates from Ark Academies and many had come to assist with the resistance," she confirmed.

"They will be used for golems," the ace said and his voice trembled slightly with rage.

"Golems? What do you mean, Kaiden?" she asked. "I thought those had been dealt with after the Gin incident."

"It looks like the AO was behind the experiment in the first place, Chi," he explained. "I fought one during my last mission and don't tell anyone this, but it was controlled by Flynn."

"Flynn! He is alive, then?" Chiyo looked shocked before worry washed over her features. "Or did you have to..." She couldn't seem to finish the question and her gaze slid away.

Kaiden tried to put the words together and looked at his clenched hands to take a moment to think and breathe. "They are using students—Nexus students, at least—as puppets. They have control over them somehow and make them go into battle using the golems. I was only able to talk to him for a few moments thanks to Chief. It's something to do with their EI connection but I'm not exactly sure what or how. We've heard that they've used the other students as soldiers, but I don't think they can control ours like that, at least for now. They've found another way, though, or maybe that was their plan and they can only use Nexus students for now. I don't know."

Her eyes half-closed, she nodded solemnly as she assimilated what he'd told her. "I see... That is terrible. I have to imagine, even if it is quite grim, that such a feat will cause issues to the body and mind after time. I don't want to think of the potential consequences."

"Agreed. Which is why we need to hurry and get them back. Your mission went well, I take it?"

She nodded. "I retrieved the keys. Cyra is examining them now. The chancellor is making final preparations with the military and our forces here. We are getting everything put in place and in record time as well. I feel safe in saying that we will attack soon."

"Then I need to get back with Desmond and Zena. They've offered to help but their forces are depleted right now as they were under attack by the Omegas when we got here. They are trying to contact other chapters to bring more in. Even if they don't get here in time, we'll head out and hope they can make it to the fight later."

"Understood. I'll pass that on to Sasha," Chiyo acknowledged. "I'll be there on the battlefield with you, Kaiden, and I'm sure Genos and the others will too."

"Of course. I wouldn't have it any other way" Kaiden smiled and went to end the call, but a quick fact popped into his head. "Oh, and Chi, make sure to tell everyone we'll arrive in an Omega assault ship."

"Wait—what?" she asked and eyes widened in humorous confusion

"We'll try to throw some Fire Riders symbols on there or something, but we have a new ship, which should prove useful. I have new armor as well. I'll show it to you at the battle."

"Well...okay then. See you soon, Kaiden." She signed off. He sighed as he leaned back in his chair. While he'd wanted to add some levity after the news, maybe she now thought he wasn't taking this seriously. No, both of them knew better than that, at this point. He was excited to retake the Academy and thought only of rescuing his friends and finally taking the battle to the AO after these months of hardship and bloodshed. On the other hand, he had begun to feel desperate. His instinct warned him that he needed to shake it off as it would lead to foolish mistakes once the battle came.

He exited the private room and walked into the lobby. Wolfson, Haldt, Zena, and Desmond stood and talked near the stairs and the head officer looked at him. "Ah, good, you're back," he said. "How did it go? Did she get those chips for Laurie?"

"Of course," he confirmed. "And arranged assistance from the Azure Halos as well. I considered giving them a call but didn't know if we had the time."

"That techie gang from the raid?" Desmond asked thoughtfully. "I guess that means the pie is divided between a few more now, but we could certainly use them given our dwindled force."

"I have two chapters on the way," Zena said. "I'll call on more but that gives us over a hundred and fifty grunts all together. Now, we only need ships to get them there."

"I've been able to secure some supply and dropships, so we're good on that front," Desmond told her. "It might be a little cramped, but I still have other calls to make."

"We need fighters as well," Wolfson added. "Ground troops are necessary, sure, but with that big bastard flying around and in enemy hands, it'll make things difficult."

"You said it didn't kill you all outright the first time," Zena pointed out. "They obviously want something from you—or the students, at least. Maybe they will keep their cannons cool."

"At some point, they will weigh their options and realize that it's probably better to simply write off the potential gain from the students and faculty and glass us," Haldt reasoned. "We need to focus on disabling it or to keep it busy while we do what we need to."

"The military will handle it from the sounds of things," Kaiden told them. "Apparently, they are itching for revenge themselves."

"How nice of them to finally join the club," Wolfson snarked and glanced at Haldt. "There have been a large number of volunteers to the resistance and many are former brothers and sisters in arms. I wonder if we can get them to join us."

The officer nodded. "They aren't in uniform anymore so they wouldn't technically be abandoning their posts. I'll see who I can find. Volunteers only, though."

"Agreed. It wouldn't feel right to force them given all the loss that has happened already," the large man said and scratched his beard. "But my guess is that most of them will be quite happy to actually take it to the enemy instead of merely defending against the attacks."

Haldt nodded and turned to Kaiden. "I should head out and see who I can enlist. Is there any word on when the attack will take place?"

"Soon. They don't want to miss their chance and potentially let the enemy sneak off with whatever they are trying to find," the ace replied. "We have no exact date yet but it wouldn't surprise me if they called at the end of the night and told us. My guess is in two to three days."

"Then I should head out immediately. I have calls to make and people to find." He turned to Desmond. "Do you mind if I borrow one of your ships?"

"Take mine, Haldt," Wolfson said. "You've proven adequate as a pilot."

"Much obliged, sir," the man answered, although Kaiden could hear a slight amount of sarcasm and had to restrain a chuckle.

"We'll try to get as many of our guys in shape as possible in that time," Zena stated. "They are a hearty group and I'm sure some want to increase their kill count if the Omegas will be there."

"I'd imagine there'll be at least a few," Kaiden assured her. "It'll be mostly those droids, though. They've crawled all around the island since the invasion."

"Annoying little bots." Desmond growled, his expression one of disgust. "They can take a beating but we have some big guns and the sky on our side. When the supply of jets gets here, we can take them."

"Then we all have work to do and only a few days to do it in," Wolfson said and folded his arms. "Let's get to work, lady and gents."

They separated and the gang leaders went to explain the plan to their members while Wolfson and Haldt left for his ship to check it before the officer set off. Kaiden made his way over to one of the sheds and opened it to see the power armor he had taken from the Omega captain. A couple of the Skyway engineers said they could probably repair it. While it wouldn't be as pretty or durable, they should be able to keep it as powerful and add a few shield units to compensate for the lower armor. He had no objections.

"It's gonna be nice to finally take it to them, eh, partner?" Chief asked.

"I felt that way after the raid. Now, it seems like I celebrated too early." the ace admitted. He drew Debonair and studied it absently. "I'll be happy to take the colossus and get Flynn, Marlo, Izzy, and everyone else off. But I won't be satisfied until I put some holes into that psychopath's head."

"Meaning Merrick?" Chief asked. *"I guess he can't expect redemption, huh?"*

He holstered his pistol as he shook his head. "Not from me. I never liked that kind of story anyway."

CHAPTER TWENTY-NINE

"So the attack was your doing, Dario?" Merrick asked and his assistant's hologram bowed.

"Of course. I felt it was best that we eliminate a potential stronghold or launch point for our enemies at the start. We acquired more test subjects to boot." The assassin smiled and straightened. "It's not exactly like we've been incognito this entire time and certainly not at the moment the way we hover above the Academy. If they come, then they come, and we shall deal with them."

"I wish you had talked to me before you revealed yourself to Nolan. I imagine he wasn't particularly happy to be spied upon."

Dario smiled and shook his head. "I don't think so either. However, he knows his place and seemed more than happy to accept my proposal. Or at least thought it the better option given that he first thought I was there to eliminate him."

The AO leader allowed himself a small smile. "The fear of mortality is an exceptional bargaining chip, as I certainly know." He looked at a monitor that observed the island and zoomed in as a group of Ark soldiers secured the bomb they had brought with them. "How long until you can make it inside the old facility?"

"That's difficult to say," the assassin admitted. "The bomb will certainly damage the door but it will take hours to prepare, in and of itself. From what I've been told, it might not destroy it completely but we have other tools to finish the job, obviously. After that, it is merely a matter of finding the serum and anything else of interest."

"If there is no attack, feel free to look around and take all that you can," Merrick ordered. "If there is, the serum is your priority, nothing else. I don't want to hear that we lost it simply because you desired a fight."

Dario nodded nonchalantly. "Of course. I wouldn't risk all you have worked for, at this point. We are quite close to achieving our end goal, no?"

"We still have much to do, Dario," his boss replied and gazed out of the office window at the stars and the edge of Earth that was all that was visible of the planet from where he stood. "But once this comes together, I will soon be able to show the world the fruits of my labor."

It had been a mad dash during the three days since the attack on the Bellingham outpost. Most prepared for battle while others made supply runs or went out for recon missions. It was good that Sasha had grown accustomed to functioning on little sleep as he had few hours to spare over the last few days.

Hartman had finally approved a military dispatch to Nexus, although under certain conditions. They would engage the colossus and hold it at bay only temporarily, but if the moment came that it could be destroyed, they would take it. The military wanted blood and a win. The commander-cum-chancellor and his team would have to work fast to make sure they could capture the ship or at least save everyone within before that could happen. It wasn't something he looked forward to telling the others.

But for now, he needed to remain calm and ready his troops. He was a commander again, even if only until this was over and he could truly take on the mantle of chancellor. They needed victory before that could happen.

On the grounds, all the students and resistance members had come together to talk strategy and go over each other's weapons and skills. It was almost like they were back in their old workshops.

Genos was with the engineers. As one of the few mechanists and therefore someone with equal combat and engineering ability, he helped to decide who should focus on repairs and droid control and who should focus on fighting. In the back of his mind, he knew he could influence their fates when he decided their responsibilities, but he saw no trepidation in the eyes of any of his fellow engineers.

Cyra, Indre, Otto, and Chiyo were in the technicians building and examined their supply of gadgets with other technicians, both military and student. They also downloaded Laurie's new security program to distribute to everyone in preparation for another disruption event or mass hacking attack.

Silas, Raul, Luke, Mack, Jaxon, and Cameron were with the soldiers, who either used the time for target practice, running drills, or preparing their weapons and armor. Anticipation filled their temporary barracks and hoo-rahs filled the air anytime someone brought up how they would retake the Academy and destroy the invaders.

Julius helped in one of the medical tents and was soon joined by Amber, who had arrived recently. When he'd been told what had happened at the Bellingham outpost, he offered to allow her to rest. Her response was that she wanted to help and that she should, exactly as he did, while she was there since she would go to battle as well.

Fritz and Kit showed off their new droids to the engineers and technicians and recruited volunteers to act as directors once the battle started. They gave them time to familiarize themselves with the mechanicals and master their abilities and controls in practice.

Haldt headed toward the base, followed by a convoy of ten other dropships, each holding between ten to twenty volunteers along with the ships' pilots. A fleet of ships bearing the Skyway Kings logo passed every now and then, and there was a report of a large carrier ship with an Azure Halo symbol headed toward Washington, although it was given clearance every time.

Zena walked out of the makeshift med-bay of the gang's base and went outside to check the troops. All were engaged in fighting practice or talked to each other about the battle and the potential for loot. Desmond flew with the jockeys, using larger jets to keep his freshly cleaned heavy armor in the air.

Kaiden and Wolfson were sparring and talked strategy

between blows. A Skyway King engineer walked up and interrupted their match to talk to the ace about the repairs to the power armor he had procured. He nodded and pointed at the assault ship to tell the man to put it on board. Several jockeys and Rider troops were busy plastering stencils of their respective logos all over the vessel.

In hangars in the United Kingdom, Canada, and the East Coast of the US, workers readied destroyers and assault ships for the fight against the colossus. They watched footage of the last battle against it to look for tactics and weak points and made a note of the damage to the side from the collision. Pilots and crewmen loaded the destroyers and carriers with fighters, interceptors, and bombers to prepare for the jump to the island in the morning.

Nolan stood motionless at the helm of his ship, confident that he'd done all he could in response to his inner sense that something was coming. He made sure to activate every droid he could, have all the golems prepped, and get every Omega and Ark soldier not assisting with the retrieval of the serum to stand ready on the island and in the abandoned city. Repairs to the colossus from the previous fight had gone slower than he wanted, but Aurora was focused on getting the power back to its maximum for shields and the main cannon. They would not be caught off guard this time.

Dario helped to escort the bomb down the long path to the hidden facility below the Academy, amused by the concerned twitches and movements of the soldiers whenever the bomb was even slightly jostled. He felt something was coming as well but was more excited than concerned, unlike Nolan. The assassin relished the forthcoming clash and had had no doubt that they would send as much firepower as they could to the island in an attempt to reclaim it. He would have innumerable opportunities to enjoy himself and only hoped he had a rematch with a certain ace.

Sasha finally stepped out of the resistance headquarters. All the troops, staff, and crew members had gathered together as he had asked. Technicians activated large holoscreens so the large group could observe the commander while he spoke.

"To all of you here, I know what you are feeling—the anticipation of battle, the anger of loss, and the hope of victory. For some of you, this may be the first time you feel these specific emotions. For others, it might be common by now. We have prepared for this fight ever since the Arbiter Organization made their appearance in the world to take our Academy—and all Ark Academies—under their control while they destroyed Terra, the world council, and took over the embassy."

Some shifted in place while others nodded. He could see the tension in all of them but with it, determination. "We will make them answer for what they have done. We will rescue those who were taken from us. All around the world, they are fighting. They will not break us. We will not let this madman's dream become a reality. This fight will be possibly the greatest challenge of your lives, but we will rise to it. This will be the battle that changes this war.

It will be the beginning of the Arbiter's downfall and a new dawn for us all!"

With that last bellow, the crowd cheered and held up fists, helmets, tools, and weapons in unison. Sasha knew he was certain of his last statement. No matter what happened, this would lead to the new dawn of an era. It was up to all of them for it to lead to something better.

CHAPTER THIRTY

"Hey, kid!" The trio of Ark soldiers turned to a group of Omegas that walked up the street. "We want to change places."

"Why?" the lead Ark asked and shouldered his gun. "Do you prefer to look at these abandoned buildings instead of your own?"

"Yours is closer to the base and closer to the food. It's easier to take a break for a while," the Omega stated, a slightly angry edge to his tone.

The Ark soldiers looked at one another. "And what do we get out of this. exactly?" their spokesman asked and tapped his suit's belt. "If you don't have any spare creds, there's enough dark allies who do."

The man snarled for a moment before a fiendish grin crossed his face. "You show much more spine than most of the other puppets."

One of the other soldiers sighed in frustration. "We're not the golems, jackass!" she retorted and pointed to the emblem on her armor. "Look for these. If we have the icon, we still have a functioning brain. The lack of one seems to be something you mercs and the golems share."

Her teammates snickered and shook their heads and turned away from the gang members, who began to reach for their blades, itching to start a fight due to their anger and boredom. Before any of them could fully grasp the handles of their knives, both groups were buffeted by a violent gust of wind that rushed from the edges of town. The dispute forgotten, Omega and soldiers alike exchanged glances of confusion and unease while others moved around the corners of the streets to get a better look.

A large flash of light was followed by several more as assault ships, corsairs, and destroyers, all flying military colors, warped in and immediately soared over Bellingham Bay toward the colossus. Many of the AO troops cried out in shock or began to fire pointlessly at the large vessels. Others looked toward the edge of town and began to shout at their teammates. Dropships and carriers approached at surprising speed with a modest fleet of fighters and bombers above them as protection. These broke away to begin to pummel the now disorganized enemy troops with laser volleys and dropped explosives.

The carriers stopped at the edge of town and the side panels opened. Troops flooded out while the dropships pushed in a little farther to deliver soldiers, heavies, agents, mechs, and even a few mech jockeys. The invaders immediately began their assault while those in occupation scrambled to meet the attack and called for reinforcements.

"Sir, we're under attack!" a crewman of the colossus called to Nolan as he walked into the command deck. Immediately after his cry, the enormous vessel rattled from a shot by one of the destroyers.

"I am well aware of that, " the general snapped and looked at one of the screens. "Aurora, what are you waiting for? Fire the cannon! We have more than enough power."

"I am attempting to, sir," the EI explained, her voice a little quieter than normal. *"I am having trouble coalescing the energy. A disturbance is blocking me from activating the main cannon."*

"Disturbance? What kind of disturbance can stop you?" he asked before he recalled how, technically, they had stalled her before during the invasion. He glanced quickly at the row of technicians. "How are our instruments?"

One of them met his gaze. The man was calm but sweat had begun to appear on his brow. "I was about to report, sir. We have difficulties establishing commlinks to other parts of the ship. Most of the main systems seem to be fine but perform at a slower rate. There seems to be some kind of disruption—" The explanation seemed to occur to the technician at the same time it did to Nolan.

The general gritted his teeth. "They are using our own device against us." He cursed and fixed the man with a grim expression. "Find out where the device is located. Make it a priority and tell me immediately so we can destroy it."

"Right away, sir." The team set to work as Nolan took

his seat. "Someone, fetch Lana. I need to know if this will affect our EI." he ordered. "Then, get down to the power room. Make sure the connection to the Academy's shield is still established and siphon the energy to our shields while we still can. We can outlast this pathetic assault."

Sasha stepped off the carrier with his rifle in hand and surveyed the battle that raged below. Their surprise attack had worked well, at least at this juncture. The shield was still in place at the Academy, and as long as it was, they wouldn't be able to set foot inside. Not only that, the enemy could simply continue to send reinforcements from within the Academy and the colossus as time went on. It simply meant the other group needed to work as quickly as possible but they were among the best, so he was confident.

He used the scope of his rifle to peer at the colossus. The hangars opened on the left side and he frowned. He'd hoped that Laurie's modified disruption device would have been more effective and shut down most of the ship, but the big issue was the cannon. That wasn't firing, so he couldn't be too critical. Craft began to pour out in defense of the massive vessel and banked toward the military fleet which sent out ships of their own.

He then looked at the bridge leading to the Academy, where a wave of droids and Ark soldiers ran to join the fray. A few mechs brought up the rear and he aimed and sniped a few bots from his position almost three and a half miles away, a personal best. He would have to commend Julio on his choice in weaponry once this was over.

That moment, however, seemed a long way from now. He glanced at the troops who acted as his personal squad. They showed their discipline and waited silently for his orders, but he could feel their desire to fight. "I have to coordinate the attack for now," he stated and pointed down to the town. "Assist in the assault. I will be fine."

The group saluted and shouted, "Sir!" in unison before the men broke away and rushed to join the combat. Sasha activated his commlink. "Kit, Felix, are you coming in soon?"

"We're almost there," she answered. "I can see the carriers. Look behind you and you should see us." He did so and stepped behind the carriers to see a fleet of a dozen dropships heading their way. "Janis is on his way, but the carrier ship is slower than we are."

"We have enough to keep things fun," Fritz declared as the dropships sailed overhead. "Now watch our new droids in action!" The bottoms of the vessels gave way and dozens of large spheres plummeted, only to unfurrow on impact and stand. The blue Azure Halo droids faced their white-and-black Arbiter counterparts. Although most did well on their own, the engineers deployed, took control of them, and were able to get far more use out of them. They increased and decreased power in certain areas to maximize efficiency and target specific enemies for better strategy.

One of the mech jockeys noticed an Arbiter automated mech. He raced forward and clotheslined it in a massive clash of metal, thrust his mechanical foot on the chest of the machine, and aimed both arm cannons at it to fire them simultaneously. It exploded in spectacular fashion.

Across town, another mech was felled by two titans who crushed its legs. It toppled and two demolitionists looked back as it fell, turned away from their opponents to walk over, charge up their cannons, and annihilate it in a joint blast from their giant weapons. Even in the heat of the fight, they took a moment to fist-bump each other before they switched their cannons' mode to laser and began to carve through oncoming bots while a few Omega soldiers ran or ducked to avoid the beams.

Sasha took stock once again. They appeared to have the upper hand and still had reinforcements on their way that Kaiden and Wolfson had recruited, as well as all the droids Janis was bringing. There was hope for further military assistance if they could get their spare ships jump-ready, but for now, they were in a favorable position. That could change if the enemy called for reinforcements or the AO learned of the attack. He was sure their response would be swift, which was why they needed the infiltration group to accomplish their mission without delay.

A message appeared in his oculars. *We're on the way*. It was short but all that was needed. He nodded and aimed casually once again to fire at a few Omegas who tried to flank around the edge of the rear buildings. The rest was up to Haldt and the students. For now, the best thing he could do was be a commander.

He saw several snipers taking up positions on rooftops, vented his rifle as he identified seven of them, and counted down from five. At zero, he slammed the vent shut and brought the butt of his sniper rifle to his shoulder. Seven shots followed in rapid, rhythmic succession and all caught the unaware snipers through their helmets and felled them instantly. He opened the vent again and walked down from the hill as he shortened the barrel of his gun for close combat. He was a commander, but he was also a soldier and it was best to remind the enemy of that.

CHAPTER THIRTY-ONE

"We're heading out now," Kaiden told Chiyo in the monitor screen as their recently acquired assault ship raced toward the Academy. "ETA is about thirty minutes. Trying to get this ornery bastard of a ship to move faster is proving challenging."

"It would probably have helped to have a crew who knew how to operate it," she pointed out. "You had Omega prisoners, didn't you?"

"They were surprisingly unhelpful," he told. "Even the ones who did talk, it all sounded like technobabble to most of us. Chief and some of the SK engineers are running it. But they can only do so much and Chief has to work off several different schematics. These guys might be mercs, but they have a hell of an infrastructure to be able to design and make their own ships."

She nodded. "I've already alerted Sasha about your new vessel. He said he's informed the others but you might not want to get too close to the military ships. Things are obviously quite hectic right now and they are preparing for Omega reinforcements."

"Noted. How are you and the others?"

Chiyo looked into the bay. All their friends were there. Genos examined his tools and Jaxon and Silas checked their weapons while Luke and Mack held an arm-wrestling contest in their suits to pass the time. The others simply sat and waited. "We're fine. Ready to get going. Haldt says we're only a few minutes out. We should have the shield down by the time you get here."

"Then good timing on our part. You guys be safe and leave me something to destroy."

"We hope to keep the fighting to a minimum for now. While we may be strong together, we are only a small group in an area crawling with enemies and they have control of the island. There will be enough for you once you arrive."

"We'll come in screaming," he promised. "Good luck. Out."

"Out." Chiyo signed off and returned to her place on the bench and filled everyone in. "Kaiden and his reinforcements will be here in thirty minutes. We should have the shield down by then."

"I would guess that is the most time we have," Genos stated. "Given the circumstances, I don't think we can get away with sneaking around the Academy for too long."

"The tiptoeing method isn't really our style," Mack confessed and pointed to himself and Luke. "Hell, even Cam is shit at it and he's a bounty hunter."

Cameron shrugged. "I've simply decided I'll bring all

my targets in dead. There's less need for sneaking around then."

"You are here in case sneaking around doesn't work," Indre pointed out. "We'll need a distraction if we are seen so we can still get into position."

"Distraction? That's way easier to do." Luke chuckled. "Can't we make that plan A?"

"It's a little late to change plans right now," Jaxon muttered. "Once the shield goes down, feel free to do as you please, but that is the main objective." He glanced at Cyra. "In that regard, is the marker ready?"

She nodded, retrieved the case, and opened it. "The marker itself didn't need much work. Most of the changes were to the satellite, which was the professor's doing." She took the device out and pointed it around. "We only need to get close to the generator in the R&D building and pull the trigger. That will send the pulse. It will shut down the generator and anything near it, which will bring the shield down and hopefully a good chunk of the bots."

"That won't affect our gear, right?" Raul asked.

Chiyo shook her head. "Assuming you have installed the chips we distributed, you should be fine. It's temporary, anyway, but with the generator down, it means most of the internal security will be compromised as well. Cyra, Indre, and I can make sure we gain control and then hand it over to the commander."

"We can still use the sat-cannon, correct?" Jaxon asked. "Or was that function lost?"

Cyra shook her head and put the marker back in the case. "Oh, we still have it. You have to let the satellite recharge for a while and flip the switch on the marker. But we only have a couple of blasts so it's best to use them sparingly."

"That sounds like a plan," Luke said, stood, and looked at the cockpit. "Hey, officer! Are we there yet?"

Haldt looked back. "As a matter of fact, we are. Get ready."

The craft descended as the officer brought it to the side of the island to hover above the water for a few moments while he activated the aquatic landing mode. It landed gently and floated in place. He retrieved his machine gun and joined the others as they opened the side door and exited, using the water carrier piers to make their way up to the Academy.

Within only a few steps, they were stopped by the shield. Chiyo looked at Indre, who pointed to the pack on her back. The infiltrator nodded and stepped beside her as the other girl pressed a switch on her wrist to open the case. She removed the draining device. "I don't want to leave this on long. Someone might notice," she explained as she approached the barrier.

"I would think most of their attention is focused on the big-ass battle in Bellingham," Cameron suggested. "But maybe a big hole in the 'impenetrable' shield would make people a little suspicious."

"More along the lines of 'impregnable,'" Indre corrected with a snicker as Chiyo placed the device against the shield and activated it. "There's a small but significant difference."

The infiltrator held the device in place as it came live. Blue lines darted about ten feet all around. The light of the shield seemed to be sucked into the lines, then traveled into the device. “That’s neat,” Luke said as he watched the decay of the small section of the shield.

Soon, an eight-by-eight-foot opening appeared and widened. “Get inside,” Chiyo ordered. The others complied hastily one after the other and all turned as she maneuvered carefully around the field until she too was behind the wall. She deactivated it and stepped back and the shield began to reform. The edges drew together, albeit quite slowly. “Even with the device, the shield is repairing itself at a very reduced rate,” she noted.

“They might be siphoning the energy from it,” Cyra suggested. “I noticed an energy transference on my tablet. I thought it might have been a conflict between the shield and the colossus, but the vessel itself might be doing it.”

“To strengthen their shields, probably, because they can’t use their cannon at the moment,” the infiltrator deduced. “That will keep the fight going but it’s all the more reason to get this done. We don’t want the military to destroy the colossus but we can’t risk them getting that cannon back online and ending the battle right there.”

“Then we should hurry,” Haldt stated. The others nodded and they made their way through the island to the Academy above, alert and watchful for droids. All they could hear were the sounds of battle outside the island and any metallic footsteps thudded away from their position and toward the gate.

“Sneaking is way easier than I thought it would be,” Mack commented.

“Normally, you don’t have as big a distraction,” Indre reminded him. “It is a nice change of pace.”

“We can’t get sloppy,” the security officer admonished.

"They are still in a daze from the blitz, but someone is calling the shots and they will realize that sending everything out there isn't a good move. Hell, they might have already and orders simply haven't carried through yet."

"So let them send some basic bots," Luke huffed. "That won't put a stop to— What's that light?"

The group looked up at a blue shimmer at the top of the stairs before a boom filled their ears and the light rocketed toward them. Luke activated his gauntlet shield and braced himself as Mack held his hands up and directed his suit's energy into the titan's barrier. The blast pounded into it, but Luke held firm. "Thanks for the energy boost," he called.

"Care to reciprocate?" Mack asked and ran to the front.

"Go for it," Luke shouted. The vanguard absorbed his shield and formed it into a ball which he threw up the stairs where another blue shimmer appeared. The energized projectile obliterated the droid at the top of the stairs.

"It looks like we already lost the element of surprise." Raul sighed.

"It didn't take long," Cameron muttered and looked over his shoulder. "What now?"

Haldt stepped forward. "You already talked about that." He readied his weapon and began to advance. "The techs need a distraction. Who will join me?"

As the officer ran up the stairs, Mack placed a hand on Luke's gauntlet to charge it as the two nodded to each other and raced up behind him. Cameron, Raul, and Silas joined them. Genos moved to follow but was stopped by

Jaxon. "Defend them, kin. I will rejoin you when the shield is down."

The engineer nodded and activated his cannon. "Of course. Be safe, kin Jaxon."

The Tsuna ace nodded and followed the others. Chiyo walked in front of the remaining group of Indre, Cyra, Amber, and Genos. "We have a mission to complete," she said and drew her SMG. "And more after that. Let's get this done."

Cyra nodded, took the marker out of the case, and holstered it on her back. "We're right behind you." They began to run. A loud rumble from above was followed by cheers and shouts from their comrades.

"I wonder if the R&D building will still be intact for us to do what we need to do," Genos said, an edge of concern in his tone.

Chiyo looked over her shoulder and although her words were serious, there was a trace levity in her voice. "Why do you think I want to hurry?"

CHAPTER THIRTY-TWO

"So what does it look like over there?" Wolfson asked as Kaiden joined him and the gang leaders on the top deck.

"Chiyo didn't know too many details. She's on a separate team to infiltrate the Academy to turn the shields off while the main force occupies the...everything else," he explained and leaned against one of the railings on the side of the deck.

"They'll have the shield down by the time we get there, right?" Desmond asked.

Zena stepped forward. "We'll go ahead and send the flyers out. They are much faster than this ship and the shuttles."

"It sounds good to me. You had those chips made, right?" the ace asked. "They'll fall victim to the disruptors, otherwise."

"We made a good number but didn't really have the set-up to pump them out," she replied. "They'll be fine. We were able to scrounge up some frequency insulators. Those should work, right?"

He shrugged. "If you say so. I guess we'll know if they stop flying and fall out of the air." He turned to face the group. "Chiyo also mentioned to not get too close to the military. Sasha should have told them about the ship but you know they can get trigger-happy at the sight of enemy vessels, even the ones with new decorations."

"I told you we should have made it more blue," Desmond muttered.

She shrugged. "Yes, make us stand out more. Do remember that the Omegas are equally as interested in killing us."

"Are there many ships besides the colossus?" Wolfson asked.

"She didn't say for sure," Kaiden replied. "But there is concern that they might get reinforcements. We know the AO has captured destroyers capable of jumping. I'm sure the Horde has a few ships to spare that can do the same."

Desmond rubbed the back of his head. "It'll be fine. We have reinforcements too, right?"

"Besides those other chapters that are lagging behind?" Kaiden asked. "If you are asking about the military, we hope they will send more. They still have to worry about all the other fights going on. Last I heard is that they've tried to hurry and install warp cores into several reconstructed or new vessels and send those over, although I'm not sure how one installs a warp core 'quickly.'"

"Basically, we are the reinforcements," Zena surmised.

"That is how I've looked at it." The ace nodded. "The hope is we defeat them before reinforcements arrive, if they do at all. They are currently jamming long-range communication, but that'll raise suspicion eventually. Hopefully, they only send a small force out to investigate that we can deal with easily instead of a fleet."

Zena sighed and joined him at the rail. "There's considerable hoping going on."

"And there's nothing wrong with hope, lady," Wolfson stated. "It's what keeps most of us going to get things done. And if it will end this battle quicker, I'd say let everyone rely on it all they please."

Kaiden nodded. "That's oddly endearing coming from you."

The head officer smirked. "Sasha isn't the only one with a knack for speeches, albeit only from time to time."

Skyway fighters activated their boosts and streaked ahead of the assault ship. The ace looked through the front of the ship but saw nothing but ocean. They would have a better understanding of how the battle was going once they reported back and hopefully, they would say the shield was down as well.

"Did they have to take the fight to the plaza?" Cyra asked as they crossed to the back of the observation building. "We would have had a straight route through there."

"I'm sure they need the room to maneuver," Genos pointed out, checked around the corner, and motioned for them to follow. "And it is likely that it had the highest concentration of foes waiting as it is close to the center of the island. Even if they were not fighting, I doubt it would have been an easy crossing for us."

"Touché," she muttered and glanced around the island, taking note of the buildings. "I guess they haven't bothered with repairs," she said glumly. The ruin and devastation were a vivid reminder of the invasion.

"There was no need. They've only had the bots guarding the area and AO soldiers who come through are only here temporarily," Chiyo replied and checked her HUD. "Make sure your helmet remains undamaged. The air in here is low since they solidified the shield. It's basically your lifeline until we take it down."

"I've kept an eye on the gauge," Indre promised. "Besides, I have spares in my pack. I'm more worried about sniper shots than a bump to the head."

Genos stopped and held a hand up. "Wait, Viola is picking something up." He pointed into an alley on the left. "In here."

The group hid hastily behind the wall and the Tsuna peeked out cautiously. Several droids appeared farther down the path, eight Arbiter bots led by two of the supers they had fought during the invasion. He looked at his teammates. "A group of bots is in the way. I shall deal with them while you keep going."

"You plan to take them on alone?" Chiyo asked.

He shook his head and showed her a nano grenade. "Of course I will not. Now go."

She nodded and led the others out as he pressed the switch when he estimated that the droids were close enough and tossed the grenade around the corner. He heard it burst and soon noticed four dots on his HUD to indicate how many he had captured. It would be enough. He held the trigger of his cannon to let it charge and when he spun out to fire, the bots had already begun to fight amongst themselves.

Luke's hammer made violent impact with the ground and triggered a wave of kinetic energy that hurled several droids into the air, all of whom were quickly finished off by Raul and Cameron before they fell.

"Ha! Like that!" the titan roared as he swiped to his left and destroyed another droid's chest. "Who's next?" His challenge was met by a mech that lumbered toward them with surprising speed from the western path.

"You can't keep your mouth shut, can you?" Cameron asked as he opened the vent on his rifle and reached for a thermal with his free hand. He stopped when Mack launched himself forward to bulldoze into the mech and release a discharge of energy that felled the giant bot.

The vanguard looked at him and held his hands up. "Cam, throw it here."

The bounty hunter complied and he caught the grenade and shoved it into one of the small holes in his opponent's chest. He powered his gauntlet and thumped it down to create a bigger explosion that he himself was caught up in.

"Shit, is he dead?" Cameron asked, closed the vent on his weapon, and took a shot at a droid that crawled up one of the buildings across the plaza.

Instead of dying, however, the vanguard appeared out of the smoke, his armor aglow as he landed in front of his teammates. "Damn, that was nice!" He balled his fist and let a sizzle of energy dart out.

"Where did you come from?" Luke asked as he twirled his hammer to let the kinetic energy accumulate. "How did you get up there?"

"A few of those damn droids got their hands on me and carried me up that building," he explained and pointed to the structure in question behind him.

"Why didn't you call for help?" Raul asked and replaced the magazine in his rifle.

"Didn't you hear me cursing?" the vanguard asked.

Luke tapped his helmet. "I guess I did but I thought it was normal war cries."

Mack laughed. "In a way, I guess so."

Jaxon, Silas, and Haldt joined them. "More are coming," the Tsuna warned and gestured to the east where at least twenty more droids appeared. A few fired a volley of energy blasts at the group that was blocked by the dome Mack created.

"Where the hell are all of these damn things coming from?" Raul asked. He opened a hatch on the top of his rifle and slid in a cartridge of ballistic rounds.

"I'm sure they have many stored in the warehouses and underground," Haldt replied. "Along with however many they have on the colossus."

Cameron, Raul, and Luke looked up. "I've kind of forgotten about that since we started fighting," the heavy admitted.

"I'm blasting my barrier," Mack called and thrust it out to knock the close-quarters bots away. Jaxon, Haldt, Silas, Cameron, and Raul all opened fire at the droids as Luke activated his gauntlet shield to protect the vanguard as he recharged.

A group of mechanicals tried to flank the group, but Raul noticed them break away. He switched to the ballistic rounds and when they reappeared from the other side of the logistics workshop, he fired twice to hit the chests of two droids, which immediately exploded and annihilated the others as well.

On the roof of the cafeteria, a lone attacker approached the edge. It's right arm assumed the form of a sniper barrel and it aimed at Jaxon and fired. The laser shot was stopped by a blue shield held up by a recharged Mack. He formed the shield into an orb and launched it at the assassin to sever its head. "I hate sneaky little bastards like that."

"I'm technically one of those sneaky little bastards, you know," Cameron retorted.

The vanguard laughed as his fists began to glow. "Yeah, but you suck at it so it's all good."

With that, he and the titan went on the offensive. As another wave of bots raced toward them, Mack vaulted up and landed with supreme force as Luke drove his hammer into the ground at the same moment. The combined force created a wave to obliterate all of the attackers.

And while they managed to keep their adversaries at bay for now, in the hangars below that used to house the Academy's shuttle, hundreds of droids began to activate.

CHAPTER THIRTY-THREE

Mack crushed an Arbiter bot underfoot and shoved another away as Luke's hammer swung in to destroy it. "Get these damn bots—" The energy of his vanguard armor flared and he formed an orb between his gauntlets as a trio of mechanicals prepared to fire at him. "Out of my face!" He cast the orb and it intercepted the shots and exploded. The cascade of energy engulfed his attackers and several around them as the Nexus soldiers backed away.

"Watch your fire!" Raul called and took a moment to open the feed of his tracker drone in his HUD. "Shit. There are more on the way and I read more energy signatures coming from below around the docks."

"You had to know they had more than this," Haldt pointed out and vented his gun.

"Do we have to fall back?" Luke asked and spun his hammer in his hands. "I'm enjoying racking up my tally. Forty-seven so far."

"Is that it?" Cameron snickered. "Fifty-eight for me."

"What the hell? How have you kept pace?" Mack asked. "Luke and I have demolished them left and right."

"That would be because Haldt, Jaxon, and I have worked almost all the other directions." The bounty hunter chuckled. "Raul's pulled his weight too, I guess."

"Uh, guys," Raul muttered and looked at them with alarm. "I'm getting signatures around almost the entire western half of the island. They just started showing up."

The group all looked at one another. "Are they coming from below?" Haldt asked and the tracker nodded.

"I would imagine they've stored many of the droids below in case of an attack," Jaxon said and closed the vent on his machine gun. "They must have activated them in response to our ambush. Either that or they are rather keen to eliminate our group."

"We must have pissed them off royally." Luke chuckled and swung his hammer before he flipped it over his shoulder. "We still have a good position and can take them, right?"

"Not a chance in hell," Raul stated and sent the feed to his teammates' helmets.

Cameron gave a whistle. "Damn, I don't do this often but I gotta agree with Luke. These guys want us dead now."

"It's more likely they are being activated to assist with the fight outside the island," Jaxon reasoned. "Although I'm sure they will deal with us along the way."

Silas checked his belt. "This place needs to get repaired anyway," he muttered and nodded to the packs on his and Haldt's backs. "We had a plan in case of overwhelming odds, right?"

"Indeed." The officer nodded, removed his pack, and

placed it on the ground. "Everyone, take some from either my box or Silas' and get the other group on the comm. Let's find out how they are progressing."

"Why are there still so many bots?" Indre shouted when another of her drones was shot out of the sky. "Dammit, there goes Too-Bee."

Chiyo closed her holoscreen. "Kaitō will have us covered here in a moment," she stated and readied her SMG. "We're so close and only need to focus on taking the lab."

"There's something ironic about destroying most of my own creations," Cyra muttered as she leaned around the corner and blasted a half-destroyed bot before she was forced to dart back to avoid several lasers. "Or at least creations I had a hand in creating. My guess is the professor would perform a eulogy or something if he was here."

"It might be a situation I'm glad he's not here for then," the infiltrator stated and frowned when she received a notification of a comm call. "It's the soldier group," she said and answered. "Hello?"

"I'm not sure if you've noticed already or not," Cameron said, "but there's a massive group of bots getting all warmed up down below and they look like they want to join the fun."

"Dammit," she whispered. "We're only a few hundred yards away. We've been held up. There was a surprising amount of security around the R&D building."

"They knew it was important, even with the professor taking most of the projects on the way out," Amber suggested.

"Well, that and the shield. That's very important," Cyra added.

"We're about to head out. We'll make it, I promise," the infiltrator assured him.

"Understood. We are gonna head toward the gate," Cameron told her. "Meet us there. Hopefully, the army in the city will reach us before we get bum-rushed, but we're taking option B right now. That'll hopefully slow them somewhat."

"But only somewhat," she agreed before she signed off. "Kaitō, are you ready?"

"I've infiltrated six units so far, madame." the EI said. *"I can gather a few more in a couple of—"*

"Time is of the essence," she interrupted him and looked at her team. "We have to go now. Let's take the lab, then we need to join Genos so we can meet the soldiers at the gate."

"You couldn't make contact with him while you hacked into the bots?" Indre asked.

Chiyo shook her head. "I think he was still busy."

The Tsuna engineer took a moment to rest against the dilapidated wall of the logistics dorm. He dragged a few deep breaths as the two nano-hacked droids patrolled around him and stepped on the various parts of the couple of dozen bots he had destroyed. They had been tenacious. He had to admire their design, but even the most well-made machine could always be destroyed or repurposed. Still, a part of him did want to examine them after this was all over. They could prove to be a good base for redesigns of the Nexus security bots. But before all that, he should probably call Chiyo and inform her he would be on his way.

A rumble under the ground curtailed his moment of rest. The bots stopped moving and stood alert as a section of the earth began to ascend and a mech emerged. It lit up and the circle on its face turned blue as it took a step forward, then craned its ungainly head to look at the Tsuna and his stolen droids. He tilted his head as the mech's arm cannon began to prime. This was an annoying predicament, but his mind began to dance with ideas. It could also prove interesting.

He would have to hold off on the call to his teammate for now, but he would come back bearing gifts if this went well.

The soldier team ran from the plaza and slapped silver boxes against various pillars, building walls, statues, and anything large along their path to the gate. Raul's drone flew overhead so the tracker could keep an eye on any new developments.

The dozens of droids that flooded out of the warehouses in the harbor would certainly qualify as a new development.

"Step it up!" Raul shouted into the comms as he sent the feed to the group again. "They are coming for real now."

"Damn. It looks like they were hiding the real shit." Cameron scowled as he slapped one of the explosives against the fountain statue. "We will need back up unless the heavies think they can hold them off with their shields."

"Hell yeah, we can!" Mack whooped as he ran down the center path to catch up with Raul and Haldt as Luke, Silas, Jaxon, and Cameron came up from behind.

"I admire enthusiasm but let's be smart about this," the officer suggested and retrieved his tablet. "I'll call the ship to meet us at the gate when the barrier goes down in case we need a quick getaway."

"Did group B tell you how long it will take?" Silas asked.

"They said they were gunning for it right now," Cameron said and shrugged. "Are all bombs in place?"

"Our section is complete," Jaxon confirmed.

"Same with ours." Haldt nodded as the entire group gathered directly in front of the gate. He held the trigger up. "Raul, let me know when."

Aside from the sounds of fighting in the distance near the R&D department, the group heard nothing but the thunderous approach of the droids. Some could be seen hopping along the remaining rooftops of the Academy buildings. Haldt held the trigger ready while Raul watched the feed and the seconds ticked by.

Cameron took aim with his rifle and Jaxon exchanged his machine gun for a rifle as well, but the officer held a hand out to tell them to lower their weapons, at least for now.

The hacker closed the feed and nodded at the security officer. "Do it!"

Haldt pressed the trigger, and the entire center of the island erupted with such violence that even the heavies felt the force through their armor. Buildings toppled and droids shattered while an enormous cloud of dust and debris hung over what was probably a large crater in what remained of the island.

"What the hell was that?" an Ark soldier asked as they continued to set the bomb up in front of the stubborn door to the abandoned facility.

"Did they get through the shield?" another asked.

Dario, with a curious frown, checked his tablet. "No. At least not yet from what I see." He put the device away and walked to the stairs. "Although I suggest we quicken our pace somewhat. It seems we won't have much time to peruse the goods like the general wanted, although we may have a different kind of fun now."

"Oh, my God!" Indre exclaimed as the explosion settled. "Aren't we trying to take this place back?"

"We can rebuild later," Cyra shouted and yanked the case off her back as she shot an approaching bladed droid. "Chiyo!" She threw the case to the infiltrator as she fired two more shots at the mechanical and walked back, taking her rifle out to assist Indre and the three remaining hacked bots to hold the seemingly never-ending Arbiter bots at bay

Chiyo unlatched the case, withdrew the marker, and aimed at the building. She walked closer as it primed. "Kaitō, assist in the connection process but don't release those droids," she ordered.

"Understood, madame. I am close to task capacity, but I shall do my best."

She looked through the scope and focused as a triangle formed in the frame. A thin line appeared that went through the building and began to expand. Soon, it encircled the building, then moved behind her and from there, around almost the entire section.

"Connection established, madame. Power at one hundred percent. You may fire when ready."

The infiltrator pulled the trigger with no apparent result. To the naked eye, there was nothing, but a bright flash blazed in the screen of the scope and immediately went dark. She checked the marker, which was still fine, but the scope had failed. When she looked back, her group no longer fired and instead, all the bots had deactivated, Cyra held a hand out, placed it against the head of one of the bots, and pushed it over. It toppled against another that fell into two more, and all tumbled without any effort to resist.

"So, it worked, right?" Indre asked. A crackle above them drew their collective attention. A trail of energy no longer connected the shield to the colossus. A hole began to form at the tip of the dome and it widened, then descended.

They had done it. The shield had fallen.

"The fighters say the shield is still up." Zena sighed, Kaiden and Wolfson frowned, and Desmond shrugged as her hand lowered from her commlink "I guess we'll have to join the main fight until—" Her hand darted to her comm again and a wicked smile formed on her face. "Scratch that. The shield is falling. We'll have boots on the ground the second we're there."

Whoops and hollers issued from the gang members. Wolfson punched a fist into his other hand and smiled as he grasped his shotgun and headed to the deck. Kaiden was happy but not elated. He had expected his friends to succeed.

It had taken them longer than he'd thought but still, they'd earned their drinks once this was over.

CHAPTER THIRTY-FOUR

Sasha had reached the city itself when Haldt informed him via the commlink that a large number of droids had been hiding under the island. It answered the unspoken question amongst them all after the battle had started as to how many droids the AO could apparently produce and made those they battled now seemed almost paltry by comparison. Janis would arrive soon and his forces had pushed to the edge of the city. The bridge to the Academy lay directly ahead. All they needed was for the shield to fall.

As the thought entered his mind, he turned to glower at the beam that connected the shield to the colossus and hope flared as it began to dissipate. The barrier began to shimmer before it faltered and holes appeared all around the dome.

He wasted no time. "This is Commander Sasha. All troops, the shield is down. I repeat, the shield is down!" He quickened his pace and was almost unaware that he ran beside other military and resistance members who sprinted down the streets of Bellingham toward the bridge. “Make sure to keep your flank covered but head toward the Academy grounds. Our enemy is awaiting their defeat!”

Cameron unlocked his helmet, pulled it up slightly, and drew a deep breath. “This is probably the first fresh air the Academy has had in months,” he commented before he slid the helmet on, turned the oxygen tank off, and opened the vents. “Man, that’s nice.”

Luke, Silas, and Haldt gestured to where dots appeared on the far side of the bridge. “It didn’t take them long to notice, did it?” the titan asked.

“It’ll still take a while for them to get here, assuming they will make their way on foot,” Silas pointed out. He watched as the destroyers swooped into the fight now that the colossus’ almost impenetrable shields had finally disappeared. “Do you think we can flag one down to help?”

“I think they have their hands full,” Haldt reasoned as their ship hovered on the side of the bridge directly outside the gate. “Contact the others and make sure they are on their way. Hopefully, there wasn’t a second wave of bots gunning for them, but we should be careful. There’s no use getting this far only to—”

“Droids!” Raul called.

Mack’s armor lit with energy. “Where?”

This was answered by a small fireball that spun toward the vanguard, who raised a hand and blocked it with a shield. “That was my drone,” Raul stated and drew his rifle. “The last image was of a group heading through the plaza

—or maybe climbing through the rubble in the plaza would be more accurate. There were others coming around the edges as well."

"I guess it would be too hopeful to think the blast would slow them enough for the others to arrive." Jaxon looked to his right as he felt an odd rumble. "Mechs!"

The group armed themselves and took defensive positions as two mechs ascended from the ground. Both immediately prepared their cannons. The two heavies ran ahead and activated their respective shields, but before either side could fire, a large blue blast erupted behind one of the mechs and it toppled noisily. The other turned to see what had happened and a large metal arm swung violently and severed its head with a single blow. The massive body stumbled and fell over the edge of the island and into the sea.

"Hello, friends!" Genos waved cheerfully from where he hung off the edge of a mech. "I'm glad to see you safe."

"Genos!" Jaxon shouted in surprise as the engineer vaulted off. The two Tsuna ran up to each other and the ace placed a hand on Genos' shoulder. "It's good to see you have fared quite well," he said and studied the large mechanical.

"Yes. I was unfortunately separated from the others, but I was able to acquire this in the hope that it would prove useful when we met again." He looked around the group. "Are Chiyo and the others with you?"

"Not yet," Luke said and shook his head as he walked over. "They took the shield down a few minutes ago so they should be on their way. We were about to try their comms before those—"

"Droids!" Cameron shouted.

"I was getting to that," the titan protested in annoyance until he looked back. A large group of droids raced up the main road toward the gate. "Oh, shit!"

The group all turned to face the advancing enemy while Genos clambered onto the mech again. "I shall go and find them. We shall meet soon," he stated as the metal beast lumbered away. A volley of plasma shots was unleashed by the droids, but his mech blocked them easily and fired two large salvos at the group to destroy several and scatter the others, which made them easy targets for the rifleman amongst the group.

"We need to get us some of those," Raul remarked as Genos headed toward the R&D section. "Damn useful."

"Wait it out until the riggers and jockeys get here," Haldt said briskly. "We have an early start, gentleman. Let's not allow our tallies to slow now, shall we?"

"The island is in sight," Desmond shouted as he stepped onto the top deck, now outfitted with his large jetpack. "Jockeys, get your asses in gear. You're heading out!"

"The sky's our land and we're the Kings!" a few of them yelled, followed by a chorus of dozens as they all moved to the edges of the ship. Kaiden looked at the shuttles that surrounded the assault ship and several began to open their side doors as more sky jockeys leaned out and waved to each other. When he gazed ahead, the silhouette of Nexus appeared between the mountains and above, several destroyers harried the colossus while numerous fighter ships battled around them.

"Man, that monster is big," Zena said, startled by her first glimpse of the vessel.

"It'll make for a nice explosion when we're finished with it," Wolfson responded, shouldered his shotgun, and nudged the ace's arm. "Will you head out with the jockeys, boyo?"

He nodded and began to walk away. "I will. I should probably get suited up."

The large man chuckled. "You'd best make sure not to scare your friends. They may blow your head off thinking you're one of the bots."

"I'll make a note of it," he responded with a chuckle. "See you down there, Wolfson."

"Oh certainly," the head officer answered, although too quietly for Kaiden to hear as he looked at the Colossus. "I'm more worried about getting up there, however."

"Indre, are you all right?" Cyra asked as the girl leaned against a wall and clutched her arm.

"It burns like hell," she muttered. "They have potent cannons, I'll give them that."

"Here, let me help," Amber offered, held her stim-ray to the agent's arm, and pressed the trigger. A green beam flooded the dark-red mark and the gouge created by the laser shot that had cut through Indre's armor. The vivid color faded as her skin repaired and filled. While the armor was unaffected, in less than a minute, the wound had healed.

Indre nodded as she moved her arm. "Thanks, doc. That thing comes in handy."

"I think so as well," the medic agreed and glanced at the stim-gun. "Although if you don't calibrate it right or use too much force in certain injuries, it can actually increase the pain and even kill nerves. it can be tricky sometimes."

"Thank God you aren't a first-year," the girl said with a smirk as Amber stowed her equipment.

"How far are we from the gate?" Chiyo asked Cyra as she joined her in shooting at the pursuing droids.

"Not too far, but the quickest way is through the path they are blocking." She ducked as a blast from one of the droid's cannons knocked rubble loose above her head.

"We'll have to push through," the infiltrator stated quietly. "The cannon is still down and all Indre's drones are destroyed. I'll ask Kaitō to try to hack some more—what?" A large mech came into view and trampled a couple of enemies as it charged its cannon and destroyed a group across the way. Several Melee droids attempted to leap onto it but it hurled them all away when it purged its shields and it took several steps forward. A few more mechanicals were crushed beneath its massive feet as it fired another blast at the fleeing droids.

Something climbed onto its shoulders and waved at the group. "Is that...Genos?" Cyra asked as they all stared in bewilderment.

"Friends? Are you there?" Genos called and the entire group chuckled and ventured out of their defensive den.

"Genos? It's us," Chiyo replied on the comms.

"Oh, good! Wonderful job on destroying the shields. I apologize for not accompanying you all the way," he stated as the mech marched forward. Despite their understanding of the situation, Cyra and Amber still fidgeted somewhat as the clearly Arbiter-made monster approached.

"Didn't we leave you with seven or eight droids to deal with?" Indre asked as the metal beast stopped in front of them. "How did you get the mech?"

The Tsuna dropped off the machine and walked up to them. "By improvising, I suppose," he said, although it really explained nothing. "The others are waiting at the gate and the army is on its way already. I suggest we join them."

Chiyo smiled under her helmet and nodded. "I agree."

Amber pointed to the sky. "Look there!"

The group looked up as several shuttles descended rapidly while all around, armored troops with jets orchestrated maneuvers to fire at the droids on the ground or that attempted to climb the buildings.

"It looks like the first part of the calvary is here," Cyra noted.

"This is Kaiden Jericho, broadcasting on…all the frequencies I can. Is anyone there?" the ace asked.

Chiyo's smile widened. "We're here, Kaiden." Hers was only the first response as Genos and most of the soldiers also greeted the new arrival. The engineer sent a ping and one of the jockeys broke off and banked in their direction. It didn't look like Kaiden's usual armor and Chiyo wondered if he had to wear a spare from one of the gangs before she realized it was much more complex than a normal suit.

He landed in front of the group, wearing a bronzed set of armor with black trim. The faceplate rose to reveal his broad smile. "Great job on getting the shield down. Now, it's my turn to get to work." He lowered the faceplate again and the eyes glowed white and Chiyo thought she could make out Chief's orb avatar in the sockets. "Do you care to join me?"

She looked at Indre, Cyra, and Amber. "Will you be okay?"

"Of course, and we'll be fighting again soon enough," Amber stated and the other two nodded.

"Then I shall," the infiltrator confirmed.

"As will I, friend Kaiden." Genos nodded and returned to the mech. "I believe this will be of great benefit as well." It lit up once again, its shields partially reformed.

"Oh yeah, that'll do," the ace said and brandished his rifle. "Now, let's go find that teleporter and get on that colossus. I don't want to keep the asshole who took our Academy waiting."

CHAPTER THIRTY-FIVE

Janis stood in the center of the command deck and one of the technicians turned to him. "Sir, Kit sent a message to say that the shield is down. They are already heading to the island."

"That quick, eh?" The Azure Halo leader took a moment to look at the land map on the technician's screen. "We're still about ten minutes out. Hopefully, they can hold on that long."

"Maybe we can send some drones to back them up until we arrive," the man suggested.

He shook his head. "They don't fly faster than the carrier unless we allow them to overclock their cores, but that would drain their energy much quicker. It won't be very helpful to send depleted drones that will simply fall out of the sky on arrival." He placed a hand on the technician's shoulder. "Don't worry, they've done well so far. I'm confident they will keep doing well and once we arrive, we'll help them finish this."

"Cannon charge at twenty percent," Aurora stated as the colossus was rocked by another blast from one of the WCM destroyers. Nolan cursed himself. He should have siphoned energy from the Academy shield to charge the cannons faster instead of empowering the shields. But if he had done that, it would have destabilized the shields. Now, with them taken down anyway, he had no alternative. So be it.

"Send out any remaining bombers and have those already deployed focus on one destroyer at a time, starting with the one directly on our port side," he ordered and studied the holographic map of the battle as he prepared his plan. "It should only take two to three runs along the ship to destroy any shields they may have. Then we'll send it crashing onto the island. Kill two birds."

"Sir, what about Dario and the soldiers?" one of the ensigns asked.

The general looked at the man. "Dario should be close to finishing his mission," he answered with a nonchalant wave of the hand. "Besides, he hasn't gotten to his current position by being easy to kill."

"Is everyone behind the shield?" Dario asked politely and the soldiers looked at one another. He made one final headcount as he twirled the trigger in his hands. "It looks like it. Very good." He held the trigger up, opened the top slot, and placed his thumb on the button as he focused on the bomb attached to the door. "You may wish to brace yourselves."

With that final warning, he pressed the button and the bomb made a loud, high-pitched ringing noise. The lights around the center and on the top turned white, then yellow, before the noise reached a fever-pitch and the lights briefly went red before the device exploded.

The detonation shook the cavern and some of the metal pillars gave way as the energy unleashed collided with the shield. At first, it seemed to hold up, but cracks formed and several soldiers began to take steps back.

The assassin frowned and shook his head. "Perhaps I may have been off on where this needed to be deployed. I thought it was fifty feet back but it might have been fifty feet up," he commented as more cracks slivered along the barrier. Three soldiers began to run away from the shield and up the stairs and he motioned for those in the back to grab them. "Don't run off yet," he stated as his gauntlets flared to life. "We still have a job to do. There's no point in dying now."

Dario released hundreds of his nanos along the shield. They landed around the cracks and began to repair them rapidly. The explosion had still not completed, and more cracks began to appear while others deepened. He continued to direct more nanos to maintain the protective barrier, surprised at how many he had to forfeit. It really was an impressive bomb.

Finally, the chaos subsided. The room was dark as the artificial lighting had been destroyed and dust whirled in the air. He waited a moment to see if anything large fell, but aside from the sound of the metal walls crackling and small to medium pieces of rubble that fell from the ceiling, it appeared the worst was over.

He instructed his nanos to form into several spheres and illuminated them as he deactivated the shield. While he released the bright orbs throughout the room to give them a path, some of the soldiers tossed lighting sticks around the area.

"There, not too bad now, was it?" Dario asked as the soldiers who tried to flee were pushed forward.

"Sorry, sir, we let our nerves get to us," one of them apologized.

Dario waved him off. "It's all right. It was something of a mistake on my part, anyway. Now then, let's see what became of the door, shall we?"

The soldiers nodded as the assassin formed one more sphere and let it guide them down the walkway and to the previously locked and impregnable door. Once they were close enough, he chuckled. "It's rather stubborn, isn't it?" he remarked. The door had been blown open but not very wide. While the gap was certainly enough for two or three people to slip through at once, given how large the explosion was, it had still held on remarkably well.

"You three—" He turned and pointed to the soldiers who had tried to run. "If you would like a chance at redemption, take the lead. Remember, everyone, we're looking for the serum or at least the blueprints or recipe. Make sure to search carefully."

The group nodded and the trio looked at one another briefly before they walked past the assassin and through the door. Others tried to follow, but he held a hand up to stop them, seemingly waiting for something. One of the soldiers inside retrieved a light stick to peer into the darkness but two red lights appeared only several yards ahead. He uttered a surprised yelp as the light darted forward and a large blade skewered the soldier's chest. His two teammates stepped back hastily and fired their weapons at the mechanical. It turned so its shields blocked the laser fire and swung its blade to hurl the body of the soldier into one of the others as it leapt forward. The heavy metal body crushed the third man beneath it before the non-bladed arm formed into a cannon and fired at the others on the ground before either could recover.

"Hmm. A Reaper droid," Dario commented and beckoned two spheres over that he reformed into spears. "I thought they would still have some tricks and traps waiting for us in here."

The Reaper turned and the soldiers behind him prepared to fight as the large droid ran to the door, moving much quicker than a machine of its size had any right to. It raised its cannon and prepared to fire as the assassin cast both spears out. One struck the mechanical's shoulder and the other the barrel of the cannon. He snapped his fingers dramatically and the spears detonated to destroy the cannon arm and blow off the other arm and a third of its chest.

He hummed merrily as the five remaining spheres gathered around him and he walked inside. The broken droid raised its head, opened its mouth, and fired several kinetic shots from a gun within. Dario formed a small shield and blocked the shots. "Cute trick," he muttered and created a buzz-saw-like blade with his nanos. "But you've outstayed your welcome, I'm afraid." The saw began to spin rapidly as he lowered it and bisected the head of the Reaper as it finally stilled.

"Well, that was satisfying." He chuckled and his tablet vibrated with a new message. Still smiling, he took it out and looked at the notification, then nodded as he put the device away. He turned to face the soldiers and completely ignored a loud thud behind him. "All right, *ragazzi e ragazze,* it appears we have less time than I originally thought." More noises from behind indicated that something was approaching. "So, your job is to fan out and find our objective," he explained, created several bombs, spears, and blades with his nanos, and turned away from the group. As he walked forward, red lights closed in. "And my job will be to keep you alive."

Another Reaper droid leapt out from the darkness and swung its blade at Dario, who parried it with two blades of his own and pierced the mechanical with three spears. He smiled as he held a hand up with his thumb and middle finger pressed together. "It's ironic if you think about it." He snapped his fingers and blew the Reaper to pieces as he simply continued his walk into the abandoned facility.

CHAPTER THIRTY-SIX

"Nice of you to join us!" Cameron shouted to several of the jockeys who landed nearby to help them keep the droids at bay. "Nice entrance too."

"They are almost here," Raul shouted and looked across the bridge. "Only a few more minutes—what the hell?" The gate to the Academy began to close and the massive doors slid together.

"Dammit, where's the gate control?" Mack demanded as he formed a large shield around himself and attempted to prevent the gates' closure. His effort was to little avail, however, as his shield held only momentarily before it snapped under the pressure and Luke hauled him back.

"Contact Kaiden and Chiyo. One of them should be able to fix it," Jaxon suggested, vented his rifle, and switched it out for his machine gun as the droids fired lasers toward him. He ducked to avoid it, but one of the shots did strike the shields around his shoulder. He retaliated with a spray of kinetic rounds that felled two of the attackers. The other jumped away but his head exploded from a shot by Cameron, who nodded to his teammate before he placed his fingers against his helmet commlink to connect to Kaiden. "Hopefully, they can do it quickly," the Tsuna ace murmured to himself as he selected his next target.

"Commander!" a soldier shouted and pointed to the gates. They had begun to close and the army was only several minutes away. Sasha grimaced but didn't slow as he activated his comm.

"Any shuttles that can break through, come to the bridge for a quick pick-up," he ordered and turned to the soldier. "Do not slow your advance. We'll climb over the damn thing if we have to," he stated. His determination inspired those around him to increase their pace as they advanced on to the gate.

Two more droids fell as a round of lasers drilled into their backs. Kaiden had eliminated seven so far and he roared as he threw another thermal at more of the advancing horde. One simply snatched it out of the air and flung it up. These bots were a nuisance. Where he towered above on his hacked mech, Genos caught the explosive and hurled it again to eliminate the mechanicals. He adjusted his seat on his metal mount and the group continued to push through toward the administration building.

The ace smiled as he fired a blast at the droids' feet. It

hurled them back and provided enough time for him and his team to get around the corner. Now that the enemy had reached them, they had actually moved back from where they had dropped in and had to weave through the grid-like pattern of the buildings for cover and distance. Chiyo stopped and turned with her SMG and pistol at the ready. The ace followed suit and charged a shot. When the bots appeared, the two teammates fired as one and destroyed their pursuers before they could respond.

"Look up!" she shouted. Kaiden did so and immediately located three of their adversaries perched on the ledge of one of the buildings preparing to fire. He swung his weapon to target them but several small explosions detonated around the mechanicals. Two fell over the side and a couple of jet jockeys soared overhead and waved at the group.

As Kaiden returned the gesture, they spun quickly in an attempt to dodge a sniper shot. One was hit in their pack, which ruptured and exploded in the air in short order and thrust the other one out of the sky. The ace grimaced and told the others to keep moving as he hurried to check on the jockey. Chiyo followed and Genos made sure to hold the line.

They reached the fallen man, who sprawled helplessly while a droid's leg crushed his chest and as Kaiden raised his weapon, it fired into his helmet. Chiyo fired first and the impact forced the droid off the fallen jockey, but it recovered quickly and moved almost spiderlike to weave around her shots and retaliate with a sustained volley. The ace grabbed her and pulled her down and the lasers streaked overhead. He fired and managed to remove the droid's legs. As the mechanical landed heavily, it pushed up and aimed at them once more. He dropped Sire and yanked Debonair out to deliver three rapid shots into its head and it fell it decisively.

He stood and helped his teammate up. "Thank you," she said and vented her machine gun.

"Kaiden, Chiyo, are you there?" Cameron called out over the comms. "The gate is closing…closed—whatever!" he stated frantically and sounds of battle were evident over the link. "The reinforcements are almost here. We need to get it open and the terminal isn't working."

"It must have locked out," Chiyo surmised. "They probably still have master control."

"If worse comes to worst, we can simply blow the gate, but I'd rather spare the ammo and time though," Kaiden stated.

She nodded. "Blowing through it would take too long if it's even possible with the arms we have."

He looked at Chief in his HUD. "We need to get it open. Where to, Chief?"

"Keep heading to administration," the EI answered. *"We can access the master controls there."*

"Can you hack into it?" Kaiden asked.

Chief's orb shook in lieu of his head. *"Probably not, but Sasha can get into it—or, rather, his chancellor code can. Even if they reset the system, they can't change or erase his codes. I'll fetch them from him."*

"That sounds good." The ace gestured for Chiyo to follow. "Let's keep going. We'll get those gates open, Cam," he hollered into the comms and switched to Genos' link.

"We're heading to the administration building. We have to open the gate first and will need cover while we work."

"Understood, friend Kaiden," Genos responded. "I'll make a path."

The two moved along a slightly convoluted route and used their knowledge of the Academy's layout to their advantage to dart hastily around corners if they were set upon by any more droids. Opening the gate took priority right now, although after the last attack, he made sure to keep an eye on the roofs as well.

As he and Chiyo turned to the right, a trail of lasers from above seared down the path they had previously run through and a fighter banked away above before it elevated once more. Kaiden was thankful but he also hoped he had actually waited until they were out of the way rather than it simply being a happy coincidence. Things had become hectic.

They reached the plaza with battles all around and the administration building only a hundred yards from them. "Chief, do you have the codes?"

"I do, and the chancellor slash commander asked for you to hurry if you would," the EI responded.

"We're working on it. How close do you need to be to access the system?"

"Get inside and head to the second floor. The console is on the fifth floor, but that will be enough for me to cast in."

"Gotcha." He looked at Chiyo, who closed a holoscreen.

"We should have assistance. Make a run for it," she told him.

"All right." An explosion made them both turn as Genos

and his mech lumbered into the plaza. "Assuming Genos doesn't destroy that assistance. Let's go."

They sprinted to the doors, which were fortunately already destroyed so they didn't have to wait for them to open. Several droids located them and tried to fire or intercept, but hacked mechanicals attacked and distracted them. The two teammates hurried inside, raced to the stairs, and ascended at a run as several Scarabs fired at them. They drew their pistols to deal with the annoying small bots.

As they reached the second floor, Chief nodded to Kaiden and disappeared to access the master system. A group of droids entered the building. Most were normal Arbiter bots but the ace noticed a couple of the enhanced bots among them. He leaned cautiously over the railing and let the HUD scan them and lock on.

Chiyo reached down to retrieve her shocks but he held a hand out to stop her. "I got this," he said quietly as the shoulder pads of his power armor opened and small missiles engaged. She crept back as he leaned away and fired the missiles up before they quickly adjusted their trajectory to the floor below.

The projectiles pounded into the targets with a series of impressive explosions. Kaiden peered down but saw nothing but parts. One of the enhanced droids sputtered, only the head and part of the torso still together, but it soon deactivated. He thought back to the time they had fought the enhanced droids during the invasion and how difficult they had proven. Now, he had disposed of them in a single attack and decided he needed to keep this armor.

"Got it," Chief declared. *"The gates are open. Let the people in."*

The main gate unlocked with several loud clicks and the two sides of the barrier began to draw apart. Mack, Luke, and Cameron whooped and several shuttles flew in over the island's walls to rain laser fire from the sides of the vessels as soldiers within went on the offensive. Sasha was amongst them and as the gates opened, the first few soldiers of the army below him made their way in, followed by the couple of hundred behind them.

It was their turn to invade now.

CHAPTER THIRTY-SEVEN

"Sir! There's an assault ship approaching," the dropship pilot called to Sasha and pointed out the cockpit window. "But it's covered in graffiti or something."

"We're expecting them," he stated and fired at one of the sniper droids on the roof. "Take us in close to the assault ship. It will be nice to finally have his assistance."

"Whose, sir?" one of the soldiers asked.

Sasha fired another shot and eliminated a bladed droid that snuck up on one of the downed jockeys. "You'll know him by the hollering."

"We're finally here!" Wolfson bellowed and placed one leg on the railing as the assault ship flew over the Academy walls. "And not a moment late. It looks like the real fighting has begun. Bring us in."

"We've flown all the way here and now, he wants to act

like the captain." Zena sighed. "Bring us into the fray. So far, we haven't been shot at by the military but the enemy will probably realize we aren't on their side soon enough. Let's eliminate all we can in the confusion and get the foot soldiers deployed."

"Right, we'll throw the ropes," one of the grunts acknowledged and hurried away as several other Fire Riders began to tie the ends of long black cables onto both railings of the deck.

"Ropes?" the head officer asked and watched in bewilderment as the grunts worked hastily.

"Yeah. Kaiden blew up their little hover chamber on the underside of the ship," Zena reminded him. "We couldn't repair it in time and didn't have the right parts anyway. This method might be antiquated but it gets boots on the ground, doesn't it?"

The giant laughed and hefted his shotgun in both hands. "I like the ingenuity and never cared for the fancy stuff anyway." He took a few steps back and smiled. "I have my own way down, though." With that, he uttered a roar, charged, and leapt over the rail to drop over seventy feet to the island below.

"He couldn't wait for thirty seconds?" Zena sighed as she snatched her machine gun from the bench and strode to the railing. "Come on, boys and girls! We can't let those military types have all the fun. We'll earn our keep today."

Genos leapt off his mech a split-second before an orb of

blue energy pounded into its side. He landed and spun as the mech walked back and a second blast destroyed its chest and toppled it only several feet away. It really was a pity, but he probably could have had more use out of it if he had been a little more aware.

He was even more disgruntled when three others entered the plaza as he had no more nano grenades. While he did have his cannon, he would have to get close to do any real damage. Before he could approach, a loud bellow distracted him and something drove into the shoulder of one of them. A figure in heavy armor simply grasped the head of the mech and pulled with seemingly inhuman strength to rip it out of its socket. He took a thermal grenade canister and threw it down the hole, then vaulted off as the two others turned and swung their massive arms in an effort to land a blow.

The large man landed and dispatched two droids with his shotgun before he raced away as the mech exploded and demolished its fellows in the process. Genos, despite his bewilderment, was impressed.

"I am Baioh Wolfson, head officer of this Academy!" the newcomer roared, took an ax from his belt, and used it to slice cleanly through the neck of an Arbiter droid. "And I'll make you *kuks* rue the day you tried to take our Academy."

"Ah, it is Kaiden's mentor," Genos muttered and charged his cannon. "Such a magnificent if reckless attack makes sense now." He fired a blast at an enhanced droid that advanced on Wolfson, but the mechanical was felled by a heavy shot from above before his could even connect. He gaped when a massive assault ship flew in. It appeared to be an Omega Horde vessel but with many odd markings along the hull.

Ropes uncurled as the ship lowered slightly and fired at any droid in the area while troops in heavy and medium armor in a fiery-red and sky-blue slid down the ropes. Some leapt off before they reached the ground and all fired at the enemy droids and shouted fiercely. He recognized them immediately as the gangs Kaiden was well acquainted with.

Genos ran to Wolfson as the ground shifted, the telltale sign of a mech being deployed. He glanced over his shoulder and, sure enough, a beast rumbled from the earth. Before he could decide whether to engage it or not, one of the gang members yelled, "Fucking get 'em!" At least a dozen Fire Riders and Skyway Kings attacked and obliterated it before it had a chance to prepare a shot.

"Ey, is that you, Genos?" The Tsuna turned as Wolfson strolled up beside him. "It's nice to see a familiar face right away."

"I'm happy you could join us, Elder Wolfson," he responded. "Are you looking for Kaiden?"

"I could always pull him up on the map but if you know where he is, I'm listening."

"Certainly." He nodded and pointed to the administration building. "He went in there to take control of the master system and open the gate. Coincidentally, we were heading there anyway as there is another way into the old facility from here that is much faster and potentially safer than using the normal route near the docks."

"Then let's get in there," Wolfson urged and tucked his

weapon securely against his chest. "Nothing bad has happened before I got here, right?"

"There were some explosions a couple of minutes ago," Genos told him.

"That sounds about right." The giant chuckled and pushed into a jog. "We should hurry."

"Why are there so many inside the building?" Kaiden shouted as he poked his head into the hall and fired a charged shot from Sire. It was dodged by most of the droids but hit one that had come around the corner at the perfect moment.

"I think they were cutting through," Chiyo told him and tapped the screen on her gauntlet. "We simply happen to be in the way." Both she and her teammate ducked into the room they hid in as three of the droids stopped moving. The others pushed past but the three began to shake and emitted a loud beep before they exploded and catapulted their fellows off their feet.

"Go!" she shouted and both entered the hall and eliminated the mechanicals before they could recover. As they made their way to the end of the hall, an enhanced droid stepped out, its cannon ready to fire.

"Shit—Chiyo, get behind me!" the ace yelled and held Sire to the side as his shields flared and she crouched behind him. His adversary fired and the bolt careened into him and kicked up dust and metal. The droid tilted its head before a bolt of green energy streaked in retaliation to shatter its chest and careen it into the wall.

"I get why it's called power armor now," he commented as he and Chiyo stepped through the smoke. But before he could fully enjoy his victory, three more enhanced droids stepped out and primed their cannons.

He scowled as he and his teammate took aim. "This might be pushing it, though."

CHAPTER THIRTY-EIGHT

"I believe we are close now, correct?" Genos asked as they ran deeper into the building. A loud explosion one floor up cracked the ceiling and dust filtered onto them before a droid plummeted from above. The Tsuna ran forward and readied his cannon, but although the enemy tried to push up, its damaged chest sparked and it stiffened before it collapsed.

"Well, that saves us the trouble," Wolfson stated and tried to reach a box on his back but his bulky frame made it difficult. "Do you mind grabbing that box for me Genos?"

"Certainly," the Tsuna replied, took the box, and placed it into the officer's outstretched hand.

"Appreciated." The large man opened it and removed several small disks as the distinctive sounds of fighting above them escalated. He tilted his head as if to listen more closely before he took a few steps forward to the edge of the hall, threw the disks onto the ceiling, and retreated hastily. "Head down!" he shouted as he fired at the disks.

They erupted as soon as the shot hit, the ceiling gave way, and three enhanced droids fell from above. Wolfson took two more disks and flung them at the pile and they stuck onto the head of one and the leg of another. He nodded to Genos, who charged his cannon as the enemy began to stand and fired a large red orb that found its target in the center droid. The resultant eruption annihilated the bots and a large portion of the ceiling.

Once the dust settled, a large figure dropped from above. Genos instinctively prepared to fire, but his companion stopped him and he realized a moment later that it was Kaiden in his new power armor.

The faceplate opened and the ace nodded a greeting. "That could only have been you, Wolfson." He chuckled and motioned to someone above before Chiyo landed quickly beside him. "You are the only one as partial to destruction as I am."

"I wouldn't say partial, exactly. I merely don't mind it," the man corrected.

"It's good to see you are unharmed, Genos," Chiyo said.

"You don't have your mech anymore, I see." Kaiden looked disappointed.

The Tsuna nodded and glanced at the giant beside him. "He is…more compact than a mech but equally as devastating."

Wolfson uttered a loud laugh. "I'm putting that on my officer ID when this is all said and done."

"This is Sasha. Are you there, Kaiden?" the commander asked over the commlink.

"Finally. It's good to hear your voice, Sasha," he acknowledged. "Are you on the grounds yet?"

"Just landed. How is your progress?"

"We're on our way and are near the center of the administration building, so we should be close to the secret room Laurie told us about," he advised.

"Who is with you?"

"Chiyo, Genos, and Wolfson." He linked the call to the others.

"Wolfson is with you?" Sasha asked. "Will he accompany you?"

The head officer looked at Kaiden and nodded. "Aye, do you need me on the field?"

"If you are going, then no. I will take charge," the commander stated. "I hoped that at least one of us could accompany Kaiden while the other handled things out here."

"You're more suitable for that anyway. I never was one for large-scale battles," the officer stated. "Well, I'll fight in one certainly, but trying to command all the moving pieces isn't much of a strong suit for me."

"I understand. Do your—" His statement was cut short by a loud explosion over the link from his side.

"What was that?" Chiyo asked.

"One of the destroyers. They've lost their shield and are taking heavy damage from the colossus," Sasha explained, his voice grim. "You need to hurry."

Kaiden nodded. "We won't let you down," he promised and cut the link as he motioned for the others to follow, holstered Sire, and looked at Chiyo. "Do you know if the enemy has opened the door yet?"

"I felt a large explosion before you arrived," she explained. "I would imagine that was the bomb they brought to open it. I don't know if it worked but they appear to have set it off."

"Then if they did make it in, they'll meet us there," the ace surmised and shrugged. "It means we don't have much time, but if we can eliminate them while we're down there, we don't have to worry about them getting the serum." The faceplate closed and he turned away. "Let's get going."

"One of the destroyers is disabled," the Arbiter technician stated. "It's trying to break away. Should we pursue?"

"Fire on it and send the bombers on their next run while we do so," Nolan ordered. "Send out any remaining fighters and drones to defend them. I'm sure they've caught on by now and will make plans to intercept the bombers." He looked at an ensign. "Are the pods ready?"

"We're at seventy-five percent, sir," she told him.

"That is enough to begin." He focused on another technician. "Mark points around the center and along the rim of the island amongst the enemy combatants. See if we can't take out some of their forces while we bolster our own."

"Understood, sir." The man set to work quickly.

The general looked at his screen. The cannon was only at twenty-seven percent and charged much more slowly now. It had been almost completely depleted when they arrived. He had to come to terms with the fact that if he wanted to destroy the enemy, he wouldn't be able to do it with his forces alone.

"Break off one of the fighters," he ordered. "Send it to

the west and once it gets outside the jamming area, have it send a distress beacon."

"At once," the same technician replied.

Nolan leaned back in his chair. He was loath to call on Damyen for anything, especially so soon after his previous assistance. But he would swallow his pride because if he failed now, he failed the organization and Merrick's plan would not come to fruition.

That was a guilt he would not be able to shake, even in death.

Sasha watched the battle above with the helplessness that came from the inability to intervene. The crippled destroyer had broken away but was still battered by the colossus' side cannons. It was now far enough away that if it did break apart, it should hopefully miss the island. He was still hopeful it could escape but it was too damaged to warp at this point.

Several objects were jettisoned from the underside of the colossus, followed immediately by many more. He recognized the pods, exactly like those that had been launched at the island during the invasion.

"We have more droids incoming!" he shouted on all comms. "Be ready. They are dropping pods so don't get trapped."

Three of them landed about fifty yards away from him. The heavies who guarded the commander looked at him and when he pointed at the hulls, they raced forward while he and two other snipers took aim. As soon as the doors opened and the droids emerged, they were beset by cannon fire, kinetic hammers, rockets, and sniper fire from Sasha's group. He would not let them take this island again. The AO might have the numbers advantage, but they were prepared this time.

Almost as if in response to this thought, Janis' carrier finally appeared over the mountains and cruised toward the island with its three-hundred-droid load. It was not nearly the end.

CHAPTER THIRTY-NINE

Kit surged forward and thumped the back of a droid's head with the butt of her rifle to knock it off the resistance soldier. They both fired on the mechanical and once it was riddled with holes, she helped him up as Fritz contacted her. "Hey, Kit. Janis is here."

She looked up as the soldier ran off to rejoin the fight and grinned as the large carrier finally advanced over the horizon. "It took him long enough." She chuckled and a small smile lingered on her face. "This'll turn the tide. Hopefully, we don't make a habit of getting into big fights like these after this, but we should look into upgrading that ship's engines once we—"

"Look out!" another soldier yelled and yanked her to the side. Before she could frame a question, a large object thudded into the place where she had previously stood. Two more landed behind them as she and her rescuer tensed and trained their weapons on the pods as the sides fell free and Arbiter droids boiled out.

"Fritz, we aren't the only ones with reinforcements!" she called as she fired on the new arrivals while she backed away a little to gain space. One of the resistance mechs ran forward and fired at one of the pods while it kicked the other into the sea. A third careened into the back of the mech and crushed it. The pilot was able to crawl from the wreckage, but Arbiter bots descended and swung their blades viciously. Kit and a few other soldiers opened fire and managed to eliminate a couple before the remainder dispersed and turned to them to retaliate, but the pilot was already dead.

"We need back-up," she yelled as more pods landed and the liberation forces were quickly overwhelmed and forced deeper into the island and away from the gate.

"Janis, what's your ETA?" Fritz demanded over the comm-link to the Azure Halo leader. "We're swarmed out there. The colossus is sending dozens of pods filled with bots and soldiers and we're now forced toward the center of the Academy. Soon enough, they'll be able to treat us as nothing more than a shooting gallery."

Janis looked at his instruments. "According to the GPS, we're another fifteen minutes out," he explained, looked at one of his crew, and gestured with his hand. "We have a few shuttles meant for evac but we'll send them now with some of the droids. I'll have to deploy the drones to keep them safe."

"I'll see if we can't get some of these jet jockeys to meet

you," the other man yelled in an effort to be heard over the cacophony. "If any can be spared."

Sasha fired three rapid shots and overheated his rifle. Three droids that attempted to leap to his position were destroyed in mid-air and he vented his rifle as Fritz contacted him. "Hey, Commander. Do you have a line to the Skyway Kings?"

"Not presently, but I should have no trouble establishing one. Give me a—" Something landed behind him with a loud clang and he spun as he drew his pistol to aim at a heavily armored figure, who held his hands up.

"It's all right," the newcomer stated and removed his helmet. "The name is Desmond—we met while taking that AO factory."

"I certainly recall you." The commander nodded, holstered his pistol, and closed the vent of his gun. "This is good timing on your part. I'm in contact with one of the Halos and it seems they could use your help." He connected the man to the commlink.

"Desmond of the Kings here. What do ya need?"

"I'm Fritz. We have reinforcements incoming, but the carrier is a slow bastard and won't be here for another fifteen minutes at least. My boss is sending shuttles on ahead with drones for defense, but we're worried they'll be targeted."

The Kings leader looked at the carrier that was still a large blob on the horizon. "You certainly won't be able to hide a ship that size once it gets in view. It may already have been picked up by some of the enemy ships. Shuttles will make for easy targets as well."

"We were hoping you have some jockeys to spare. Some fighters and interceptors will probably try to engage the shuttles. The drones can deal with most of them but some assistance would be nice."

"Agreed." Desmond nodded briskly and looked at Sasha. "I was about to ask if you had anything in particular for me and my Kings, but this'll do."

"Take what you need," the commander told him. "We'll hold no matter what."

The gang leader smiled as he put his helmet on. "I like that confidence, Commander." His jets began to prime. "But we work fast and will be back before you know it." He launched off the edge of the building and circled while close to twenty jockeys fell into formation behind them.

As Sasha watched them depart, a droid snuck on top of the roof and crept up to him. The marksman simply raised his pistol to his left and fired two shots into its dome. It collapsed and he returned to his perch and began to select and eliminate his targets with practiced precision.

"Is this the room?" Wolfson asked and when Kaiden nodded, he lifted a massive boot and kicked it in.

"We have the access code, you know," the ace muttered and scowled at the door that now hung by only one hinge. He noticed that the metal blocking bar had been engaged when the man had kicked it. Being able to kick a door in with a blocking bar could only be with the help of the armor, right?

The four walked into the storage room and Chiyo hurried to one of the back walls. "There's a second door..." She looked around and Kaitō scanned in her helmet and located a small crease along the left side of the wall. "Here."

Kaiden nodded and approached. "Upload, Chief."

"I'm already on it. We're in."

The false wall pushed out, then slid aside to reveal a metal door. Metal unwound within, followed by a hiss as it unlocked and opened to reveal a hatch inside.

"It seems small," Wolfson muttered.

Kaiden knocked the back of his hand against the head officer's chest. "Suck it in, big guy."

"We can close this door once we descend, correct?" Genos asked.

"Yeah, I still have control and even if I didn't, the door closes automatically after five minutes."

Chiyo retrieved a small cube and tossed it onto the ceiling where it attached and opened to reveal a camera. "To make sure we're not followed or warn us if there's something waiting on the way back," she explained quietly.

"If all goes well, the plan was that we will take the transporter into the ship," Genos reminded her.

"We want to actually invade the ship," she said. "I am realistic in saying that I doubt the four of us could take it alone."

"I could take it myself," Wolfson and Kaiden boasted at the same time, which drew an amused gurgle from Genos while she shook her head.

"If we can take the transporter up top so we can actually seize the ship with a significant force, I think that would be for the best," she reasoned.

"I'm not sure that's much of an option," the head officer replied dubiously. "Although I'm not too familiar with much inside the old facility. It was basically a vault for this stuff and not examined very closely. But I do know that the transporter requires its station to work properly. We can detach it but without the station, it'll lack the power to function properly."

"And how heavy is the station?" Kaiden asked.

The man gave him a sidelong look. "Let's go with 'hefty' and the four of us won't be able to carry it even if we took it apart."

"We need to get down there," Genos said cautiously. "I'm sure our enemy is already making headway. Whatever advantage this hatch may give us will be made moot if we take too long to descend."

The ace frowned but nodded. "Agreed. Chief, send a message to our group to get their asses over here when they can make a break for it and make sure to open the door when they do."

"Gotcha, partner."

"In the meantime..." He knelt and undid the latch. "Let's get down there and stop those bastards." Once the hatch was open, they were greeted by darkness. There appeared to be no ladder, pole, or even rope to climb down.

Kaiden looked at Wolfson, who knelt and flipped a switch on the underside of the hatch lid. Blue lines appeared in the tunnel that traveled all the way down. "It's a gravity well," he explained. "Who's first?"

The younger man stood and rolled his shoulders,

stepped onto the ledge of the hatch, and gave a quick salute. He uttered a surprised yelp when he descended much faster than he thought he would.

"I probably should have mentioned it takes a while for it to warm up," Wolfson commented cheerfully as he looked at the other two. "All right, who's up next?"

CHAPTER FORTY

"The shuttles are away, sir," one of the Halo crew stated, "and the drones are deployed as well."

"Good." Janis looked at his monitor. "Let's see how long it takes for enemy fight—"

"Enemy ships are coming to intercept the shuttles, Janis!" one of the techies cried.

"Rather quickly, apparently." He sighed and leaned back in his chair. "Get the carrier's guns ready. I'm sure they'll target us eventually as well."

"What about the shuttles?" the crewman asked.

He studied the monitor for a moment. "Fifteen shuttles covered by over fifty drones and I see only six enemy fighters going to engage."

"There are more on the way, sir," the man informed him. "It will be sixteen enemy ships in total. It takes three to five drones to combat an enemy fighter effectively."

"Then I suppose it is a good thing the Kings will join us," he replied, although he typed a hasty message to one of the bays to prepare more drones in case.

"Hey, boss!" one of the Kings shouted over the comms. Desmond looked in the direction in which the jockey pointed. "We have incoming."

A group of fighters streaked toward the shuttles in a direct trajectory, which meant they were too focused on trying to destroy the shuttles and their cargo to see him and his jockeys.

The Skyway King leader smiled. "All right. boys. Head up and flank them," he ordered and the group elevated and began their maneuver. "Let the drones slow them, pick 'em off, and let's get back to the real battle."

His team cheered as they circled to one side to position themselves behind the enemy fighters. Desmond would admit the Azure Halos were good with robots and tech, but when it came to the skies, they should leave it to the professionals.

Two of the Arbiter interceptors raced to destroy the newly arrived Halo shuttles. They fired the moment they were in range but their blasts were diverted by several drones as the remainder broke away to engage the Arbiter ships. One of them was able to roll out and immediately gained two pursuers that fired small laser shots at it. The other wasn't so lucky. One drone crashed into its wing but didn't break apart and instead, took hold of the wing. The barrel of its gun switched from a wide-mouth to a small, more focused barrel and it directed a concentrated beam into the wing in an attempt to cut it off.

The pilot pressed a switch and a small turret activated on the upper back of the ship that immediately turned and fired on the attacker. The mechanical withstood the first couple of rounds but was only able to slice through about a fourth of the wing before it was finally destroyed. The pilot pressed another switch to activate a small Scarab droid that popped out of a compartment under the turret. He traced the damage on his monitor and sent the Scarab to repair it. When he looked up again, he was face to face with a drone that glowed red. He pulled his yoke to the side in an attempt to fling it off, but it exploded before he could make even a half-roll and it set the cockpit and pilot on fire as the craft plummeted to the streets below.

An Arbiter fighter came through and launched a missile that broke apart to release dozens of tiny replicas that marked and followed various drones and destroyed them with ease. Before the pilot could gloat, however, a thud on his craft caught his attention. He activated the outer turret, but it had already been destroyed and in the next moment, his ship rapidly lost power. A blue-armored jet jockey knocked on his cockpit and waved at him, a detonator in his hand. He responded with an obscene gesture but the man was already out of sight. As he tried frantically to restore his systems, an explosion ripped through the top of his craft and it spiraled in flames to join the interceptor below.

Desmond used a different approach and bided his time while a fighter prepared to fire another missile. He drew his machine gun and fired at the projectile before it had a chance to uncouple from the host. It exploded and devastated a good third of the fighter along with it and the gang leader smirked before he received a warning in his HUD that he had been targeted. He spun, located an interceptor on a direct course toward him, and immediately elevated sharply as it fired several shots. The agile vessel was able to change directions quickly and pursue him.

He pressed a button on his gauntlet and two flare grenades dropped out of his pack behind him, detonated, and created a bright light. The interceptor fired seconds before the vivid flash of illumination, hit him, and shattered his shields as it flew past.

"Are you all right, boss?" one of the jockeys yelled and approached on his left.

Another hovered above and held a launcher up. "Do you want us to wreck him for you?"

"Hell no," Desmond yelled as he righted himself and exchanged his machine gun for his launcher. "That bastard is mine." He raced forward and pushed his jets to their limits in an attempt to catch up to his attacker. Finally, the interceptor turned and gave him his opportunity. He checked his launcher to confirm the chocks were currently loaded. While he preferred to see the bastard burn, these would do.

The Arbiter vessel fired, but with far more grace than one would expect in heavy armor, Desmond swerved easily around the shots and fired as the enemy passed him. The grenade struck home and bathed the ship in electricity. Several eruptions of sparks followed in sequence as various instruments overloaded on the craft. The pilot seemed to try to control the ship and activate something to disperse the electricity, but his instruments began to fry in his cockpit and smoke billowed from both the ship and in the cockpit as he fumbled under his seat for the ejection lever. The craft tumbled end over end to Earth, the pilot unable to eject. "Ya got what was coming to ya," he muttered and shouldered his launcher when the ship blew up on impact.

"Boss, we have more incoming," a jockey notified him. He scanned the sky around him and located five more ships coming down from the fight above.

The shuttles were now in the town and only a minute or so from dropping the droids off. "Now they are being petty," he mocked.

"They still have drones around, so maybe we can tell the Halos to take care of them?" one suggested.

"Hell no. That's not how we do things and you know it," he snapped and pressed the side trigger on his launcher to switch the payload to chasers. "Some of you have shield deployers, right?"

"Here!" a man shouted and flew closer.

"We got you, boss." another said as he and a teammate flew up on his right.

"I need to get in close so shield me until we are in range, but when I tell you to break, then get the hell out," he ordered. "These little puppies aren't picky, so dead-drop if you have to."

"Understood," one said and the other two nodded.

"Let's get them, boys!" Desmond roared as the four set off. His men took their place ahead of him and he held his launcher up and focused on the ships through his scope. The three jockeys activated their devices to create a large shield that covered the space in front and around them as the fighters opened fire to pummel the combined barrier.

"The shields are losing power fast," one of the men warned as they continued their ascent.

"We're almost there," Desmond replied, his voice low as the yellow numbers that counted down in his scope went from two-hundred feet to zero in seemingly no time at all, the distance swallowed hungrily as they raced up and the fighters streaked down. "Break!"

His team deactivated their jets and plunged earthward as the shield collapsed and their leader fired three rockets. These broke apart like the fighters' missiles, but each held three mid-sized salvos instead of dozens of small ones. At this range, they acquired their targets easily. Only one of the ships was able to escape before the other four were destroyed by the missiles. Desmond hovered in place as he watched two of the projectiles trail the ship until they struck the back of the fighter and thrust it into a wild spin for a brief moment before it erupted.

The other jockeys joined him and cheered in victory. "They'd better remember not to mess with the Kings of the sky!" the leader shouted.

"The sky is our domain!" the others chanted. They turned as the carrier passed and Desmond waved nonchalantly at the command deck window.

"Good job, gents," he told his men. "Now, let's get to the real action before all the Halo bots steal the good fights."

CHAPTER FORTY-ONE

"I'm having flashbacks!" Luke roared as he drove his hammer into the side of one of the pods. The blow thrust it several yards away and it toppled a group of bots before it thumped into the side of a building.

"Are you freaking out?" Mack asked as he swung a glowing fist into the chest of one of the enhanced Arbiter droids and flung it aside.

"Hell no!" Luke growled as he rolled his hammer in his hands. "I'm getting more pissed off."

"Guys, check your HUDS," Indre stated over the comms. "Chiyo sent us a message."

"I'm a little busy here!" Cameron winced as he kicked a bladed bot off him and fired several rounds from his pistol into its chest.

"Sure, take your time," Silas replied sarcastically as sounds of gunfire came over his link. "We can wait."

"What? I'm the designated reader or something?" the bounty hunter asked as he fired two rounds from his rifle at the heads of two bots that swung their cannons toward him.

"You are the only one who can actually break away from the fighting right now," Raul pointed out patiently.

He shook his head but when he looked at the ridge of one of the buildings, he saw no droids waiting—which didn't necessarily mean there weren't any. He sighed as he raised his arm. "Give me a minute and keep fighting."

"That was the plan. I like living," Mack declared as his suit glowed with energy and he rushed into a group of droids that approached from an alley.

"You won't hear an argument from me," Raul concurred and flung a net grenade at two droids that bound them together and began to crush them.

"If you could hurry, it would be appreciated, Cameron," Jaxon added as he stood and fired back to back with Silas. "As exhilarating as this may be, I would prefer to be of more use."

"Yeah, because demolishing a robot horde is merely a simple task for us," Cameron muttered.

"It kind of is at this point," Silas commented.

The bounty hunter made no retort and instead, fired his grappling hook to strike the rim of the roof of the building and pulled himself up. He landed rolling, his pistol at the ready as he crouched and scanned the rooftop. Fortunately, he had a brief moment of reprieve as the only droids on the roof were already deactivated by well-placed shots to the head or core. He remained low as he opened the message and read it.

"They are in but said they won't be able to take the teleporter out, though. They want us to join them so we can all head into the ship."

"Join them?" Jaxon asked and glanced at the main building. "I am not opposed to that, but we've been forced away from the building since they went in. We'll have to make our way there."

"I thought we didn't go with them to make sure no one followed?" Raul asked.

"It says nothing here about that, so I guess we did what we could," Cameron reasoned. "The Halo droids are coming in. That should make up for us not being here."

"So we're worth about a couple of hundred enhanced droids?" Luke asked and held the trigger on his hammer as he swung it into the ground again. Several droids were catapulted away by the kinetic energy dispersed. "I'm not sure if that is a compliment or insult."

"Keep in mind I include myself in that," Cameron replied. "I'm for it. I'd rather take this fight to the asshole controlling these things than keep dealing with the horde."

Suddenly, another person joined their link. "This is Commander—Chancellor Sasha. I received a message from Chiyo."

"We got it, sir," Jaxon replied. "We were discussing heading out."

"Go. I'll cover your flank," he stated. "I must remain here to help coordinate, so help end this in my stead."

The bounty hunter snickered. "I guess there is no more debate. That was an order."

"Agreed," Jaxon acknowledged. "Let us join our friends."

Genos was the last to fall down the tunnel and when he landed, he was greeted by Chiyo as the two men talked to one another on a private link. Although he couldn't hear them, from Kaiden's angry gestures, he seemed to be rather annoyed about the head officer's little prank.

The large man waved dismissively and Kaiden shook his head as they rejoined the team link. "Are you guys ready to go?" Wolfson asked.

Chiyo nodded and made another study of their surroundings. "This seems to be a cavern."

"A tunnel, technically. The remnants of the abandoned facility are back that way." The large man pointed down the long corridor. A very soft light illuminated the mouth of the tunnel. "Turn brightness on in your visors. Let's avoid using flashlights or anything like that until we make sure we're clear."

The group made their way cautiously to the end of the tunnel. All listened intently for unusual sounds, but it was silent except for a low hum that grew slightly louder as they approached.

"I would guess that is from the main generator that powers the island," Chiyo suggested.

Wolfson nodded. "Aye, it's located above this cavern and keeps some of the gadgets and whatnot powered in here as well, but in a rest state."

"I do not hear any footsteps or fighting," Genos said, his head tilted and his expression serious. "I hope that means we are still ahead of our adversaries and that they have not already recovered their target."

"Hopefully, they are dead," Wolfson muttered. "They came in through the main entrance. This place may not have been in use, but it was guarded well. Really nasty droids called Reapers guarded the front."

"Reaper droids?" Chiyo asked.

Kaiden looked at her. "Is something wrong Chi?"

"I...no, it's only a coincidence," she replied.

The head officer increased his pace once they drew near to the end of the tunnel. He stepped through the exit and perched near the lip of the ridge outside. The three joined him quickly and were stunned by what they saw below.

The floor was metal, laid out almost like a maze or unfinished building. Some areas were completely enclosed and metal cubes sealed away whatever contents lay within. Large metal cables protruded from the floor and wound up through the earthen walls of the cave, stretching to the very top of the cavern and into the metal base of the Academy above. One large orb in the middle of the area was what emitted the dim light. It was enhanced by the crystals that adorned the walls and were scattered along the floor.

"It is...quite immense," Genos stated quietly.

"It's almost the size of the island itself," Chiyo said where she knelt beside Wolfson. "Why is it designed like this? Is this another way to trick potential intruders?"

He shook his head. "This was going to be the Academy —not as grand as it is now, of course, and almost spartan by comparison from what I've been told. The plan was to make super-soldiers. It was in the beginning stages of being built after we made first contact with—" He paused and glanced at Genos. "Our now friends the Tsuna."

"Humans can be quite prepared, it seems," the engineer

mused. "Looking at it now, it is quite amusing to think that I am now a part of the Academy that was originally designed to fight my people."

"Amusing is one way to put it," Kaiden said. Suddenly, there was an explosion below and to their right. The group fell prone and crawled forward cautiously to peer over the edge. A hole had been blown into the area and several soldiers in dark-gray armor, tinged an odd teal color by the light of the orb, rushed in with their guns at the ready.

"The Ark soldiers." Wolfson grunted. "I guess we did beat them, but only barely."

The ace shrugged as he retrieved his rifle. "We have to eliminate them. It shouldn't be a big deal. I only count about six…eight…twelve… Dammit, I thought those Reapers were supposed to be invincible, Wolfson."

"I don't see any droids with them," Chiyo pointed out. "Maybe they were lost to the Reapers while the soldiers took them out?"

"Or they came down here with a platoon and this is all that remains," Wolfson added. "It looks like nineteen in total—a pain in the ass but they don't know we're here yet so we still have the element of surprise. Even if we didn't, I'm sure we can—"

"There's one more," Genos said and pointed to a figure with a long coat who strolled casually behind the group.

Kaiden zoomed in with his visor and noted the man's elaborate garb and the armor beneath that looked much like his outfit. His smile was a little carefree and almost mocking and was very familiar. It took a moment to put it together but the heat of anger followed immediately.

"It's that asshole from the factory," he stated coldly and

Chiyo and Genos glanced at him. "Dario." He looked at the others. "Our plan is to kill them, right?"

"I don't think a simple chat will suffice here, boyo," Wolfson replied.

"Good." The ace stood and with a stern voice that was more rage than authority said, "Target whoever you want, but that bastard is mine."

CHAPTER FORTY-TWO

"It seems to be clear sir," one of the Ark soldiers said as Dario sauntered nonchalantly into the main chamber of the old facility.

"No more droids and turrets? I'm almost disappointed." He chuckled as he walked farther in and stopped at a large metal wall with two large doors that blocked their path to the prize within. "It has a nice ambiance, I must say, but the décor leaves a little to be desired." He held two fingers up and made a beckoning motion. "Demolitionists, this would be your time to shine."

Four of the soldiers stepped forward and each drew their launchers as they stood in front of him and aimed at the door. One began a countdown from five and at zero, they delivered their salvos simultaneously, which struck the large frames with an explosive punch. They waited a moment to let the smoke clear and studied a few breaks and a large dent in the doors. Clearly, they weren't sufficient to enable their team to make their way through.

The assassin sighed. "Fire again." He waved his hand

carelessly. "And again and again if need be. We haven't come this far to give up due to stubborn doors, my friends."

The demolitionists nodded and took aim once again. After another countdown and a round of fire, the doors bent a little more and a section came loose to expose a white, chalky substance beneath. The men didn't wait for the next order and another countdown began, but this was interrupted by two bright lights that rocketed from above, one green and the other red.

These orbs streaked toward the demolitionists. Dario's eyes widened momentarily and he summoned his nanos hastily to shield himself as the projectiles collided with two of the men, detonated, and killed all four when their weapons exploded and scattered their remaining teammates.

The Ark soldiers scrambled to their feet and tried to determine who had attacked. While they attempted to regroup, they were bombarded by small missiles. Some destroyed shielding devices while others struck the floor and erupted to damage the metal and make the cave shake.

"It would appear we have company," Dario muttered as his nanos dispersed. He looked at one of the soldiers. "Send for the remaining droids at the entrance. They shouldn't have a problem getting here now unless they trip over the broken parts along the way."

The soldier nodded and pressed a switch on his gauntlet as another charged shot seared from above. The assassin's frown turned to a puzzled expression when four figures leapt from a ledge near the top.

He studied them quickly and identified each one by

their armor. The one with the insulator was obviously a Tsuna, the heavy one who wore an older armor model could only be Baioh Wolfson, and the female was Chiyo Kana, the infiltrator he fought at the factory. The final figure wore power armor and looked familiar. He was sure he had seen a set among several of the Omega Horde, although in different colors.

A thought occurred to him as he considered who this might be. Chiyo had been at the factory, along with two Tsuna, whom he had to believe both worked with a certain ace. A smile settled on his lips. It appeared dear Kaiden had finally sought him out after all this time.

The man also aimed at him right at this very moment. He once again drew his nanos around him as the ace fired a charged shot at the Arbiter assassin. The explosion was enough to dismantle his defense but he leapt back and formed three spears that he hurled at the man one by one. Kaiden shot the first two and rolled out of the way of the third. Dario snapped his fingers and the spear began to glow, but before it exploded, his adversary took flight using jets on the back of the armor.

The chaos of battle began around him as the newcomers attacked the remaining soldiers. He simply frowned as he watched the soldier soar above him. "Jets? This will be tricky."

A heavy Ark soldier raised his kinetic hammer, but Wolfson punched him in the face before the blow could be delivered. He then thrust his shotgun into the man's chest and fired before the man could recover, spun with surprising speed, and shoved a vanguard back with the side of his gun. He drew a plasma ax and lodged it into the side of the vanguard's helmet and the man promptly slumped as blood drained out of the wound.

The head officer looked at the heavy, who had thrown his hammer at him. There was no time to avoid it and the weapon careened into his chest. As the energy inside released, it hurled him back about thirty yards before he impacted with the side of one of the walls.

"Cheeky little bastard, aren't ya?" He grunted as he stood but the heavy's only response was to draw a heavy pistol and aim it at him. The man tried to fire but the pistol flared and exploded in his hand while the Wolfson drew his own weapon and fired five shots into the already compromised chest plate of his adversary, who immediately toppled. The head officer looked at Chiyo, who nodded at him, and he nodded in appreciation as two more heavies advanced. He holstered his pistol, retrieved his shotgun, and roared a challenge as he went to engage them.

Genos flipped over a large rock and a group of Ark soldiers opened fire at his surprisingly fragile blockade. He began to charge a shot and noticed a round stone nearby. He picked it up and flung it at the soldiers.

"Grenade!" one called frantically and the firing ceased temporarily.

The Tsuna simply smiled as he darted from behind his shelter and fired a blast from his small cannon to catch two of the soldiers in its blast. He drew his repeater pistol and fired at the other two to destroy their shields so they were forced to retreat and hide behind another large rock. Now, it was his turn to be the attacker and made a mental note to not confuse rocks with explosives as he charged another shot.

"I can't see!" one of the soldiers called when Chiyo darkened his visor, having hacked into his armor's systems. Two others echoed the cry and they all began to fire blindly. A direct battle was not her strongest suit, but she had no trouble ducking under their laser fire as she made her way around and fired into the backs of the three enemy soldiers. She then noticed that her own HUD had begun to distort and realized that apparently, they also had a hacker among them. It did not, however, need her personal attention. "Kaitō, please clear the nuisance," she requested.

"At once, madame." Only two seconds later, the HUD returned to normal and the hacker had been purged. *"I traced the culprit, madame. He is to your left, seated on the ridge."*

"Appreciated." She raised her gun arm to her left and fired her SMG to force the hacker out of hiding when his shield shattered. He tripped and rolled down the ridge. Chiyo walked over as he tried to stand, aimed her gun, and pulled the trigger once more to finish him.

Dario continued to pursue Kaiden and hurled nano-made spears, blades, saws, and bombs at the airborne soldier, who was able to outmaneuver them or was relatively unaffected by the explosions thanks to his strengthened shields. The assassin heard a soldier cry out and realized that his force had been quickly whittled down to about seven remaining soldiers.

"I can see why we need real Ark Academy soldiers," he grumbled as he raised his hands into the air. "Damyen needs a talking to." A multitude of nanos condensed upon themselves to create a giant orb above him and he cast it down as it began to glow with the tell-tale sign of a growing explosion. "I have to handle everything myself, it seems," he said with a dark chuckle as he watched the bomb descend on Kaiden's team. He might lose the rest of his men too but at least he could have a proper fight with ace thereafter.

CHAPTER FORTY-THREE

"Chief, do it!" Kaiden shouted as he raced toward the bomb. It began to glow brightly and increase in size. Dario smiled with smug anticipation, both enjoying the sight and seemingly oblivious or at peace with the fact that he would blow up his own men.

"It's a good thing he made something so big," the EI commented. *"It makes this easier. Uploading Kaitō's diffusion program."*

The bomb's glow reached its apex but the giant orb simply fell to the cave floor and broke apart to litter the ground with thousands of tiny nano machines. The assassin stared, his expression perplexed, and Kaiden took the opportunity to fire several shots. While the man dodged most of them, one struck his left ribcage and another his right thigh to thrust him back, although they inflicted no particular injury thanks to his armor.

The ace landed in front of him and his adversary leaned against the wall and simply stared at him as he aimed his rifle into his face. "You put up a better fight the first time."

"I've had a long day." Dario chuckled, moved one leg back, and rested his arm across the knee. "So, you've come all the way down here for me, *mio amico*?"

"I didn't even know you were here," he retorted. "I'm simply lucky that way, I guess."

"I suppose we both are." The assassin stretched his gauntleted hand forward and rummaged it through the nanos. "Let me guess—a diffusion program?"

"Chiyo made it after our last fight," Kaiden said as his finger tightened on the trigger. "You're not that tough without your tricks."

"It's why I try to not let those who see my work live long enough to talk about it," Dario replied with a grin. "That and being an assassin, but I can tell I'm not the only one who didn't learn well enough after our last fight." He raised his hand. "I can control my nanos in a couple of different ways if you recall."

"Kaiden!" Chiyo called before an Ark soldier with a sword swiped at her and forced her back. The ace turned and cursed as the previously deactivated nanos now rose and formed into a large tendril. It whipped at him and he elevated sharply with the tentacle in pursuit.

Dario stood, brushed himself off, and walked casually toward him with one hand raised. He controlled the nanos using the unique magnet setting of his gauntlet as he hummed snatches of an unrecognizable tune. "You should also remember to end the fight before gloating. But I suppose I have that habit too."

The infiltrator dodged another slash from the soldier and fired her SMG at the assailant, who raised his other arm and created a medium-sized shield to block the shots as she pushed in closer, slashed viciously, and cut her weapon in half. The swordsman kicked her back into the cavern wall and stabbed the blade at her chest. Chiyo's shields temporarily halted the blade as she drew her pistol, but they broke and the blade sank into her chest plate. Before it could touch her skin, however, the swordsman was blasted off her and she slumped to her knees and yanked the blade out once she'd caught her breath.

"Are you all right, Chiyo?" Wolfson asked and held his hand out.

"I am, thank you," she said as she took it and he helped her up.

"I'm only returning the favor," he replied and both turned at a thump behind them. The two heavies he had fought stood several meters away.

"You haven't beaten them yet?" she asked.

"I thought I had," he admitted somewhat sheepishly as he rubbed the back of his helmet. "Tough bastards."

There was the sound of a blade drawn to their left and they looked at the swordsman who was back on his feet and had drawn an auxiliary blade.

"Dammit, he's still alive too?" Wolfson brandished his weapon in frustration. "I'm losing my touch."

"You know," Chiyo began and studied their opponents. "Heavies have more systems in place and are easier to compromise and I don't think that swordsman can stand up to your armor and shields."

He caught her meaning immediately. "Shall we switch partners, then?"

She nodded. "I think it would be best."

The head officer grinned, nodded, and roared a challenge as he attacked the swordsman, who jumped back in surprise. The two heavies began to give chase, only for Chiyo to toss a shock grenade at their feet. It stunned the two briefly and she had Kaitō accessed their suit systems quickly to deactivate the weight distribution mod. The two men regained the ability to move only to topple due to the weight of their own armor.

"Come here, you!" Wolfson snapped as his opponent jumped and darted constantly around the larger man. He was finally able to catch hold of him when the Ark soldier ran up a wall and flipped to attempt a strike from above. The head officer dropped his shotgun and stopped the attack by grasping both his hands in one of his massive armored gauntlets. The man was at his mercy as he dangled in the air, and he lowered him slowly.

"That was a bad move on your part, idiot," he said mockingly as he drew his other arm back. The soldier flinched a second before his fist ground into his face and launched him against the cave wall. The man fell and his sword clattered free. The large man broke the blade under his boot and retrieved his gun. As he walked away, he looked back, lifted the bottom part of his helmet, and spat on the ground in front of the man before he replaced his helmet and shook his head. "They always gotta try to be fancy with it, those sword guys."

"I would highly recommend you give up now!" Genos shouted as he continued to adjust the settings on his cannon. The only response was a concerted volley of enemy rifle fire from across the cavern. Both he and the four remaining soldiers had barricaded themselves behind large piles of rocks and crystals, though the Ark soldiers did far more shooting than he did.

"Are you all right, Genos?" The Tsuna looked up as Chiyo crouched beside him, holding a pistol. One of the soldiers lobbed a thermal grenade and it exploded a fair distance behind them.

"I am doing quite well, friend Chiyo, considering the circumstances," he replied and nodded, finally finished his work, and settled into a crouch as he prepared to stand.

"Is there anything I can do?" she asked.

He considered it for a moment. "I suppose they might try to flee. If any make it out, please attend to them," he requested and fired his cannon, which now delivered a single long beam instead of charged shots. He moved it across the enemy barrier and it bored through the rocks and into the men behind, who yelled in pain and shock. As Genos had guessed, one was able to scramble out of cover and raced across the cave away from the beam. Chiyo was ready and with several well-placed shots, the soldier fell in mid-sprint and laid unmoving.

"I believe that is all of them," the engineer said smugly, turned his cannon off, and vented it. "We should help friend Kaiden now."

She nodded. "He might not be happy about it but we have a more important mission."

Dario glanced over his shoulder and sighed. All his men were now dead or disabled, Kaiden had proved to be a rather slippery target and his friends were about to join the fun. He checked his gauntlets and grimaced at the seventeen thousand, eight hundred and forty nano count. He was running low and it didn't help that a good seven thousand were effectively worthless on the floor—or were they?

He ceased his pursuit of the ace and brought the tendril toward him as he raised his other arm and transformed the remaining diffused nanos on the ground into a spiraling tornado that he directed at the approaching Nexus soldiers. They were forced back and Wolfson and Genos fired at the swarm as Chiyo retrieved her remaining shock grenades.

The assassin wound himself in the tendril and used it to take himself above and onto the top of the building. When he looked down, he almost giggled when he realized that despite its massive size, it was certainly not complete as many areas had no roofing. He landed on one section that did and looked at the glowing orb. He didn't know what it was but he had no use for it so turned the tendril into a spike and aimed it at the sphere as he glanced at Kaiden, who flew toward him.

"Come on then, Kaiden. Make this all worth it," Dario said, his tone too low for anyone to hear other than himself as he cast the spike at the orb and destroyed it to plunge the area into darkness.

CHAPTER FORTY-FOUR

"I*'m hitting the brights,"* Chief warned and Kaiden's HUD adjusted to the darkness. He scanned the building quickly in search of Dario. He was no longer on the roof, which meant he had to have jumped down into it.

"Do you see him, Kaiden?" Chiyo asked.

"Not yet, but he can't have gone far." He descended slowly into the building. "I'll go after him."

"We should accompany you, friend Kaiden," Genos protested. "He seems to be a devious foe, and we no longer have enemies of our own to—"

"Look out—bots!" Wolfson yelled. A group of Arbiter droids had entered the cavern from the entrance Dario had blown open with the massive bomb. Wolfson, Genos, and Chiyo all fired at the enemy and the mechanicals immediately retaliated with laser blasts and energy shots. The teammates dispersed to find cover.

"Do you guys need help?" Kaiden asked, his attention divided between them and inside the building.

"Get after him, Kaiden," Wolfson ordered. "We can deal with the junkers. Go and stop him."

"Please be careful," Chiyo warned.

The ace nodded. "I'll get him, then we'll find the transporter and end this fight," he promised as he used his jets to slow his fall. When he landed, he looked around warily. He knew Dario's nanos glowed when activated—except when he used the magnetic function—but he could only make simple shapes in that form and those wouldn't do much damage. They could, however, catch him off guard and maybe keep him in place as the man made another bomb to blow him away.

"Keep an eye out, Chief," he asked as he readied his rifle. "He's waiting for us. I don't think he'd he'll simply take the serum and run."

"Agreed," Chief said with a nod of his avatar. *"You seem to attract the crazies."*

"No kidding," he answered as he continued down the corridors. The building was remarkably well preserved aside from dust and rocks everywhere, which he had to assume came partially from time and partially from the big fight that had taken place. If it wasn't for the fact that it had only been partially completed, this could have made an impressive Academy.

Although this supposed super-soldier idea unnerved him. That was what the Animus was for, wasn't it? If they weren't considered super-soldiers, what the hell did they intend to try to make there?

"Kaiden, I pick up a faint energy reading. Beyond those doors to the left."

The ace approached the doors and confirmed that there

had been a lock but it was now blown apart. If his quarry wasn't in there, he had certainly gone through. "Is this a trap?"

"Obviously. The reading was a flare, basically like he sent out a signal for us to find him."

He sucked in a deep breath. "We have one more group of missiles left in the suit, right?"

"And that energy cannon too, you know. You haven't really made use of that," the EI reminded him.

"I know. I've been saving the energy," he confessed.

"Saving it? For what?"

"For what is probably about to happen." Kaiden kicked the door in with his gun at the ready. The room was a large chamber with nothing in it but a large metal plate in the middle attached to the ground. Dario stood on the far end of the room with his arms at his sides but gauntlets activated.

The assassin looked at him, his ever-present smile on his face. "You know, I've never been one for history. I'm more future-minded myself," the man said as Kaiden took a few steps closer. "But I know what this place could have been and it really makes one think. This room could probably have been the main training area for the future of humanity."

"Did you get what you came for?" the ace asked and glanced casually around the room to identify any potential attack.

"The serum?" Dario gestured behind him with his thumb. "It's back there in the room behind me from what Merrick said. But it has a little trap I have to get through before I can take it. Otherwise, it will destroy itself. It's very delicate work and all that so I have to deal with you first."

"And my friends," Kaiden corrected.

The man chuckled. "I feel I can take them rather easily."

"Your grunts couldn't," he retorted.

The man placed a hand dramatically against his chest. "You wound me—or would have, except I didn't train them. I'll pass the compliment along to Damyen when I see him."

The ace sighed and lowered his weapon slightly. "What the hell are you guys actually after? Your boss says he wants to save the planet. By killing millions? Enslaving the rest?"

"It's temporary," the assassin replied, although he took a moment to think about it. "I suppose the deaths aren't, but *mio capo* is no megalomaniac. He has an odd way of doing things, but they always come out for the better. This serum?" He pointed behind himself again. "We'll mass produce it and it will help to initiate the next step for humanity and turn us into the apex race of this entire sector. That's worth it alone, right?"

He felt his blood boil, took aim at Dario once again, and began to charge a shot. "To hell with you."

"Kaiden, energy is flaring up all around us," Chief warned.

The ace identified small pockets of yellow light that began to glow, more and more by the second. "Begin charging the shields. Chief. Prepare to burst."

"So this is it, eh?" the assassin asked, took a few steps forward, and held a hand up. He placed his middle finger against his thumb. "You were a good fight. I don't get many of those these days. Most of my work is taking care of dignitaries, politicians, CEOs, and the like. And it is wet work, but I have to usually make it look like an accident or an internal rupture or something. I guess that's why I was so excited when I met you—you made me try again."

Kaiden remained silent and simply stood tall and lowered Sire while he stared coldly at the man.

Dario's smile softened as he studied the soldier. "It's not my style, but that armor looks good on you." He glanced around as the orbs began to move slowly toward Kaiden. "It's fitting that you be buried in it," he added and snapped his fingers. The orbs glowed brightly and rushed closer.

"Burst, Chief!" the ace yelled. The armor glowed with a white light that surged free and collided with the orbs, which exploded on impact and created a chain of detonations that rocked the cave.

The assassin stumbled back, blinded by the white light and shaken by the wave of force. He gathered what remained of his nanos and drew them close to him as he looked at the smoky area.

A brief glimpse of green light, darkened by the smoke, began to glow. His eyes widened and he made a shield as the light careened toward him and broke against his shield as another swept in behind it, then another. Each blast depleted what was left of his small number of nanos. One final shot followed before something clattered. He took a moment to steady himself before he broke a small part of his shield to look out at Kaiden, who stood before him with his rifle on the floor.

Dario stood tall and his nanos separated and swirled around him. "Crafty. I certainly have to give you that, although you now have no shields."

"And how many of those little bugs do you have left?" the ace asked.

He raised his hands, rolled them effortlessly, and created a dozen lances that circled him before they pointed directly at the other man. "Enough."

"Mark 'em, Chief," Kaiden stated and a small line ringed each spear. He smiled under his helmet. "I hope this is worth it, Dario."

The assassin shook his head in confusion but quickly realized that his adversary must have heard him before. He smiled as he held a hand up. "It was entertaining, Kaiden," he stated and pointed forward to launch the lances.

The shoulders of the ace's armor popped open and a dozen missiles streaked out and intercepted each spear to create another chaotic blast that Dario shielded himself with his jacket. A rush of air indicated Kaiden's jets activating. He looked up as the soldier attacked with a blade that emerged from the gauntlet of his armor.

Dario brought his hand back instinctively to retrieve his nanos, but he heard a warning beep—one he hadn't once heard as long as he had used them—to let him know he was out. As his adversary reached him and drew his arm back, he looked up and the surprise on his face turned to a grin. The ace thrust the blade into the assassin and the jets drove them both into the back wall, where Dario's head thumped against the metal plating.

The jets died and he withdrew the blade and looked at the man's body. Blood poured from his sternum with another small trickle down his mouth and droplets on the back of his head. He had no final retort and no movement, and Kaiden himself had nothing to say. He didn't even gloat.

After a long moment, he approached the door the assassin had indicated and slid it open. A small table stood inside with a cylindrical case that housed a vial of blue liquid. He walked up to it and stared at Dario's supposed prize, the next step of evolution.

The two machines beside it seemed to be nothing other than monitoring equipment. He touched the case tentatively and both monitors went red. A gas filled the case and the liquid turned from blue to white, then become muddied and thick.

"The gas changed the structure of the serum. It's basically toxic waste now," Chief said, more formally than anything else and sounded almost robotic for the first time.

"Whoops," Kaiden said flatly and turned away. "I'm sure they have a recipe somewhere."

"Maybe. But it requires the right environment to make and many of the ingredients are basically blacklisted nowadays," the EI informed him. *"A pity for whoever."*

"It's a pity we didn't make it in time to stop him from tampering with it, huh?" he asked.

Chief nodded and turned an amused pink. "*Yeah, and it's sad that I had a glitch and didn't catch a recording of it either.*"

CHAPTER FORTY-FIVE

"Kaiden?" Chiyo called over the comms. The metal of a droid's head crunched behind her as Wolfson trampled a still fidgeting bot with his boot.

There was no response and Genos frowned while his fingers tapped his chest plate as they looked at the massive doors.

"Do we have another way up?" Wolfson asked as he sauntered up to them and studied the barrier.

"I have some line," the Tsuna responded and removed a spool from his belt. "I don't think it is enough to reach the top, however. If our friends arrive soon, Cameron has a real grappling hook. Perhaps Luke and Mack can help break down the rest of the door."

"Do you think he's all right?" she asked, concern evident in her voice, but a small amount of fear had crept in as well.

"The boy is fine," the head officer said almost off-handedly. "It's not like he hasn't made it through any number of explosions. I'm sure it was merely a desperate last ploy from that assassin."

"That's a damn good guess," a voice replied over the link. "Although it was more his main strategy than a last-ditch effort."

"Kaiden!" Genos answered. "I'm glad you are still well."

"What of Dario?" Chiyo asked.

"He won't bother us or anyone ever again." The ace's voice held the dispassionate tone of someone who had answered a simple trivia question. "Sorry for the blackout. I had to purge my shields and my energy has been wonky since. I'm looking for the teleporter now."

"Chiyo has a map," Wolfson pointed out. "Come and get the doors, boyo."

"They are busted," Kaiden answered. "It's not like much in this place seems to work in general. I already thought of trying to carry each one of you, but these jets are meant for one and I'm already putting a strain on it with this power armor. I'm not sure if I could carry Wolfson, anyway."

The large man huffed, leaned back, and shouldered his shotgun. "What the hell is that supposed to mean?"

"I think he was referring to your heavy armor, Head Officer," Genos interjected. "I don't think it is a matter of your normal weight. I am almost equal to that in my armor."

Wolfson waved it off with a vague gesture before another voice joined the link. "Woo! That was a long way down. These anti-gravs always make me feel tingly."

"Luke?" Chiyo asked.

"The one and only," he replied. "The rest are on their way down. Did you guys leave some enemies for us?"

The Tsuna looked around and kicked a robotic arm off the rock he stood on. "Not here, no, but I'm sure there will be sufficient even for you once we arrive on the ship."

"That's good news, there! And we can get all the others back too," Luke said. Chiyo looked up as the heavy made his way out of the cave above.

"Kaiden's looking for the teleporter but we can't make a way in," she told him. "We could use your assistance."

"Sure, where ya at?" he asked.

"Look down and to your left," Wolfson answered. The titan did so and waved at the group.

"All right, we'll be there soon. The others are all almost down the shaft."

"Yeah, I see the problem," Mack commented and studied the damaged door. "But it shouldn't be an issue."

"Do you think you can blow through that?" Indre asked as she and Chiyo looked at a holoscreen to see if they were still operational and hackable.

"I'd like to try but time is of the essence and all that," the vanguard stated and walked closer to the hole the Arbiter demolitionists had already made. He stuck a large hand into it, formed an orb of energy, and stepped back slightly but left the orb in place. His attention focused, he brought his hands together and began to separate them slowly, and the sphere increased in size. He began to strain once it reached the edges before he uttered a loud yell and forced it to grow even further and make the hole in the door bigger. After a moment, the orb collapsed and left a much bigger opening.

"Nice work." Silas placed a hand on the vanguard's shoulder.

"It won't be a graceful entrance but we can get in," Mack responded.

"And we can get to that teleporter," Cameron stated.

"Oh, I forgot to send the map to Kaiden," Chiyo realized as she shut the holoscreen.

"No need, I think," the ace replied.

"What do you see, Kaiden?" Wolfson asked as he motioned for the rest to enter.

Kaiden gaped at the sheer size of the teleporter. Several screens were active as the large pad on the ground pulsed with a teal light. Four large power cables went from the walls into the pad, and the console was in rest mode. "Something I can say we definitely can't carry up."

"We'll get over there on the double," the head officer stated as the group nodded and began to sprint.

"I'm in a domed room in the...uh, back right I guess," he responded.

"Look for his dot on the map." Chief sighed.

"I have a question, Kaiden," Genos began.

"Shoot."

"There is no need for that right now. There are no enemies present. Were you able to find the serum the Arbiter Organization wanted?"

"I did."

"Do you have it secured?" Wolfson asked.

"It is destroyed," Kaiden answered.

"What? By wh—" Cameron began.

"It's a real shame about that but sometimes, unfortunate things happen on a mission," the head officer responded and cut the bounty hunter off. "Don't beat yourself up over it."

"I'll try not to," the ace replied dryly. "So, should I hold off on touching anything until you get here?"

"I think it is recommended that Chiyo or Indre works the machine," Jaxon suggested. "Unfortunately, Cyra could not join us as she wanted to take the R&D building and make sure they do not reactivate the shields. But she was sure we could manage it."

"Gotcha. Chief downloaded games for my HUD so I'll wait for you guys to get here."

"We can do that?" Luke asked with a glance at the only faculty member on their team.

"It's not exactly regulation," Wolfson muttered and passed the titan. "Now move it!"

"That's a big boy," Mack said and studied the teleporter. "Otto would be all bubbly with even a peek at this."

"Why isn't he here?" Kaiden asked.

"Julius got hit so he's watching over him." The vanguard sounded solemn.

"Is he gonna be all right?"

"He is a medic, after all, so it's kind of his bag to heal, especially himself. I offered to stay, but they both told me to go on and be the representative for our team."

The ace smiled in his helmet. "Good choice."

"We have it online," Indre announced and the entire group approached quickly.

"Do we simply step onto the pad or what?" Raul asked.

Chiyo shook her head. "The console is online but we can't establish a target. It says there is an obstruction in the way."

Jaxon and Wolfson both leaned in to look at the monitor. Genos looked up at the roof. "Perhaps that is the obstruction?" he suggested and pointed above.

Everyone looked up and for the first time, noticed lines across the ceiling—not decorative but indicating separate panels. Kaiden and Genos looked around and the ace nudged his teammate when he located a lever. The Tsuna nodded and they both walked over. "It appears safe," the engineer said after he'd examined it for a few seconds.

"Or it's a self-destruct switch," his friend answered jokingly.

"It is doubtful. Those are usually buttons."

Kaiden chuckled to himself as he extended his hand and pulled it. A shimmer traveled along the roof as a shield was deactivated before the wide expanse separated into four pieces and pulled back. The teleporter pad began to glow brightly as six panels came to life and spun around it before taking their places along the sides.

"It's asking for a target," Indre stated.

Chiyo looked down and pressed a few keys. "From our position, we are directly under the Academy fountain," she said and tapped the *enter* key. "So it's a direct line."

A beam began to form in the center of the pad, expanded out to the rim of the circle, and streaked into the large hole in the cavern above.

"It says we need to deactivate the outer layer," Indre advised them.

"That must be the fountain. The underside must have a shield like the dome did," Chiyo reasoned.

"So we simply step into the beam?" Cameron asked. "Does that mean anyone who does so will be transported?"

"It seems that way." The infiltrator nodded.

He sighed. "We came all the way down here for nothing."

"It was just in case," Luke reminded him and clapped the vanguard on the shoulder. "And Mack helped."

"I'm deactivating the fountain shield," Chiyo said. "Are we ready?"

"I'll send a message to Sasha to let him know," Wolfson told her. "Other than that, let's go do what we do best."

"Damn straight," Kaiden agreed, his weapon in hand. "Do it, Chi."

The infiltrator looked down and pressed the *enter* key once again. The beam brightened slightly as sunlight from above poured into the cavern. She looked over at Kaiden and nodded as she drew her pistol. He looked at the others, all of whom were ready.

"Let's get our friends," he said and his grasp tightened on his weapon. "And make those bastards pay!" He ran up the pad with Genos and Chiyo behind him, his blood pumping as he vaulted up and into the beam.

His vision went white.

CHAPTER FORTY-SIX

"Sir, do you see that?" a military trooper asked and pointed to the center of the island. Sasha noticed that the fountain had moved several feet and more importantly, a large blue beam now seared through the sky and into the underside of the colossus.

In that moment, a message popped up from Wolfson to advise him that the beam would take anyone into the ship who stepped inside. The man smiled as three blue orbs traveled into the massive vessel, quickly followed by several more. He recognized the moment of choice and looked hastily at the battle below. With the aid of Janis' droids that had now joined the fight, it had swung their way but they couldn't afford to lose focus. His gaze returned to the enemy flagship and determination won through.

"Soldier," he said to the trooper beside him, "can the military handle it from here with the Halo, Rider, and King assistance?"

"We'd fight on with or without them, sir," the man responded with no hesitation.

The commander nodded and activated his comms. "All resistance members...Nexus students and faculty, if you can pull away from the fighting, head into the beam. It will take you to the ship. As chancellor, I will go to retrieve those taken from us. I feel most of you will wish to join me."

In no time, dozens of messages of affirmation were sent to his HUD and he had to block the rest to avoid being overwhelmed. He holstered his rifle on his back and looked at the trooper. "Fight on. We will end this soon."

The soldier saluted. "Don't be in a rush. I'll be glad to have more personal time taking it to the enemy."

Sasha chuckled before he turned away, leapt off the building to land on the Academy grounds, and sprinted toward the beam.

When Kaiden's vision returned, he stood in an ornate bay, the floor made of a silver material with black and gold walls. A few fighter ships were visible nearby and more importantly, droids.

"What the hell?" an Ark soldier demanded and scrambled for his pistol. The ace whipped Debonair out and fired several shots to eliminate him as Genos and Chiyo finally appeared.

"Heads up—enemies!" he warned, holstered his pistol, and charged a shot in his rifle. Genos charged a shot and tossed his spare machine gun to Chiyo. She snagged it in mid-air and fired on two advancing droids. The Tsuna fired at one of the docked ships, which immediately erupted and knocked over troops that surged forward as well as a crewman as he bolted away. Wolfson, Jaxon, Luke, and Raul were the next group to appear.

"Can't I even stretch after having my body turned into atoms?" Luke complained, activated his bounce pack, and leapt into the fray.

"I'm not sure if that's exactly how it works," Raul muttered as he released another tracker drone and directed it to find the captured students while he took aim with his rifle and began to destroy the turrets above.

"I, for one, have cooled enough," Jaxon stated and fired his machine gun in controlled bursts at enemy soldiers. "I am more than prepared to continue the fight."

"Get out of the way!" Wolfson bellowed and blasted an enhanced droid in its chest. It wobbled as its core began to glow from the damage, then exploded. The man simply raced through the blast and drove a large gauntlet into the helmet of an enemy soldier.

The rest of the team soon followed. Indre appeared and flung several disks that attached to cases and the wing of another ship. She made sure she was clear and pressed a switch on her gauntlet that detonated them to scatter droids and troops as the vessel flipped and crushed several others.

Silas and Mack teleported in together. The vanguard created a wave of energy that hurled Ark soldiers into pillars and walls as the enforcer ran up to an activating mech, shot out the safety glass of the pilot's seat, and lobbed a thermal in as he ran past. The jockey was unable to toss it out in time and the huge mechanical toppled when the grenade went off.

Cameron and Amber were last. The bounty hunter fired at the ceiling with his hook, hauled himself up, and swung around the hangar taking shots at anything his scope targeted. Amber eliminated a couple of droids with her pistol and a well-aimed shot shoved another off Mack's back that had tried to force the vanguard to the ground. She drew an arc pistol and placed it against the generator on his armor, fired it, and charged him.

Mack looked down and nodded appreciatively. "Hell yeah!"

"Medics are here to make sure soldiers are at their best," she stated. "Sometimes, that is healing and at other times, a quick burst of energy."

He created a giant orb. "I feel great now," he shouted as he hurled the orb at a craft that tried to take flight. The energy enveloped the fighter and crackled before it exploded.

"Do you think more will join us?" Luke asked as he pounded his hammer into the leg of an enhanced droid, then lifted his weapon up as his opponent fell and brought it down on its head.

"Oh, I'm certain of it," Wolfson acknowledged as he thwacked an attacker with its own arm that he had ripped off. "We're not the only ones who want to see these bastards fall."

"Then let's clear the room!" Kaiden shouted and fired a charged shot at a barrel of spare energy cores that resulted in a massive eruption that destroyed a good fifth of the bay.

"Sir, we're under attack!" a technician shouted up to Nolan.

"I am well aware of that," the Arbiter general retorted. "Where the hell are you, Dario?" He hissed in frustration. The monitor read no life signs but that couldn't be right. The idiot must have damaged his armor's OS. He couldn't have fallen now—not at this crucial moment.

"No, sir, not the destroyers," the technician explained. "I mean inside the ship itself. There is a battle in progress in the hangars."

"What?" He looked at the man before he glanced hastily at his map of the ship. The section marked *Hangar Six* blinked red. "How did they get on board?" he demanded.

"Some kind of transporter, sir. We're trying to shut it down but we haven't seen a system like it before. It's not like other teleporters and has created a direct link into the ship."

"How many?" Nolan asked and stared at the techie. "How many are on board?"

"A small group right now, sir."

"Right now?" he asked. "Are there more on the way? How many?"

"Well, sir, we don't know. But from what we can piece together of this transporter, anyone can travel through it. We could potentially talk the entire number of enemy forces."

Nolan's heart stopped for a moment. This battle had still been theirs to win in his eyes only a couple of minutes before. Now, he felt a dread he hadn't experienced in quite some time.

The feeling that he could lose chilled him to the bone.

Sasha appeared inside the hangar, his rifle at the ready, but what greeted him was fire, damaged droids, and moaning Ark soldiers. "They work quickly," he commented dryly and took several steps forward. "Any units that join me inside the colossus, the first team has cleared the entrance. You have free access to the ship. Focus on finding the hostages and bring them to safety, taking out any hostiles that get in your way."

"On it, sir." While only one voice replied, at least thirty resistance members stepped through behind him and more appeared on their heels. "We've waited for this."

The commander nodded and moved forward to follow the mayhem. "I've expected it."

CHAPTER FORTY-SEVEN

General Hartman watched as dozens of orbs streaked into the colossus. "It appears they made it," he observed and a small smile settled on his lips. "It was a long-shot plan at best, and they still completed it without a fuss. Nexus students are something to admire."

"General, the other destroyers are ready to warp in," an ensign notified him. "Should I give the order?"

He turned and nodded. "Bring them in just in case but have our forces focus on defense. Destroy the enemy fighters and assist with the fighting on the ground. Let's let the resistance take care of the colossus. We might even get a new ship out of it if I know the commander."

The ensign saluted and ran off and Hartman continued to observe the fight. "Of course, he's a chancellor now and this menace attacked his students. He may want blood more than a ship."

"Raul, Indre, have you had any luck?" Kaiden asked as he took shelter behind a pillar. Genos moved out of his cover to fire a beam at oncoming assault droids.

"My drone is still looking and also dodging shots—much like I am," Raul replied and fired at an enemy sniper on one of the rails above.

"I haven't been able to get into their systems yet," Indre explained. "How about you, Chiyo?"

"I haven't found any maps," the infiltrator stated. "But I have some weird readings from a large room above us. Some of them are similar to medical equipment we would use in the med-bay. Do these mean anything to you, Amber?" She sent the readouts to the battle-medic.

Amber scanned them quickly. "It looks like equipment we would use for life-support. While it could simply be their med-bay, there are way more here than would be practical for even a crew of this ship's size."

Chiyo nodded and marked the location on the map. "Raul, I'm sending you the coordinates. Take a look."

"On it," the tracker replied and blew the head off an Arbiter havoc droid before he ducked and took manual control of his drone. He found a small space he could fit the flying machine through and directed it to the floor above. It darted around troops that raced through the corridors to join the fight and when the door to the room opened as several men in white coats ran out, his drone flew in. "I see… Good God, dozens—no, hundreds of pods." He looked at Kaiden and Genos. "They look like Animus pods."

The ace thought of his confrontation with Flynn's golem and how they made that work, and a perverse corruption of the Animus system made sense. "Call it a gut feeling, but that's where we need to go."

"These guys don't let up!" Mack called as his shields began to falter under the relentless assault of the Ark soldiers and Arbiter droids.

Luke ran ahead of the vanguard and activated his gauntlet shield. "Focus on powering mine up!"

His teammate nodded and used one hand to maintain his barrier while the other faced Luke's as energy flowed into it to increase the titan's shield power and size. It would keep them at bay but they needed a way through.

Dozens of rifle shots came from behind, followed by hundreds of laser rounds and even two large blasts. The group looked back as resistance soldiers strode up the hallway. Sasha was in the lead, flanked by several other marksmen, numerous troops, and even a couple of mechs. One of the jockeys waved nonchalantly through his cracked window.

"Hell, it's about time," Wolfson snarked over his shoulder as he caught an Ark soldier by his arm, pounded him against a pillar, and let the body fall.

The commander knelt beside Kaiden as the soldiers began to force the Arbiter forces back. Most of the original group joined them in the assault. "It's good to see you doing well," the chancellor stated. "Have you had any luck finding the hostages?"

"We have a theory," Chiyo told him.

The ace pointed up. "A big room above us has life-support equipment and hundreds of units that look like Animus pods."

"I see." Sasha nodded grimly. "From what you have told

me about their golems, it would seem likely that they based the technology on the Animus golem link we had a hand in."

"I had the same thought," he replied.

"More are coming," Genos informed them. "We should head up before they concentrate on this floor."

"There are more resistance members running through the ship. It wouldn't be a smart tactic to simply focus on one area," the commander stated. "But we should get a move on, you are right."

"Do you think we can break through?" Kaiden asked as another large blast from one of the resistance mechs went off.

"I don't see why we couldn't," he responded. "Are you saying you would have been stuck here without our help?"

"Of course not," he retorted with a smile. "But it will be much faster with the extra help."

"Hey, are you coming?" Wolfson shouted at the group as he and the other troops had pushed all the way down the hall by this point.

"Then let us proceed." Sasha stood and immediately fired at an enemy demolitionist who had his launcher trained on one of the mechs. Kaiden, Genos, and Chiyo followed as they made their way to the stairwell.

"Lena!" Nolan yelled into the comms. "How are things in your sector?"

"There are enemy soldiers in the hall," she stated. "They

are destroying everything. We only have several bots here and a few soldiers, and the EI chamber will be compromised soon."

The general shook with rage. Most of his forces were on the ground or dealing with the military ships. He didn't have the forces to quell these resistance troops who had boarded. He was coming to the realization that the colossus was compromised and would potentially fall into their hands now that his military ships were focused on the defensive. They would let the resistance capture it to gain not only the colossus but also all the information on board.

They were lost if this continued, but it didn't mean he had to let them win either.

"Have Aurora activate the rapture protocol," he ordered. "Then escape. Don't allow yourself to be captured."

"The rapture— That will…I guess we have no choice at this point," she admitted. "But I can't get through, not with that many enemy soldiers outside."

"I said don't allow yourself to be captured," he ordered. "They could still use that mod in your head to stop the protocol. Do you believe Merrick would forgive you for that?"

Lena was silent before she took a shaking breath. "I understand. I will begin the protocol and they will not get me."

Nolan nodded. "Understood. You have been an asset to the organization and will be remembered for it." He signed off, checked to see if Damyen got his message, and instead, saw several messages from Omega commanders telling him they were on the way and were gathering together to warp in. He shut his monitors off and picked his rifle up from the side of his chair. "The rest of you, activate automated defenses and get to escape pods if you can. This ship will go down but it will be by our hands."

CHAPTER FORTY-EIGHT

"Sir, we have to go!" one of the lab techs shouted to the lead technician, who was busy working on the golem stasis program. "Enemy troops are already on the floor and heading this way."

"Activate the turrets and bar the doors!" he shouted in response. "I have to purge the system."

The technician recoiled. "That will kill everyone in the pods, sir," he stated, aghast. "I know they may not see reason, but are we the monsters they believe us to be?"

"This is war, boy," he said dismissively. "We are not to let them have any advantage. We do this for the good of the future of humanity—gah!" He fell, shot by a drone above. His colleague ran to help him up, fired a pistol with trembling hands, and finally knocked it out of the air. He helped the man up and blood poured down his leg down as he tried to apply pressure. The lead technician pointed at the console. "Finish it!" he ordered.

The technician looked up and frowned at the orange

screens with a *lock-out* notification saying . "I c-can't sir!" he stammered. "I think it's been hacked."

An explosion twenty yards away from the two at one of the front doors to the room ended the matter. Two other doors to the rear and western entrances soon followed and Nexus soldiers filed in. One stepped through the front entrance, dressed in blue light armor with mods and gear that clearly indicated an infiltrator.

She walked up to the two technicians and aimed a machine gun at them. "Don't move," she ordered, held a hand up, and waved it for a moment. The lock-out vanished as she controlled the console remotely to open the pods.

The resistance soldiers ran around the room to help those in the pods out. The captives all seemed exhausted, and some drew deep breaths as liquid drained out of the pods. Amber raced through the rows of units and helped whoever she could while she searched frantically for her friends. Silas, Raul, and Jaxon also helped in the search as Kaiden, Genos, Sasha, and Wolfson finally reached the room. Taller than the others, the head officer noticed a large man with a shaved head. "Marlo!" he called and pointed to the fourteenth row. Amber saw him, darted to the row, and almost fell as she knelt to help the demolitionist up.

"Marlo! Marlo, are you all right!" she asked.

He spat some of the liquid from the pod, shook his head, and placed a large hand on her back as Raul ran up to help him stand. "I had a...had a hell of a nap," he wheezed as he spat a little more of the liquid. "How...you guys... doing?" he asked, a small smile on his lips.

She returned it. "We're here for you."

"Thanks for coming." He chuckled but the sound was weak.

Silas raced through the chaos with Jaxon behind him. The Tsuna noticed a figure stumble against a pod six rows down. "Silas!" he called and pointed. "Look there."

"Izzy!" the enforcer cried and rushed toward the scout, who leaned against a railing and tried to wipe some of the liquid off her hair and arms.

"Si?" she muttered, turned, and almost fell before he caught her.

"Take it easy," he said and eased her into a seated position. "Are you all right? Did they do anything to you?"

"They carried me here with a mechanical bug, which wasn't fun," she moaned and brushed the liquid in irritation. "I don't remember much after that. Did you guys get here quickly?"

"As fast as hell," he said, glanced at Jaxon, and nodded. The Tsuna ace returned the gesture and raced away to help others. "You couldn't have waited a couple more days to get up here, huh?"

She uttered a small laugh. "It's not like I was doing much anyway."

Kaiden shoved and bulldozed past others as he searched for Flynn and finally found someone on the floor with three others around him, two medics among them. He caught sight of long blond hair and heard an Aussie accent reply to their questions.

"Flynn?" he asked and pushed forward.

"Where?" Marlo demanded as Amber and Raul supported the heavy who insisted on moving forward.

The ace didn't answer and instead, hurried to confirm as the large man forced himself into a jog. Amber tried to keep pace and prevent him from falling. Kaiden moved to the left of the medics and knelt quickly. It was Flynn, but he was rather pale and coughed up liquid.

"What's wrong?"

"He's weary. They all are, but he's been put through the wringer," one of the medics answered. Marlo leaned against a pod as Amber retrieved her stim-ray and knelt beside their friend, adjusted the settings, and pressed the trigger. A small beam formed, and she passed it over him several times. Flynn finally took a normal breath and his mutterings stopped as his eyes blinked open.

"Wh-where am I?" he asked and tried to move, but his arms simply fell back.

"We're here, Flynn," Amber said reassuringly and took one of his hands.

"Are you all right, mate?" Kaiden asked.

The marksman rolled his head over to look at his friends and a small smirk appeared. "That's my line, mate," he replied.

"We're gonna need some drinks after this, huh, buddy?" Marlo inquired as he knelt clumsily and hovered over Flynn.

"No kidding," he responded and his eyes closed. "I could use a shower first…and another nap."

"We just got woken up, Flynn." the heavy chided.

"I had bad dreams, plus this bastard woke me up once." He looked at the ace. "I can't say it was exactly restful before then."

"Do you remember anything?" Amber asked and glanced from one to the other.

Marlo shook his head. "Nothing really, only blackness until I dropped out of there."

"I remember seeing Kaiden. My body felt like I had been run through a wall," Flynn recalled. "I think we were fighting? It's probably more accurate than I realize."

"It's all right, man. You weren't you, in a couple of different ways." Kaiden replied.

The marksman shook his head and several globs of liquid splattered. "You gonna need to expound on that at some point. For now, get me a rifle."

"Like hell," the ace retorted. "We're getting you out of here."

"These guys locked me and my comrades away for... who knows how long," the man protested with a trace of anger in his voice. "I want payback."

Kaiden drew Debonair and placed it on the ground beside his friend. "I'll get you that rifle if you can pick up and fire my pistol."

Flynn opened his eyes to glare at him, reached over slowly, and took hold of the grip of the gun. He was only able to raise the butt of the pistol up a couple of inches before it fell out of his hands. "Point made, but you're still an asshole, mate."

"And you can bitch about it more later," the ace promised, retrieved Debonair, and holstered it as he stood and looked around. "There are so many people here and we'd be lucky if a fourth of them can move on their own. I don't think we can take them all back to the teleporter or if that is even safe."

"Hey, Commander," Marlo said and gave Sasha a weary salute as he strode toward them. "It's good to see you."

"At ease, Demolitionist," Sasha said. "It's good to see you as well as Flynn, both safe if rather fatigued."

"No kidding," Kaiden said and the marksman mumbled something unintelligible. "How do you think we're gonna move all these people, Sasha?"

"Out through there," the commander said and pointed behind the ace.

He turned with a frown. "Uh...Sasha, that's a wall. If you're talking about what is behind it...I think the sky."

"Exactly." The man clasped his hands behind his back. "I've been in contact with Zena and General Hartman. She will bring the assault ship around and will make precise strikes against the wall to blow it open. The military vessels will provide cover, but they've focused on the enemy ships below and have destroyed most of the colossus' outer defenses in this section already. Once the hull has been breached, shuttles can be dispatched to assist in recovery."

"Quick thinking," Kaiden complemented and drew his rifle. "Make sure everyone gets out."

"And where are you headed, then?" Sasha asked.

"Someone has to find the head asshole in charge," he explained. "And I'll be the one to do it."

"Assuming he is still on board."

"Either way, there is still Aurora to recover if we can," the ace reminded him. "Besides, we've come this far so might as well take the ship. Even if it's too damaged to be of use after this it has to have important intel."

"It's a good thought," the commander said with a nod,

"but my guess is that they have already begun to purge all their data at this point. And we can't simply believe they planned to do this alone once we showed up. They probably have reinforcements on the way."

"I'll work quickly," he promised and turned.

"Alone?"

"Shouldn't most stay behind to help?" the ace asked.

"There's no use getting all happy with a reunion if you're gonna set off and get shot, Kaiden," Flynn protested.

"Kaiden," Chiyo said over the comms. "I have a map. I can take us to the command deck."

He nodded and thought it over. "There are still other resistance members onboard, right?" he asked and the commander nodded. "Chiyo, send the map to everyone you can. Sasha, have them head toward the command deck. We'll push through."

"Very well, Ace Jericho," Sasha said with a small nod and activated his commlink.

"Chiyo, Genos, you're with me," the ace said and headed to the doors. "Let's find Aurora and make this ship our ship."

CHAPTER FORTY-NINE

"Do you have that door open yet?" a raider asked the demolitionist as he stood and dusted his hands off.

"It'll be open in no time," the man replied and held the trigger as he stepped away from the explosive-riddled door. "You might wanna get back."

"How far back?" a marksman asked.

"Way back." The demolitionist, now in a jog, counted down from ten. At zero, he pressed the switch and blew the doors wide, and the soldiers raced up to the now open doorway with their guns at the ready. Apparently, there had been Ark soldiers waiting, but they were now strewn about the room due to the force of the blast, although one body moved in the back.

"Don't move!" the marksman ordered and aimed. When he looked through his scope, he saw the woman had a gun pointed not at them but at herself. Before he could utter another word, she pulled the trigger and the lights in their hallway began to fade in and out.

"What the hell!" a cry sounded over the comms and caught Kaiden off guard.

"Hey, who's hot-micing?" he demanded.

"Holy hell! She shot herself and this sector is losing power. What's going on?"

The ace glanced at Chiyo, who opened a map and traced the comm. "It's coming from the front portion of the ship near the command deck. According to the map, it's an area called the EIC— Wait, EI? A ship like this would need its own room to monitor the EI necessary to control it. That could be where Aurora is."

"Among other things," Genos pointed out.

Kaiden frowned as a few resistance members pushed past them. He looked at Wolfson. "Should we go?"

The head officer thought for a moment, then nodded. "We're closing in. I think we have enough numbers to take the ship or at least fight our way in. You should check the area. If Aurora is there, I think only Chief would be able to interact with her given that they are almost the same model."

"Laurie didn't have to stick a chip in his head to get her to work," the ace quipped. "Although I suppose I never asked if he tried."

"What? You don't wanna feel special anymore?" Chief snarked.

"Head on over, we'll—" Wolfson was interrupted when shots were fired and were audible over the open comm-link. Some of the other soldiers nearby heard it and spun with their weapons at the ready, thinking they were under attack.

"Shit, let's move!" Kaiden said as he, Chiyo, and Genos sprinted toward the EI chamber.

"The rest of you get it together," the head officer ordered. "Let's go take that bridge!"

Kaiden had to force the stairway door open and walked into a darkened hallway. It was eerie, going from all the noise and commotion below to the almost silent space with the only disruption being the hum of the ship itself.

"Keep your guard up," he warned as the trio walked in. "Brights on."

"I can't read the soldiers any more," Chiyo said. "I don't have any energy readings. If they were taken out by droids, they aren't here anymore."

"Do you think it was a group of Ark soldiers?" the ace asked. "Maybe they got careless after clearing the room, some came back and got the drop on—" Blasts from above stuck his armor. Chiyo aimed upward and fired, and Genos charged his cannon as a figure darted on the ceiling and jumped between the pillars and walkways above.

"Chief, fire missiles!" Kaiden shouted.

"You don't have anymore, remember?"

"Dammit, right!" He fired several shots from Sire and only managed one hit, but it was enough to damage the attacker's shields, which shimmered briefly. The man was thin and a little pale with slicked-back dark hair. He turned and fired again and several orbs dropped.

"Shocks!" Genos called as he and Chiyo stepped back. Kaiden ran forward and when the shocks detonated, they covered his power armor. The absorbers activated and the power surged into him.

"We still have those gauntlet blasters, right?" he asked.

"Yeah. Do you wanna give them a try?"

Their adversary fired another volley, some at the ace and others at his teammates. "Do it." He held a hand out and when a red orb appeared, he lobbed it at the roof and although it missed the assailant, it exploded on impact with the ceiling, enough for the attacker to be dislodged. The man landed and rolled to his feet to sprint into a room. The ace landed a couple of quick shots with Sire and shattered his target's shields before he disappeared from his line of sight.

He followed with Genos and Chiyo at his heels, prepared another blast, and spun around the door and fired. The blast almost blinded him with the brights still on in his HUD. When it subsided, he walked in and scanned the room.

"Careful with those blasts. The instruments in here are already precarious enough," a man warned. Kaiden turned quickly in the direction of the voice and located the thin man perched on a railing that ran along the top of the room, his rifle aimed at him.

The three Nexus teammates all had their weapons trained on him. "Who are you? Another assassin?" the ace asked.

"My name is Nolan. I was the commanding officer of this ship—the general of the Arbiter Organization," he announced and leaned against the wall. "Now, I'm merely a desperate man."

"You'll be a prisoner soon enough," he threatened and held Sire's trigger to begin charging a shot. "Or simply dead if you try to fight."

"I'm dead either way, really," Nolan stated with a shrug. "I had no plans to live after today."

"You'd die for this mess?" Kaiden winced. "How the hell are any of you sociopaths lucid enough to have made an army like this?"

"Dedication and vision," was the man's reply as he moved his weapon to each in turn. "Merrick's dedication and vision. I believe in what he is trying to do. It was honestly why I was so supportive of the Ark Academies—the original version at least. Humanity needs to evolve and the normal means don't cut it anymore."

"And do you believe we're all doomed as well?" Chiyo asked.

He exhaled a long sigh. "I'm not sure. Our leader seems quite sure of it himself. When he's spoken about it to me, it shakes him, which in turn terrifies me."

"For being so humanitarian, you don't seem to have much faith in us," the ace remarked caustically.

The man stood and Kaiden warned him by following his movements with his rifle. He stretched his arm out and let his weapon drop. "Faith cannot make real change, only inspire those to follow ones who can. And I have done my part. The rapture protocol is ready."

"Rapture what?" he asked. A blue light formed on his left and he turned to see Aurora's face. "Aurora?"

"Rapture protocol initialized," she announced and her

voice glitched as her form began to disassemble. *"Purging systems. Destruction commencing."*

"Aurora!" the ace called. "Chief, get in there and—"

"Look out!" Genos warned and Kaiden looked up. The man was now aglow in red light. He wore a vest lined with explosives and his face revealed determination and rage as he cast himself at the group.

"Chief, shields!" Kaiden shouted and spun to cover his allies as the Arbiter general's vest erupted and covered them with a fiery blast. The power armor's shields activated and blew outward to protect them from the main blast, but even with the increased energy, they had not recovered enough and the three were thrown into the walls of the room. Chiyo's and Genos' shields were also destroyed.

"The power armor is compromised, Kaiden. I'm disengaging the locks," Chief notified him.

"Stop Aurora!" he ordered through pained groans. "She said destruction, didn't she?"

"I read a large influx of power into the central core," Genos warned and helped Chiyo up before he moved to Kaiden. "You know what that means, Kaiden."

The pieces of his power armor gave way as he rose and left him in his normal armor with no helmet. "I do. This ship will explode and take everything around it with it."

CHAPTER FIFTY

"You thought you were so smart, didn't ya?" Wolfson mocked as he marched around the AO captives on the bridge. "I'll give it to ya that the invasion was a pain in the ass, but you didn't think we would strike back and come for our own? You're nothing but a group of idiots, I'd say." Warning sirens activated and the captives looked frantically at one another. "What the hell is that?" he demanded.

"The ship is going to blow," one of the Arbiter technicians said. "You have no hope of stopping it."

"What the hell are you talking about?" He sneered at the tech. "We have gifted technicians of our own, you know. This last-ditch attempt—"

"They cannot stop it. This is the rapture protocol," the man responded. "The OS is the first thing to purge, then the master EI. There is nothing that can stop it. This is our final solution."

The head officer's eye widened and he looked at his troops. "Get out of here!" he ordered.

"Useless." The tech laughed, clearly hysterical. "Do you know what powers this ship? The amount of energy that will be expelled will cover at least fifteen miles and destroy anything in its path. How many do you think you can evacuate in that amount of time?"

"Shut your trap!" Wolfson roared and delivered a kick to the tech's jaw before he activated his comms. "Sasha, we have a problem."

"So I've gathered," the commander replied and frowned at the blinking red lights as another group of Nexus rescues was loaded into shuttles. "What's going on?"

"Some kind of failsafe, apparently. One of the technicians says the ship will blow in a fifteen-mile spread," Wolfson explained, hauled a couple of the other captives to their feet, and shoved them out of the command deck.

"Can we stop it?" he asked.

"I'm going to check, but he says the OS and EI are already gone so there is no way to access the systems that would let us do that."

"Damn it all." Sasha growled his frustration. "I'll get every shuttle and carrier to move in and retrieve everyone we can. What's the ETA?"

"I can't tell…looking around." Wolfson ran up to a lone chair in the middle of the deck—the captain's seat most likely—and turned on every monitor he could. He immediately noticed messages on one. "What's this—ah, hell, Sasha. We have Omegas incoming!"

"How many?" the commander asked as he sent

messages to all the gangs and military leaders to begin evacuations.

"A fleet, it looks like, mostly made up of stolen vessels. That Damyen bastard is leading them. They'll mop up any who get away and head to Seattle to retaliate." Wolfson slammed his fist down, hit a keyboard, and activated another monitor. He looked at it and clenched his teeth in a grin. "I have access...wait—shit, it's locked out!"

"No hackers nearby?" Sasha asked.

"No, and you shouldn't risk sending any," he replied and sat in the chair. "I'll figure it out and see if there's still some kind of auto-pilot. Maybe I can get this ship out of the area in time before it can do real damage."

"Check for a warp engine," the commander recommended and ran out into the halls to guide the other soldiers to the shuttles and to the beam in the hangar. "And I think I know of a way to gain access to the system."

"I said don't—" Wolfson began.

Sasha cut him off. "I'm not sending someone. I'm sending an EI."

"I can control basic systems but there's nothing I can do about the core," Chief explained as Kaiden and his team continued to search the room.

"Kaitō can't manage more than the closest systems. There is no central OS anymore," Chiyo stated. "We need to leave."

"Judging from the size of this ship, the expected blast of this vessel once it destructs will be...quite immense."

Genos said and looked at his teammates. "I am unsure if we can make it to safety in time."

"Like hell are we dying here!" Kaiden retorted. "Chief, controlling what you can, do you think we can—"

"Chiyo, are you there?" Indre shouted into the comms.

"I'm here, what do you need Indre?" the infiltrator asked.

"I still have access to the teleporter so I can widen the beam and teleport the rest of us out of here, but we need to get back to the station to mark a new location."

She frowned. "That will get us off the ship but I'm not sure if we can work quickly enough to move the new location sufficiently in time. We were lucky in that our initial target was right above us." She took a deep breath. "But we have few options. We should try."

"Kaiden," Sasha interrupted. "I need you to send Chief to Wolfson. He's using an EI pad borrowed from one of the soldiers. I'll give you the ID."

"Wolfson doesn't use EIs. What's going on?" Kaiden asked as the pad ID appeared in his HUD.

"Wolfson is on the command deck and says he can control the ship but the manual controls are locked out. Chief should be able to open them, correct?"

"I can, with a link. Getting me on the pad will speed it up," Chief affirmed.

"Get on it," the ace said,

The EI nodded. *"I'm heading out, partner. I'll be back soon."* He disappeared from the HUD and Kaiden stood.

"Let's get going."

Chief appeared on the pad. *"Howdy."*

"There is no time for pleasantries, bubble boy," Wolfson retorted and cast Chief into the system. "Open this thing up!"

"Roger that." He set to work and the system activated in only a few seconds. "It's open but there is no autopilot."

"Ah, hell, things can never be easy. can they?" The head officer took hold of the controls. "I'll get this sucker as far away as I can. Look for a warp system while you're in there. We can set this ship to jump and bail out."

"On it."

He began to force the controls forward. While there was significant resistance, he felt the ship move. With little time at his disposal, he aimed toward the ocean and hoped to get it out far enough that the only casualties would be the guppies.

"There is a warp system but with how much power is being siphoned, it would blow almost immediately after the jump."

"That's fine by me," Wolfson replied. "I'll set it for some remote location."

"You can't. The warp requires manual control as there is no EI to control it. I tried myself but it seems Aurora fried the systems before deactivating. I can't insert myself." He began to blink red. *"I sense a warp marker. More than a dozen ships will be headed here in about fifteen minutes."*

"Right, the Horde and the AO cronies," Wolfson said in a low tone. "Even if we get everyone out, they'll push through and more will die. Then they'll head to Seattle and more will die there too…far more than only one."

"Only one?" Chief asked and his eye widened. *"Wolfson, you can't mean to—"*

"You're an advanced intelligence, right?" the man remarked. "Can you think of something better?"

Chief's eye shrunk. *"To my knowledge, this would actually be the best outcome, especially if you were to warp to these coordinates."* A map appeared on another screen and the man glanced at it.

"What's this?"

"The location of the warping fleet."

The head officer looked at the map again, smirked, and finally uttered a howl of a laugh. "You are Kaiden's EI, aren't ya?" He chuckled. "Speaking of Kaiden, he can't hear us, can he?"

"Not at present, no," Chief admitted. *"Do you want me to open a channel so you can—"*

"Nah, there's no use for that right now. I know how that goes in these times," Wolfson said calmly. "But I do have a message. Can you record it for me and give it to him after this is done?"

"I promise I will," the EI said in a solemn tone.

"Good, now listen up, blinky..."

Kaiden reappeared on the Academy grounds and watched the ship clear the mountains. "Do you think he'll make it out in time?" Chiyo asked.

"Of course he will," he said firmly. "He's a little thick but hardly too reckless. He wouldn't risk doing something that wouldn't help." He took a couple of steps forward and the colossus blocked the setting sun before a glow appeared.

For a moment, he thought it was the sunlight but it began to cover the ship. "He's warping?"

"He shouldn't," Genos protested. "Warping drains too much energy. It will lead to a premature explosion."

The ace frowned. "He'll make it out," he said but his tone held less conviction. The ship began to shimmer, about to jump. "Chief is with him. They'll think of something. Hell, Wolfson will probably jump out the windows on the bridge."

"I'm afraid not, partner," Chief said and reappeared in his HUD.

"Chief—wait, what's going on?" Kaiden began to panic and sprinted to the edge of the island. "Wolfson!" he shouted as the colossus began to vanish and finally disappeared.

"Are we ready to depart?" Damyen asked the Omega Horde captain as he lit a cigar and took a few drags.

"As soon as we know the area is clear, we will jump," the captain stated. "We'll take care of this mess and gain a foothold in the region while we're at it."

"I'm sorry about this." Damyen chuckled. "Our general is smart if a little too feisty. I believe we can—"

"A ship is warping in," a technician notified them. "The colossus."

"Nolan made it?" the chancellor mused as he looked out of the HQ window. "I always pegged him for the go down with the ship type. Running away is quite out of character for him.

The colossus appeared directly over the base. "I read a huge energy spike!" the technician yelled. "It's going to blow."

The cigar dropped out of Damyen's mouth. "What?"

"God, I hate warping," Wolfson muttered and glowered at the many consoles on the bridge that now sparked ominously. Panels fell from above as electrical fires began to erupt around him. He looked at his map to confirm that he was over the base, leaned back, and drew the flask out of the compartment of his leg to take a swig. "Here's to your future," he mocked the Omegas and Ark soldiers below with a toast. "You group of idiots."

The colossus erupted, destroyed the base and the Arbiter fleet below, and blinded the area in a large sheet of white energy. When it finally settled, nothing remained.

CHAPTER FIFTY-ONE

There were sounds behind him—the last blasts of the battle against the Arbiter droids still on the island, more like a hunt at this point, and cheers of victory. Soldiers called their command to check if it was really over. It was all dulled to Kaiden as the realization of what had just happened sank in.

He felt like he was about to fall, staggered, and reached his hands blindly to grasp the mostly broken railing. After a moment, he was able to steady himself as he drew a deep breath. He should have paid more attention to his surroundings. The main threat was gone but there could still have been enemies about. While he knew that on some level, he couldn't focus.

It honestly shouldn't have come as a surprise. He'd known since day one that this was always a possibility—hell, he had thought he had grown used to the idea of losing friends by the time he joined Nexus. But for the man to sacrifice himself, to be gone in a matter of moments… Kaiden had difficulty coming to terms with it all.

A hand settled on his shoulder and he turned to Chiyo, who stood beside him with her helmet off and her eyes filled with concern and understanding. She closed the distance between them and held him and Genos stepped behind her to take hold of the ace's arm. The remainder of the group looked on, some of them in as much shock as he was.

"Could we have done anything to prevent it?" he whispered, more to himself than as a question. "Been faster? Focused on fixing Aurora before anything else? Dammit…" He leaned his head into Chiyo's hair and gritted his teeth. "Dammit."

"We're sweeping up now, Commander," General Hartman said briskly. "A good number of the droids deactivated before the colossus made the jump. They must have been connected to the ship itself and when the OS went out, so did their control."

Sasha nodded and only partially paid attention to the general's explanation in the comm.

"You led your team well. I see your years as a teacher have not dulled your ability to command. We always have a position for someone with your talent if you'd like to return."

"I decline," he replied and drew a deep breath. "We may have won a victory here but many were sacrificed to make it so, including a soldier better than I could hope to be."

The general remained silent for a moment and took a deep breath of his own. "I understand. I suppose the sad fact is that I've grown...I wish to say accustomed, but it is probably more like callous to the loss of life working in the military. You have much to process, I'm sure."

"When will we take the embassy?" the commander asked. "I cannot begin to rebuild the Academy while the Arbiter leader continues to breathe and plan. Will we have to wait for another half a year to even have a chance to take action?"

The general's tone became gruff and no-nonsense. "I cannot promise immediate action, believe it or not, and the embassy may be much, much harder to take than the Academy was. But given the success here today—and remember, that is what this is—I can promise I will hoot and holler to make sure you are a part of the planning. You've proven yourself to me and any naysayers, commander. If we can come up with a plan to attack tomorrow, I doubt there will be many objections. But we have to be prepared."

"I am aware of that," Sasha stated. "We have much to discuss, then, but for now, I have to tend to my students."

"Agreed. The recovered hostages we have onboard will be taken to the nearest hospital. We will also take the captive AO members to base for interrogation. I will fill you in at our next contact."

"Thank you, General." The commander signed out. His shuttle touched down on the Academy grounds and the side door opened so he and more than a dozen soldiers could file out, including Izzy, Silas, Marlo, Flynn, and Amber.

"Are you sure you're all right to walk?" Marlo asked the marksman.

"I'll be fine. When I crash, it'll be for a while," Flynn assured him and looked around. "For now, let's find the others."

Desmond and Zena looked at the Academy from their assault ship, which approached the side of Janis' carrier. "Is that the end of it?" he asked.

"It looks like it," she said with a nod as she leaned over the railing. "We should probably get out of here before they start making trouble."

"I think the WCM would be more grateful than that," he chided. "It's not like they can enforce laws without a WC anyway."

"I'm not sure that will hold up in court," she retorted and focused on Janis' ship. She contacted him through the commlink, changed to a private channel, and added Desmond. "So, what will the Halos do now?"

"Repair and make new droids from the looks of things," Janis replied as he gazed at their much smaller vessel from the bridge windows. "And what are your plans?"

"Nothing concrete at the moment," Zena replied with a glance at the Skyway Kings leader. "There are still a number of Omegas about. I don't know if the loss of that big ship will change much, but they've taken too much of our gangs' turf over the last few months. After a little rest and recuperation, I think we may take it to them instead of sitting around waiting for them to attack us."

"The Halos don't exactly have turf. We have a junk town—a rather nice one, actually," Janis told them. "But they have raided our stores and vaults. Trying to recover some of our equipment was how we ended up in this fight, really. Am I correct in thinking you are trying to arrange a mutually beneficial arrangement?"

"She doesn't really use fancy words like that all too much." Desmond snickered and received a glare from Zena.

"I think we both have a similar problem and I think it would be mutually beneficial for us to solve it together since you're here," she said bluntly.

"Do you have a place for my gang to hide out while we're in town?" Janis asked.

"There's a Ramses warehouse available. It's not like the big wigs are around to object," Desmond told him.

"A warehouse?"

"I imagine a decent warehouse is better than a junk town, however nice it might be," the Kings' boss said jokingly.

The Halo leader chuckled. "You haven't seen the basement," he countered. "But we can at least discuss the possibility. Send me the coordinates and I'll talk to my co-leaders on the way."

"Done," Zena confirmed and gave a mock salute as she and Desmond walked to the bridge. "They have three leaders in one gang, right?" she asked. "We're both leaders of different gangs but we work together all the time."

"We've been over this," Desmond said with exaggerated patience. "What would we change the color to—purple? It doesn't look good."

"And baby-blue does?" she retorted.

"It's cyan," he countered and looked at the pilot. "Tell everyone we're headed back and to find a shuttle or walk."

"Are you gonna be all right, mate?" Kaiden raised his head to where Flynn and the others stood on his left.

"Yeah, eventually. It's mostly shock." He straightened and Chiyo and Genos stepped away as he faced his friends. "He would probably kick my ass if I got too down anyway."

"That is accurate." Genos nodded and Jaxon smiled slightly despite the seriousness of the moment.

The ace chuckled and his gaze drifted beyond the group to the island, which was mostly rubble. "It'll be a hell of a job to repair everything now that it is our responsibility again."

"Are you kidding? I bet we can fix it all in maybe a month," Luke said and folded his arms as he studied the destruction. "It needed an update anyway. Maybe we can add a few new improvements."

"It's something to consider," Jaxon said with a nod. "For now, we should celebrate and rest."

"Besides, we still have one more objective," Silas added and everyone looked at him. "We heard the chancellor talking to one of the generals." He pointed skyward. "We can't start rebuilding while a certain bastard still wants this place."

"Right." Kaiden balled his hands into fists as he looked up and envisioned the embassy in the stars above. "He won't have it—or anything else now. And I'll do my damnedest to be the one who ends it all for him."

CHAPTER FIFTY-TWO

They couldn't contact Damyen's HQ, there was no connection to the colossus, and Dario did not respond. While they still attempted to piece everything together, things looked rather bleak. And yet, despite it all, Merrick seemed rather calm—almost disturbingly so, at least to the Omega commander, who stole glances at the man as he and the crewmen and technicians tried to gather intel.

The AO leader leaned back in his chair, seemingly lost in thought, his arms folded while one finger tapped his arm. The commander had seen guys like him before. This was the metaphorical calm before the storm when the leader saw a failure in their plans and tried their best to hide their displeasure before they erupted in anger and a flurry of vulgar language. But they always showed signs before their rants—veins throbbed or they muttered to themselves, perhaps even a darkening of the skin as anger took hold—but none of that was apparent with the man he now watched cautiously.

"How many?" Merrick asked and finally opened his eyes. "By your best estimate, how many would a total loss cost us at this point?"

The commander looked at one of the technicians, who simply shrugged. "My guess would be tens of thousands if the main base was destroyed," the Omega leader said finally. "A considerable number of droids as well, the loss of the Ark students captured over the last few months, either by rescue or lost in the fight. This would compromise our hold on the planet."

"But the forces up here?" the other man asked. "Your space forces still remain?"

"Obviously." He nodded. "And we've been able to capture stations Icarus and Zeta. We should still be able to capture a third and possibly a fourth station before any retaliatory strike occurs."

"Which would give us control of four of the six stations around Earth," Merrick said, more to himself than anyone else. "They would need to capture those stations, both for a foothold and to rescue any inhabitants. That would buy us time as we consolidate our forces." He turned his focus on a row of technicians. "Losing Aurora hasn't compromised our hold on the embassy, has it?"

"Somewhat, sir," one of the men admitted. "But the internal defenses are still under our control. Any security access we have lost should be under our control in only a few days. Those are the priority. Everything else should be back in our hands within the coming weeks."

"I see." He nodded, stood, and walked to the consoles. "We'll need to be ready for their eventual assault. For now, any remaining destroyers should be recalled. Let the ground forces keep the assault ships and any smaller craft. We'll focus on guerilla tactics from here on to hobble them. I'll have all the equipment taken from the tower and brought here for further experimentation. I'm sure that today cost us many potential soldiers but we'll still need all that we can to be prepared for the future."

"Yeah, sure." The commander nodded and for a moment, Merrick looked at him, his eyes narrowed in a fearsome glare at his apparent nonchalance. This caused a brief moment of confusion and surprise in the battle-hardened Omega leader, but Merrick simply turned away and continued to walk forward and scan the various holoscreens that displayed maps and video feeds.

"Change is difficult. I'm sure almost everyone realizes that at some point in their lives," he said with a sigh as if he'd had to adjust to that realization himself. "None have seen what I have. They fight because they see me as the enemy, a title I am willing to carry for now. It is better that than to be called a horror." He paused when a new screen activated with the feed from the main base. The colossus appeared and then exploded, and the resultant energy destroyed buildings, men, and ships before it engulfed the camera and the screen went black.

"Shit." The Omega leader sighed and turned away.

"It appears Nolan started the protocol and they found a way to use it to their advantage. That is very resourceful." Merrick looked at the commander, who tried not to make eye contact. He almost wished Merrick would fly into a rage like most others did—he knew how to deal with that. "Commander, you have the orders. I wanted to add one more thing, however, before you begin."

"What's that?" he asked. Merrick held a tablet up and flicked it in his direction. The commander received notification of a message with a list of names. They were familiar and he recalled a couple as those who set their alliance up in the first place.

"Find those people, the other members of the organization," the man stated and drew a deep breath. "If any are on stations, make sure they are well defended. Those on Earth...I need them disposed of."

"Disposed of?" The commander looked at the AO leader once again. "Don't you think we have lost enough forces?"

"The ones we still have are precious. I can promise you that the ones I have asked you to take care of can certainly not fight. I have no doubt that the military will attack us, but they will want as much intel as possible. Maybe they find out about the other members and interrogate them, or the others become skittish and try to strike a deal. I cannot let either possibility come to fruition."

The commander nodded slowly. This man was cold but thorough. He had heard that a couple of other leaders in the company were contemplating leaving the partnership with the AO but at this point, they were too deep. What would they say if they did break away and the military came for them? Sorry about the small genocide? If they had a path, it was with him now.

He only hoped his own name wasn't on the next list.

Kaiden walked into Wolfson's dojo and paused to look around. It was remarkably well-kept, albeit in comparison to everything else. In addition to three large holes in the ceiling, most of the furniture and items not nailed down or to a wall were scattered and overturned and there were scratches and burn marks on the wall, but everything was still standing. It seemed to be a good metaphor for its former owner.

He walked to the far end of the room, flipped a bench onto its legs, and took a seat. He would only be there for a moment as many of the other Nexus students had begun clean-up efforts. It would only be for a short time and certainly not long enough to get much done, but it was more symbolic than anything, something to help them feel they had reclaimed their Academy after all the effort it took. While they waited for the way forward to present itself, the activity also provided a way to unwind before they took to the stars later.

"Are you really all right, partner?" Chief asked and appeared above him, glowing a muted blue.

"Like I said, eventually." He sighed. "To think that the first time I met him it was because he literally dragged me here and tried to force me to be his protégé. I guess he got what he wanted in the end. It's fitting in a weird way that one of the men I grew closest to was as stubborn as I am."

"Yeah..." Chief made no effort to complete his response and instead, descended slowly to look at him. *"I planned to save this for later, but I think you should at least know about it and make the decision yourself."*

A small circle appeared as an attachment to a message in Kaiden's vision. "What's this?"

"A recording from Wolfson. He made it for you before he jumped."

Kaiden's lips pursed and he stared at the message as he thought it over. He nodded. "Go ahead, Chief. You know I'm not patient."

"Are you— No problem, partner."

The message opened with no video, which was somewhat disappointing but he reminded himself that he didn't actually want to see Wolfson surrounded by the signs of a ship about to explode.

"Hey there, boyo, sorry for the ruckus in the background," the head officer began. The creak of metal and sizzle of electrical explosions were audible as he spoke. *"I told the bauble I didn't want to call you before this thing went up. It didn't sit right, but as I'm talking to you now, I have to say maybe I should have— Well, it's too late for that now, I suppose. I told you once that the thing that hurt the most about being a soldier wasn't the physical injuries but the loss of others you had grown to befriend and care for. But that is also the driving force to what we do. The best soldiers have that in common—not fighting for themselves or even their planet as a whole but fighting for those dear to them to make sure they don't lose them. Making the decision I have now...it's a pain in the ass, certainly, but I can tell you it was still easy. I've lived enough, as it were. You and the rest have many years to catch up and make a legacy half as good as mine."*

Kaiden smiled when Wolfson chuckled. *"Not to mention the body count. If all goes well, I'll take a few thousand of these bastards with me and probably a few more fighting on the way up or down, whichever. So don't worry about me now. I have no regrets—actually, I have one, but I think you can help me with that."*

Kaiden straightened and listened closely. *"I won't be able to finish this with you, but you were my most promising student. I still had the wins in our little brawls, but who knows what would have happened in another year or two...or ten really, but I'm willing to give you the benefit of the doubt. You would have surpassed me. Honestly, boyo, you have already in some ways. You have grown from a punk who was good with fists and guns to a punk who's good with fists and guns and getting the job done. You've become a capable leader despite your kicking and screaming all the way there, and you've grown to understand the importance of fighting for more than kicks. I hoped to see what would become of it all, but I have a gut feeling—the most accurate feeling, I might add—that you would come out of it all a better man than I."*

There was silence for a moment before Wolfson drew a short, hesitant breath. *"I suppose I've been ramblin'. I mean it all, though. As I said, I have one request. I won't be there but I know you will. You would fight through hell to finish this. And when you bring this home and finally stare at that idiot Merrick, place a couple of extra holes in him for me."* He chuckled. *"It's an easy request, I reckon. You will probably melt that bastard as it is. Even when I'm gone, know that I'll be looking after ya. Not even the devil could stop me doing that. Kaiden, take care. I'm proud of ya."*

The message ended and he lowered his head. Silence settled over the room and a few tears fell while the ace sat unmoving.

"Maybe it was too soon to—" the EI began.

"No, it's fine." Kaiden looked at Chief and swiped his arm over his eyes. "That was needed, really." He stood, looked around the room once, and fumbled for his pistol. It was the one Wolfson had made for him, designed after the one from his Animus sessions—a gift, something practical as he called it.

"He was right at the end of it all," he said and traced his fingers over the weapon. "I intend to blast that bastard apart anyway but now, I'll end it with this, for him." He holstered the gun and moved to the door. "A good soldier completes the mission. A great soldier does it for duty," he recalled and considered Wolfson's ideology. "The best soldier does it for those he cares about."

ANIMUS ON AUDIO

Kaiden and friends are now available in audio at Amazon, Audible and iTunes. Check out book one, INITIATE, performed by Scott Aiello.

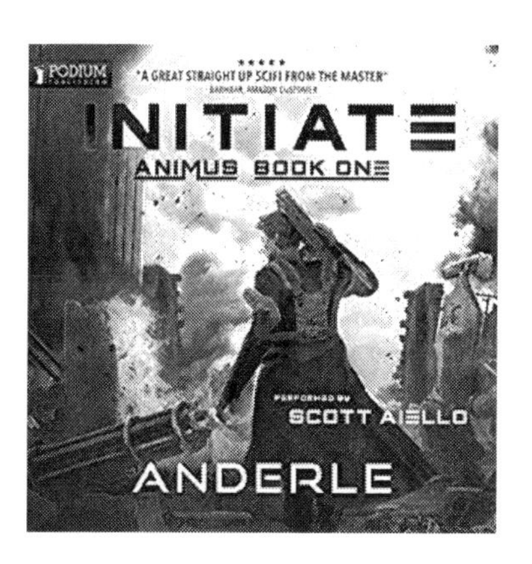

Check out book one at Amazon

(Books two - five are also available in audio, with more coming soon.)

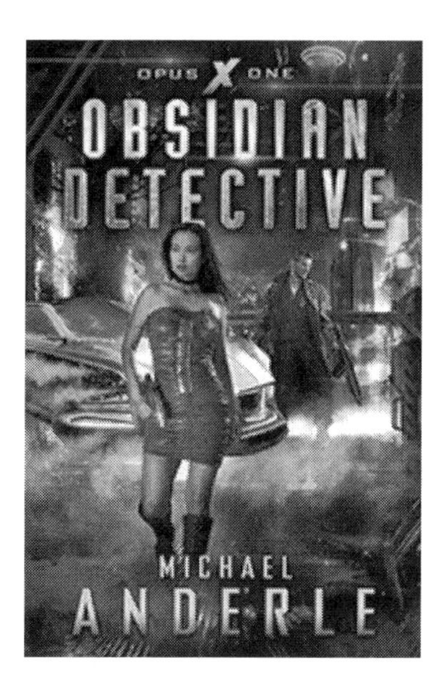

Available now at your favorite ebook stores.

Two Rebels whose Worlds Collide on a Planetary Level.

On the fringes of human space, a murder will light a fuse and send two different people colliding together.

She lives on Earth, where peace among the population is a given. He is on the fringe of society where authority is how much firepower you wield.

She is from the powerful, the elite. He is with the military.

Both want the truth – but is revealing the truth good for society?

Two years ago, a small moon in a far off system was set to be the location of the first intergalactic war between humans and an alien race.

It never happened. However, something was found many are willing to kill to keep a secret.

Now, they have killed the wrong people.

How many will need to die to keep the truth hidden?

As many as is needed.

He will have vengeance no matter the cost. *She will dig for the truth. No matter how risky the truth is to reveal.*

AUTHOR NOTES - MICHAEL

FEBRUARY 11, 2020

Thank you for reading our Animus stories!

Joshua is hard at work finishing the last book in the series, and he's working on a couple of shorts we are going to give away for other projects.

Then, he and I will be starting another project that he has mapped out already.

For those of you who have grabbed the audio, THANK YOU. For those who did not know Podium has been producing the audio for the books, well, go check them out!

Here is the link to the first book, *INITIATE*: https://www.audible.com/pd/Initiate-Audiobook/1772309362

Diary, February 9th – 15th

So, it's Monday the 10th at the moment, and I'm already up to a few shenanigans that are cool.

At least, in my opinion.

A few weeks ago, we did a model shoot for one of our series. During that shoot, we took some special headshots of the model to allow us to see if we could map a real face to a 3D head. Now, that doesn't seem like anything special.

Except, we are a publishing company (trying to become an entertainment company.)

We type—a lot—and edit and publish and all sorts of things related to putting out books. Having said all that, we have been working towards 3D bodies / heads / video clips for three (3) years, and recently, Reallusion (https://www.reallusion.com) has released a way for us to use our modeling images / cover shoots for a bit more.

Take a moment (or twenty) to see the product Reallusion has released (link above) to map a face to a 3D model. I think you could have fun with it. Imagine taking a picture of your grandparent, or mom, or friend and placing them in a short animated video.

Can you *IMAGINE* the mischief you could get into? It would be *FANTASTIC.*

Now that you have the power, don't do anything evil. (I can't say "don't do anything I wouldn't do" since we all know I'm an author. *I'll absolutely do something you shouldn't do and laugh maniacally as I do it.)*

Even if you don't have the time right now, use your phone to capture the images of your friend/loved one/person you hate ranting about a subject. You will be able to use the voice to match the lips of the 3D character in the future. You just need the photos and audio at the moment. Use them when you get time.

Or, someone on Fiverr (www.Fiverr.com) will eventually offer it as a service for $50.00, I believe.

Consider it the not-very-fake deepfake (https://en.wikipedia.org/wiki/Deepfake) – the cheap version.

I'm so happy to be back in Vegas!

I'm back from the #Superstars Writing Seminar in Colorado Springs, Colorado. The people were fantastic, the relationships I formed spectacular.

The lack of oxygen was suffocating. (PUN, PUN! Wait, is that considered a pun?)

(*Editor's note: No.*)

It might surprise you to know that Las Vegas is about a half-mile above sea level. So, while I came down from on high, Vegas isn't exactly brimming with oxygen. This might also explain why some casinos (rumored?) pump oxygen into the casino area itself to keep people awake.

I think I might go visit the Aria to work. Maybe I'll be pumped full of oxygen.

Dammit, I need a nap, and it's only 10:30am in the morning. This jetlag is STILL kicking me in the ass.

Do enjoy your week. I'm going to go pretend to be an old man who needs his late-morning nap.

Ad Aeternitatem,

Michael

BOOKS BY MICHAEL ANDERLE

For a complete list of books by Michael Anderle, please visit

www.lmbpn.com/ma-books/

All LMBPN Audiobooks are Available at Audible.com and iTunes. For a complete list of audiobooks visit:

www.lmbpn.com/audible

CONNECT WITH THE AUTHORS

Michael Anderle Social

Website:

http://lmbpn.com

Email List:

http://lmbpn.com/email/

Facebook Here:

https://www.facebook.com/OriceranUniverse/

https://www.facebook.com/TheKurtherianGambitBooks/

https://www.facebook.com/groups/320172985053521/ (Protected by the Damned Facebook Group)

Printed in Poland
by Amazon Fulfillment
Poland Sp. z o.o., Wrocław

56406124R00249